The Heart Remembers

A NOVEL

Jan-Philipp Sendker

Translated from the German
by Kevin Wiliarty

Polygon

First published in paperback in Great Britain in 2021 by
Polygon, an imprint of Birlinn Ltd
West Newington House
10 Newington Road
Edinburgh
EH9 1QS

1

www.polygonbooks.co.uk

ISBN: 978 1 84697 582 0
eBook ISBN: 978 0 85790 447 4

Originally published in German as *Das Gedächtnis des Herzens*
in 2019 by Karl Blessing Verlag, Munich

Translation copyright © 2021 Kevin Wiliarty
Lyrics on pages 49 and 330 from "Heart of Gold," written by Neil Young.
Reprinted by permission of neilyoungarchives.com and Hipgnosis Songs.

British Library Cataloguing-in-Publication Data
A catalogue record for this book is available from the British Library

Typesetting by Jennifer Daddio, based on the original design by Cassandra Pappas

The
Heart
Remembers

JAN-PHILIPP SENDKER, born in Hamburg in 1960, was the American correspondent for *Stern* from 1990 to 1995, and its Asian correspondent from 1995 to 1999. In 2000 he published *Cracks in the Wall*, a non-fiction book about China. *The Art of Hearing Heartbeats*, his first novel, is an international bestseller. He has also begun a trilogy set in Hong Kong and China; the first book, *Whispering Shadows* is also published by Polygon. He lives in Berlin with his family.

KEVIN WILIARTY has a BA in German from Harvard and a PHD from the University of California, Berkeley. A native of the United States, he has also lived in Germany and Japan. He is currently an academic technician at Wesleyan University in Middletown, Connecticut, where he lives with his wife and two children.

For Anna, Florentine, Theresa, Jonathan, and Dorothea

Part One

Chapter 1

LOVE, MY UNCLE SAID, plays a part in every story, however grand or simple, however beautiful or otherwise. You will find love in the stories that make us cry, just as in the stories meant to lift our spirits.

We were sitting on the kitchen floor. Night had fallen, and it was cooler now. My uncle shivered. I went to get a blanket and wrapped it around his shoulders, then sat back down.

The fire crackled. I gazed into the embers as I listened, even though I wasn't entirely sure I understood what he was saying.

Be they conceived hundreds or even thousands of years ago in some strange and distant land, or just last night in a little hut across the river, all important narratives have just one theme: the human need for love.

Are you listening, Bo Bo?

I nodded.

There is no greater power than love, he continued quietly. She has countless faces and complexions. No other subject has ever so occupied the poets, and no other subject ever will. Rightly so, for we are otherwise apt to forget.

Seeing my puzzled expression, he leaned forward as if to disclose some great secret, only to decide against it after all.

That was just like him. The past few weeks had been full of fireside tales, all of which had invariably trailed off at some point.

Tales of the time when he was still small and the world was still big, a time when there were neither cars nor televisions in Kalaw.

Stories of a wife too young to die.

Stories of a mother who could conquer great distances without taking a single step.

And stories of a boy who could reportedly distinguish butterflies by their wingbeats.

Quite a lot of it was baffling, frankly. Who can hear a butterfly in flight? But it was never dull, and I hung on his every word.

There I go again, I heard him mumbling. Where is it going to end? What am I talking about? What does a boy your age know of love?

How was I supposed to answer that? What *does* a twelve-year-old know about love?

Nothing.

Or at least not much.

Or maybe more than he suspects?

Our conversation ended on that note, and I was disappointed. I would gladly have gone on listening. My uncle has a wonderful voice. Once he gets rolling I find myself forgetting all the cares of the day. Just like when he used to sing me to sleep.

How could I have known that this was all just the beginning of a much longer story? And that when we got to the end I would finally understand what he had been trying to tell me in all kinds of ways for the past few weeks, sometimes with words, sometimes without?

The next morning my uncle started telling me about his little sister. Now *that* was unusual.

He was stretched out on the couch under a light blanket. I had propped up his head with two little pillows. I made him some tea and sat down on the floor next to him. His eyes were closed and his mouth was open. As if he had fallen asleep. The rain had stopped, and the birds were singing. I was just thinking I might as well head into the yard to feed the chickens when he whispered my name.

"Bo Bo, are you there?" he asked.

I took his hand. I do that a lot. It was so warm and soft. He smiled without opening his eyes. I held on firmly. He liked that, especially when he was tired or when he couldn't sleep.

And he was tired a lot in those days, especially in the morning. Sometimes I worried that he was getting sick, but he told me to stop fretting; it was just a question of age. A man of nearly eighty years would feel tired from time to time, after all. I don't know if that's true, because I'm only twelve, and he's the only eighty-year-old I know. Or at least the only one I know well.

Neither of us said anything for a while. In the yard the bamboo creaked in the wind. A few flies buzzed around us. The delicious smell of a neighbor's curry drifted in. U Ba squeezed my hand and started his story.

His sister had a big heart, and she was the most beautiful woman he had ever met, aside from his wife, of course. And his mother. She had the elegant, graceful bearing of a dancer, eyes that flashed with an uncommon intensity, and laughter that would warm your heart.

I can't say whether he was exaggerating. I hadn't seen her in ages. I can't even remember what she looked like, or what her laugh sounded like, never mind whether it would warm your heart.

"Do you and she look alike?" I wanted to know.

He thought about it for so long that I started to think he wasn't going to answer.

"Yes and no," he said at last. "It can be like that with siblings. In some ways they can be so close, while in others they may be so distant that it hurts."

I don't have any brothers or sisters, so I can't really say whether he was right. I have U Ba, my uncle, and he doesn't feel distant, at least not in a way that hurts.

"How many children does she have?" I asked carefully.

U Ba cocked his head from one side to the other and wrinkled his brow without saying a word. I had no idea what that was supposed to mean. Grown-ups are not always so easy to understand in my experience.

There was so much I wanted to ask him about her. Whether she was healthy, for instance. How she was getting along. Whether she might be able to come visit us sometime. But I knew I'd get no answer.

To keep him from falling utterly silent, I went and sat next to him on the couch and started massaging his feet. He liked that, and it generally made him more talkative.

"Tell me more about her, U Ba," I pleaded, hoping to learn something new. "Tell me her story."

"Perhaps some other time," he yawned.

"No, no, tell me now. Please."

But he was finished. He opened his eyes briefly and smiled at me. He looked exhausted.

Soon enough his head was lolling to one side on the pillow. A fly landed on his cheek and was crawling its way to the tip of his nose. I brushed it away.

"U Ba," I whispered. "U Ba." But he didn't stir.

So as not to wake him, I sat there for a few minutes. At some point I got up and went into the yard, where the usual chores were waiting: chickens and a pig to feed, laundry to wash, weeds to pull. Today I also had to fix my bicycle. I must have picked up a piece of glass or a nail while riding through the mud.

Sometimes I don't know what to make of U Ba. What had prompted him to mention his sister that morning? It was very unusual. I think he was afraid it would make me sad.

My uncle has only the one sibling, you see, and so, logically, she is my mother.

Chapter 2

THE HUNGRY CHICKENS SCURRIED impatiently about my feet. The minute I tossed them a bit of food, they descended on it as if they hadn't eaten for days. Two hens quarreled greedily over a handful of grain. I stepped in and broke it up.

Hungry animals put me on edge. Even chickens.

I tried not to think of my mother while I was doing the chores, but my thoughts had a mind of their own.

All the kids I knew lived with their mothers. Almost. Ma Shin Moe's parents had died in a bus accident last year. Ko Myat's mother was working in Thailand. But she visited every year. Or at least every other year.

Thinking more carefully about it, I also came up with Ma San Yee and Maung Tin Oo, twins whose mother had died giving birth to them. Their father had a new wife, and so they at least had a stepmother. She wasn't particularly kind to them, but she was there.

The only things I knew about my mother were that she lived in Yangon and that she wasn't well. But I didn't know what exactly was wrong with her.

I had no idea what kinds of things she enjoyed or worried about. Whether she preferred rice, like me, or noodles, like her brother.

I had no idea whether she was a sound sleeper, or whether she was like U Ba. Did she wake in the night and call for me, only to find I wasn't there?

I had no idea what she smelled like. What her voice sounded like. Whether or not I took after her.

I couldn't even remember when I had last seen her.

U Ba used to have a photo of her that served him as a bookmark. She, my uncle, and I were all standing on a snowy porch bundled up in hats and mittens. My mother was holding me in her arms. I was still just a baby wrapped up in a blanket. We all gazed intently into the camera.

One day he left his book in the yard, where the pages and the photo both got drenched in a downpour. Now my mother was just a particularly beautiful smudge of color amid the other smudges.

In order to drive thoughts like that out of my mind, I started counting out loud. That's a habit of mine. Whenever there's something I don't want to think about, I just start counting. And if ever I feel especially threatened or worried, I start counting things I can see. The fruits on an avocado tree, for instance. The blossoms on a hibiscus bush. The spokes on my bicycle. Or even just stairs.

One, two, three, four, five, six, seven, eight, nine, ten, eleven, twelve, thirteen . . .

But today I couldn't put the troubling thoughts aside.

I couldn't get my mother out of my head.

I walked past the chickens to the remotest corner of the yard and sat down by the anthill.

Thousands of ants crawled in two black columns along the base of the bougainvillea bushes to the papaya tree, where, for no reason I could see, they made a sharp turn and disappeared under the hedge and into the neighbor's yard.

I liked to watch the ants. They were living proof that strength had nothing to do with size. They could carry leaves, needles, and pieces of bark much heavier than themselves.

If ever I put a stick or a stone in their way, they would stop for a moment, probe it with their tiny legs and feelers, and then walk right over it, or under it, or around it, no matter how tall or wide it was. They were single-minded animals, and nothing would keep them from pursuing their goal.

I found that thought reassuring.

And they never showed any sign of fear. I could approach them and stamp my feet; they would just go about their business. They were not like the beetles, worms, or pill bugs that would flee in all directions when I lifted up a stone.

I sat there looking at the ants, focusing on their hustle and bustle, until I lost track of the time.

Eventually I felt better and went back to the house.

On the steps lay a couple of my uncle's shirts, the two green longyis for my school uniform, and a bundle of T-shirts. Next to that was the rake I was supposed to use to clear weeds. I had absolutely no interest in doing the laundry or crawling around in the muddy garden, so instead I just went to look for U Ba.

He was still lying motionless on the sofa. His blanket had slipped onto the floor. I picked it up and folded it. It was warm out now.

Instead of fixing my bike, I took the spare and rode into town.

It was market day, and the city was more crowded with people, cars, and motorbikes than usual. I needed to be on my toes; a moped nearly ran me off the road.

According to U Ba it wasn't so long ago that there were no cars or motorbikes at all on the streets of Kalaw. People went everywhere on foot, by bike, or in one of the many horse-drawn wagons. They would turn off the electricity at nine o'clock, and a lovely quiet would settle over the place. Those who could afford it would light candles. Those who couldn't would go to bed. There were no computers or telephones and no foreign visitors.

I can't imagine it. These days all the grown-ups are obsessed with their cell phones. What did they used to do with all the time they had?

At the market most of the stands had tarps for shelter from the rain. Underneath the tarps it was always packed with people. You could smell the dried fish, the coriander, and the fresh-ground chili peppers. I gave the meat vendors a wide berth, though. I couldn't stand the stench of disemboweled animals. It would cling to my nose even hours later.

Among all the people of various ages I felt as if I saw only mothers with their children. Some mothers had set their little ones on their bellies between piles of carrots and potatoes; others had strapped them to their backs or were carrying them in their arms. Women cuddling their children. Feeding them. Singing them songs or rocking them to sleep.

The sight of them made me sad again. I wandered aimlessly from stand to stand. More than anything, I just wanted to go back home to my uncle, to lie down on the couch with him, but he'd asked me yesterday to buy him some tea and a pack of cheroots. I also picked up some eggs and vegetables for our lunch, a bag of pastries, and two bunches of yellow and white chrysanthemums for our altar. I bought two pieces of milk cake for my uncle from a vendor who was selling sweets. He never asked for these, but I knew how much he liked them. I got back on my bike and rode over to Ko Aye Min's.

His office is on a side street not far from the market. There's a sign out front: "Adventure Tours with Aaron." He goes by Aaron because he's worried that his clients won't be able to remember his Burmese name. He works as a tour guide, which is to say that he gets money for walking around with other people. I've asked him more than once what kind of a strange job that is, walking around with visitors, and how it is that he gets paid to do it. It seems like the kind of thing you ought to do just to be friendly, or to be helpful when someone is lost. He says it's called "tourism" and maybe I am too young to understand it.

It's a mystery to me what exactly is so adventurous about hiking around to the Pa-O, Karen, Danu, or Palong villages that surround the city, but loads of foreigners come to Kalaw during the dry season, and Ko Aye Min is very busy. Sometimes he's away every day for weeks at a time, and I don't see very much of him. In the rainy season, on the other hand, we don't get many visitors. He doesn't have much to do then but sit in his office, and he has plenty of time for me. We play chess or talk about soccer. He's not married and he doesn't have kids. Until recently he had a girlfriend, but she lived near Mandalay. She didn't want to introduce him to her parents, so they didn't see much of each other. Whenever she was in town, Ko Aye Min wouldn't have much time for me. But that was fine. She never stayed long, and at some point she stopped coming at all.

Ko Aye Min is like a brother to me, even if he is somewhat older. I guess about thirty. It doesn't matter. We've got plenty to talk about, and if we aren't in the mood for conversation, like today, then we've got plenty to say nothing about.

He knows exactly what he can and can't ask me. I think there are some people who just know more than others, even without being told.

He's never once asked me about my mother.

He's never once mentioned my scar.

Not like the kids or the teachers at school. My scar is dark red, as wide as a matchstick, and it stretches from the left corner of my mouth nearly up to my ear. U Ba thinks that I don't see it very often just because we don't have any mirrors in the house. He's wrong about that. I see it every time someone looks at my face.

Some days I feel a tugging in my scar. I know then that the weather is going to change.

Other days it hurts and burns. I know then that I'm going to have a rough patch.

Ko Aye Min was happy to see me. He was sitting at the back of his office reading a book. There were unopened letters on his desk, a few newspapers and maps. He held a half-empty bottle of Coke between his legs.

He put the book aside. "Hi, Sherlock." He's called me that ever since we watched a couple of Sherlock Holmes movies together. He claims I remind him of the detective because I'm always asking questions and have a sharp intellect. "Nice to see you. How's it going?"

"All right. You?"

"All right."

That was a lie. He was feeling blue, and not just a little. He couldn't fool me because I have a gift, one that's a little creepy even for me. Whatever a person is feeling, I can see it in their eyes.

I'm not talking about knowing that someone is sad because their eyes are full of tears. Anybody can do that. I can tell that a person is sad even when they're laughing.

I can tell that someone is getting angry, even if they pretend that everything is fine.

I can tell when rage is a mask for fear.

I can sense the uneasiness behind a friendly voice.

Your eyes will give you away. They can't pretend. They can't lie, even when they want to. Often they tell me more than I really want to know, and that can be unpleasant. It's hard to watch somebody lie.

That's why I tend never to look anyone in the eye for too long. Better to look away.

If there's no getting around it, I've found that I can look without seeing. It's like when you listen to a person without really hearing them.

My uncle is the only one who knows about my gift. When I told him about it, he sank deep into thought, puffing absently on his extinguished cheroot, shaking his head now and then as if he could hardly believe his ears. And yet I could tell that he did not doubt me.

One time he interrupted me to ask whether I might by chance also have exceptional hearing. I have no idea where that came from. In the end he wanted to know how I could recognize the various emotions. I wasn't able to answer. I can just tell. For me eyes will flicker or twinkle or glow like embers in a fire. They'll shine or quiver, shrouded one moment in shadows only to be nearly transparent the next. Sometimes a person's eyes are as empty as a dead bird's. Or they practically pop with fear, the way a chicken's do before the slaughter. Eyes can be dull like the water in a mud puddle, or they can blaze like the sun. Every expression has infinitely many gradations, and each one has its own particular meaning.

My uncle claims that infants have a similar ability in the first few months of their lives. They can read their mother's eyes. Maybe I just never unlearned it. We only talked about it that one time, but I get the sense that there are times now when he would rather not let me look him in the eye.

U Ba says there are one or two people in Kalaw who can read minds. The old astrologer, for instance. Probably also the old gray monk in the monastery on the hill above the city. I don't know if it's true. I can't read people's thoughts, at any rate. Even when they come out and tell me what they're thinking, I often find it difficult to understand what they mean.

I could see in Ko Aye Min's eyes that something was weighing him down. Now I just had to figure out what it was. That's the problem I run into all the time. I can tell when a person is down or happy or worried, but I have no idea why. Sometimes they'll claim that they're doing well even while I can see that they're not. I used to put more stock in their words than in their eyes, but I know better now.

Ko Aye Min was quiet for a while, then took a sip of soda. "Would you like something to drink?"

"No thanks." I stared for a while at the big map of Burma that hung behind him on the wall. "Do you have anything new for me to read?"

He stood up and went to the cabinet where he kept his books. The people he hiked with were always leaving books behind when they were through with them. Of course the Finnish, Korean, and French editions weren't much use to us. But that just made us happier to get our hands on the English ones. You wouldn't find them anywhere else in Kalaw, and we were both big readers. He tilted his head and examined the spines carefully. At last he pulled one out and handed it to me.

"International bestseller," proclaimed the bold print on the cover. By John Green. Not someone I'd ever heard of. I glanced at the title: *The Fault in Our Stars*. "No thanks," I said, handing it back to him. "I'm not interested in astrology."

"That's not what it's about. Really, it's good. I promise."

I tucked it into the bag with the groceries. "Thanks."

"Do you want to mess around on the computer?"

I shook my head.

He's got a computer that he lets me use when he doesn't need it. We don't even have a television at home, never mind a computer. Our telephone is very old. You can't do anything with it but make calls.

Nobody ever calls anyway, and there's only one number in the contact list.

U Ba says we don't need a modern phone. His heart is not big enough to let the whole world in. And my heart is too young.

"How about a game of chess?" I asked.

Ko Aye Min nodded. He took the pieces out of a display case along with the new board I had given him a few weeks earlier. I made it out of teak with U Ba's help. I cut the pieces and then glued them together and painted the squares on it. His old board had been made out of plastic, and rats had chewed through it one night. He put the timer on the table while I set up the pieces. We played two quick games. He won both easily.

"What's gotten into you?" he wondered. Usually I was a good player but today my mind was elsewhere.

How gracefully did a dancer move?

How beautifully can a person's eyes flash?

What kind of laugh would warm a person's heart?

"Nothing," I replied. "Nothing."

Chapter 3

"SCARFACE. You ugly scarface."

I turned around. It was Soe Aung. He disliked me as much as I disliked him. He was a loudmouth, and everyone was afraid of him because he had two older brothers who were just as bad as he was. Now he was furious with me because I didn't let him cheat off me for the English test.

"Scarface."

"Say it again and I'll smack you." For just one moment I thought of U Ba and his rules: be friendly toward unfriendly people, he always said; they need it most of all. So much for that.

"Scarface." He made a nasty face.

I struck faster than he could duck. That slap of my hand on his cheek felt good. You could hear it halfway across the schoolyard. He tried to grab me and throw me to the ground, but I was stronger and got him in a headlock. The other boys swarmed around us. He moved in and tried to bite me and scratch me and pull my hair. We'd scuffled before, but this was more intense. Unfortunately, whenever we fought, it was only a matter of time before someone called in the afore-mentioned older brothers. I felt their powerful hands on my shoulders now. They yanked me away from him and punched me in the stomach and chest and pushed me around until I fell lengthwise into the mud and cut my lip.

One of the teachers broke it up. The three of them got off with a warning, as usual, while I had to go to the headmistress.

She was an old woman, not much bigger than me, with a cold, sharp voice. Things weren't looking good for me. I saw it in her eyes: they smoldered with rage.

"You again," she spat.

She expected me to bow my head, but I couldn't do it. I stood right up, back straight, eyes fixed on the wall in front of me.

She got her cane from the corner. I had to raise my longyi up over my hips. I closed my eyes and pictured a mango tree. Silently I counted the fruit.

One.

Two.

Three.

I winced at the first blow. Also at the second. After that I hardly felt them.

U Ba was sitting on the top step behind a curtain of water that spilled out of the overflowing gutters. Next to him was our radio. He had taken to letting the wide world into his heart once a day after all. He listened to the news from the BBC. His expression darkened every time. I wondered why he would do something every day that invariably put him in a bad mood.

He saw my wet, muddy things, my torn shirt splotched with blood, and he knew right away what had happened.

I slunk past him into the house, changed quickly into a clean longyi and a dry T-shirt, and went back out to sit with him.

My uncle turned off the radio, put his hand on my knee, and said nothing. A gecko scurried past us, followed by another. They were going into the house to get out of the rain.

"Are you hungry? Should I make us something to eat?" He didn't understand my questions. I leaned over and repeated them a little more loudly.

"No, thank you," said U Ba. "I am fine."

Fat drops splattered on the corrugated tin roof and on the leaves of the banana trees in the yard. It was hard to have a conversation above the din. That was fine by me.

"Was there trouble at school?" he asked after a long silence.

"Yeah, Soe Aung, that..." I bit my tongue and quickly added: "He called me an ugly scarface."

"Is that a reason to fight?"

"No. But if I always just put up with it, then...," I replied softly.

"Then what?"

"Then, then..." Yeah, what then? I didn't know, either. I knew only that I had been filled with rage and that I couldn't even claim to be sorry about it.

"Must I now go to the headmistress?"

"I think so. This time it's serious."

"Just as I thought," he sighed. Not another word. He pressed my knee gently, rested his head in his hands, and gazed mournfully at our saturated yard. His shoulders were stooped, his torso bent. I realized for the first time that I was bigger and stronger than he was. It had probably been that way for a while already, just without my noticing. I glanced at the withered skin on his thin upper arms, saw how his spine stood out through his T-shirt. I felt ashamed at the thought that I was stronger than the uncle who had taken care of me for as long as I could remember, who had kept me from harm. Of course I knew it wasn't my fault, that it was just the natural way of things. Still, I didn't like it.

I thought about the chess game we played last week. He had been careless and lost a knight early on. Then a pawn. The longer we played, the more clearly I could see what an effort it was for him to understand my moves. I lured him into a trap; we were just seven or eight moves from mate, and suddenly something inside me revolted. I had never beaten him. I started to make intentional mistakes. I sacrificed a bishop, then a pawn. U Ba was happy enough to take advantage. In the end I wasn't sure what bothered me more: the fact that I could have beaten him because he was getting old and forgetful or the fact that I let him win and he didn't even notice.

Now I find myself looking for excuses whenever he suggests a game.

I scooted two steps down and took his feet in my hands. The skin was rough and hard. Like the bark of a tree. His feet hurt often, and that makes it hard for him to walk. He'll just sit on the couch, then, or on the top step, and I'll massage them.

I pressed hard with my knuckles into his soles.

"That feels good."

It wasn't hard to make my uncle happy. There are many keys to happiness, he always said. Modesty is one. Gratitude is another.

His toenails were too long. I got the clipper and trimmed them for him.

U Ba lifted his head and looked me right in the eye. I got the feeling that he wanted to tell me something. I could see in his eyes that something was on his mind. They looked uneasy. A profound discomfort. They flickered slightly. There was no shine. They were flat, dark, blunt. They reminded me a little of the calluses on his feet. I could read U Ba's eyes better than anyone else's.

I felt a sense of foreboding.

"Are you going away?" I asked as casually as I could.

He pursed his lips, then nodded silently.

Once a year my uncle would visit his sister. He would be gone for several weeks, usually at the start of the dry season in the fall.

I knew he found it difficult to leave me. I didn't want to make things harder on him, so I always did my best to hide the fact that I was sad, too.

But there was also a silver lining: Whenever U Ba went away my father would come to visit.

Chapter 4

EVEN BEFORE SUNRISE I could hear my uncle banging about with pots and dishes in the kitchen. Soon enough the first twigs were crackling and the scent of burning wood was wafting through the house. He hadn't gotten up this early in months.

When I came into the living room he was cutting fresh flowers for the altar and filling a small bowl with rice as an offering for our Buddha. Next to it he put two bananas. I knew his routines inside out.

My uncle always traveled light. Everything he needed for the next few weeks fit into a green satchel of artificial leather: a spare longyi, some underwear, three shirts, and a notebook. At home he would read for several hours a day, even with his failing eyesight, but he wasn't bringing any books. That surprised me. A life without books would be pretty empty for him. He found comfort in them when he needed it, or distraction, as the case may be. He explained to me once that some of them were like compasses for him. Without them he would not be able to find his way in the world or in his own life.

We didn't talk much while he was getting ready to leave. He's like that. Even when he goes to the provincial capital, Taunggyi, for a day he gets very quiet before he leaves. He always says that the soul can travel no faster than a person can walk. It's much slower than a train or a bus. I get the feeling that he likes to give his soul a head start, maybe so that he can be a whole person when he gets to wherever he's going.

I fetched water from the barrel in the yard and heated it in a kettle over the fire so that I could wash his hair. My mind was whirling with all the things I wanted to say and ask before he left, but my mouth felt as if it had been sealed shut. In the end I said nothing.

Just before we got to the station a military jeep drove past, slammed on the brakes, and then backed up until it was even with us. In the passenger seat I recognized a soldier who had often come to our place during the past few months. The first time I saw him standing in our yard I wanted to crawl under the house and hide with the pig. He was bigger and tougher than any other man I knew, and he had an ominous look. His uniform was decorated with colorful badges and his epaulets were embroidered with three stars and two leaves each. He was no ordinary soldier but a some-kind-of-colonel-or-other, U Ba later told me.

"Where's your uncle?" he barked at me.

I backed away and pointed mutely to the house. He marched up the steps, leaving an odd smell in his wake.

Whenever he came by, U Ba would send me away. Surely I had some kind of work to do in the yard, he would say.

It was not like him to do that.

Overcome with curiosity, I had crept closer to the house, where I could eavesdrop on them through cracks in the planking. It turned out my uncle owned some fields on the outskirts of Kalaw. They had belonged to his wife, now long dead, and the soldier wanted to buy them. Immediately.

When he had gone, some of the neighbors explained that the properties were part of an area slated for new development: villas, shopping centers, a golf course, a hospital with a helicopter landing pad. U Ba had rented the fields many years ago to some farmers from a neighboring village. They paid him with a small portion of their rice harvest. He had no desire to alter anything about those arrangements, no matter how much the value of the land might have risen or might still rise, and he told the some-kind-of-colonel-or-other as much every single time he came to visit. Sometimes in more words, sometimes in fewer.

But the colonel didn't listen, or didn't understand, or understood but didn't take it seriously. At any rate, he increased his offer with every visit.

"People hear only what they want to hear," U Ba groaned after their last conversation.

Now the soldier was leaning out the car window and regarding my uncle with displeasure. "Going somewhere?"

"Yes," replied U Ba without slackening his pace so that the car had to roll along beside us. That was not very polite and very unlike him.

"Can we give you a lift?"

"That is extraordinarily kind of you. Thank you for the offer. I will be taking the train, and my nephew will accompany me to the station. Happily we are almost there."

We walked beside the jeep, our eyes fixed firmly ahead.

"Have you thought it over?" the soldier asked.

"Your offer is very generous," U Ba replied. "Indeed, it is so generous that I cannot accept it."

"You let me worry about that."

U Ba was now walking so quickly that I could hardly keep up with him. Again and again I had to break into a run.

Suddenly he stopped in his tracks so that the jeep too had to brake abruptly. "I humbly request your pardon if I have somehow given a false impression during our previous conversations," he began. "It is not my intention to leave you in the dark about my plans. As it happens, I was inclined to take you up on your offer after your last visit." U Ba paused. The soldier watched him intently.

"Since the fields in question belonged to my wife, however, I have sought the advice of Than Win. At my request and thanks to his singular abilities, he has contacted her, or her ghost, if you will, and he has asked for her permission to sell the properties in question. Sadly, my wife did not wish to grant such permission. She was even, if I may say so, incensed by the very request. I cannot go against her wishes on this matter, as I am sure you will understand. It is out of my hands."

I looked into the some-kind-of-colonel-or-other's eyes and turned away aghast. My uncle says that some people's hearts are full of vinegar.

"I'm surprised that you believe in ghosts, U Ba." The scorn in his voice. Even I couldn't miss it.

"Don't we all?" my uncle countered. "Each in our own way."

The soldier replied with a short, angry snort. "Have you stopped to consider what all that money could buy for your nephew?" When we did not react, he continued: "I'm afraid you're making a big mistake. You won't get a better price."

"I know, I know." He leaned toward the window as if confiding in the some-kind-of-colonel-or-other. "I tried to explain that to my wife." He sighed deeply. "To my regret, it did nothing to persuade her. Now, if you will excuse me."

With these words my uncle set off again while I hurried behind.

The jeep rolled along beside us for another few yards. I felt quite hot from the rage in the soldier's eyes. Then the motor roared and the car tore away.

As soon as he was out of sight, we slackened our pace again.

"What a patient man," U Ba said softly, as if to himself.

"He didn't look so patient just now," I objected.

"You know, Bo Bo, it is not so long ago that he would not have offered any money for the property."

"What would he have offered?"

"Nothing. He would have taken it."

The train was already waiting at the station. Merchants were hawking tea or coffee in plastic bags. Kids I knew from school were carrying baskets of bananas, apples, or pastries on their heads. Stray dogs were rummaging through the scraps. Suitcases, boxes, and babies were handed through the windows. We got on board and I tried to find a place for U Ba to sit. It was the time of the Thadin Kyut festival, so the cars were all packed. There were passengers sitting in the aisles, between the seats, in open doors. The son of a neighbor spotted us, and he offered U Ba his seat. My uncle gratefully accepted. I stood beside him for a while, saying nothing.

With a mighty jolt the train lurched forward. Some of the vendors jumped off; others jumped on.

U Ba pressed my hand without a word. That was our sign. But today I was finding it hard to leave him. When I finally started to pull away I felt how he clung to me.

Kalaw was already behind us by the time we both managed to let go. I climbed my way to the door over baskets of cauliflowers, potatoes, carrots, and chickens. I turned to look back. U Ba had turned his head to the side and was staring out the window.

I waited.

He didn't move.

I waited.

Still he didn't move.

I climbed to the lowest step and jumped off. I ran beside the train for several yards, not letting it out of my sight. When it disappeared around the next bend I turned around and headed back to Kalaw. I liked walking between the rails and jumping from tie to tie.

Grown-ups, I thought, are such a puzzle.

Chapter 5

WHILE U BA IS AWAY, everything is different.

Our house is suddenly bigger.

The nights are colder. And darker.

The rain is louder.

The quiet quieter.

The emptiness emptier.

And even though I was really looking forward to seeing my father, the quiet got quieter and the emptiness emptier with each hour my uncle was away.

It sounds strange, but it's true.

One time I asked U Ba if he felt the same way whenever I was gone.

He thought about it for a minute. "No," he declared. "You are never gone for more than a few hours." He could see that I was disappointed, so he added: "But of course I miss you, and if you were ever away for longer, I would feel exactly as you do."

Maybe I just don't like to be alone.

From outside I could hear the voices of the kids in the neighboring yards and houses. Some of the boys were playing chinlone. The sound of their laughter didn't make anything easier.

I turned on U Ba's old cassette player. True, it warbled, and we had only three cassettes of piano music, but it was still better than the voices outside and the silence in the house.

I cleaned the hearth, swept the kitchen and bedrooms, took the Buddha from the altar and wiped it thoroughly with a damp cloth. While I was dusting the shelves I came across Ko Aye Min's book. I sat on the sofa and started to read it. After just a few pages I closed it again. My mind was elsewhere, and if you're too distracted to follow a story, then you have no right to keep reading, says U Ba.

The first day was always the worst.

My scar felt tighter than it had for weeks.

I walked back and forth in the house and started to count.

One-two-three-four-five . . .

At a hundred I was calming down and by five hundred I was feeling better.

I looked around our living room with its bookshelves that reached from floor to ceiling. We owned more books than the bookstore that opened a few months ago down on the main street. They were spilling out of the shelves. They stood in piles on the floor, next to the couch, at the foot of the bed.

Many of them were in terrible condition, and U Ba had taken it upon himself to restore them. When I was younger

I used to spend entire evenings lying on the couch and watching him work until I fell asleep. It typically took two or three months to finish a single book, sometimes more, depending on how thick or thin it was and what condition it was in. It had been a long time since I'd seen him restoring a book. His eyesight was failing and his hands were getting shaky. He complained that restoring books was now more tedious than ever.

I know how much that bothered him. In his opinion we were the richest people in Kalaw, if not in the entire Shan State. We were surrounded by wisdom and knowledge, by beauty and imagination. Who else could make such a claim?

Maybe it would be a nice surprise for him if I carried on his work in his absence. I pulled the cardboard box with the tools off one of the shelves. It contained a little jar full of tiny pieces of white paper, another jar of grayish glue, a pair of tweezers, and several black pens. I set the things on the table, grabbed a random old book, and opened it. *The Stranger* by Albert Camus. I liked the title, and it was a nice, slender volume. Worms, moths, termites, and humidity had all taken their toll on the yellowed paper. There was hardly a legible sentence in the first few pages.

With the tweezers I delicately took a bit of paper, dipped it in the glue, and placed it over one of the holes, then pressed it with my index finger. As soon as the glue was dry, I traced the letters carefully with a fine-tipped pen. I turned "S an er" into "Stranger." "M th r" was restored to "Mother." With some effort I managed to convert "c dol n s" into "condolences."

It turned out to be harder than I expected. I kept running into words or phrases I didn't know and whose spelling and meaning I had to look up in our old edition of the *Encyclopædia Britannica*.

"Casket," for instance. Or "private life." There was no word for that in Burmese.

Chapter 6

"*MUCH MONEY*, not *many money*," I whispered. Ko Thein Aung, who was sitting next to me, just looked at me.

"What did you say?" he asked softly.

"It should be *much money*, not *many money*," I repeated.

He chuckled while the class had to repeat five times in unison: "I do not have many money."

I sighed, said nothing, and stared out the window. It was raining. I tried counting the drops that splashed onto the window in front of me. That was just as pointless as this English lesson.

"*Three people*, not *peoples*." This time I said it so loudly that nearly everyone had heard. The room suddenly went quiet. Everyone was watching Daw Myint Naing, our teacher. It had just slipped out. Not on purpose. Like a candy that drops out of your mouth by accident.

"What did you say?" She walked swiftly from her desk right over to me. She was holding a long wooden ruler, the kind that would leave red welts on your hands.

"Nothing," I replied.

"You're lying. I heard it clearly."

So why are you asking me, I wanted to answer, but I was in enough trouble already.

"What did you say?" she repeated in a sharp tone.

I suppressed a quiet groan. "I was just talking to myself."

"Bo Bo, I'm asking you for the last time," she hissed.

"I said that there can be no plural of *people* because it's already a plural. The correct form is *three people*, not *peoples*."

Daw Myint Naing can be strict. She can be unfair. She can hit your fingers so hard that they bleed. She can't speak English.

I can, though, and she has a problem with that. U Ba speaks only English with me, so I'm as comfortable in that language as in Burmese. I had to promise the headmistress I wouldn't correct my English teachers in front of the class. To save my corrections for private conversations after the class. Otherwise the other students might lose respect for the teachers. I could understand that, but sometimes temptation got the better of me. Especially with Daw Myint Naing. She's the wife of an officer stationed in Kalaw, and her youngest son is in my grade. He's pretty much an idiot with the brain of a crab. She never calls on him in class because she knows he can't answer her questions. But he still gets top marks on all his homework and tests. On his report cards, too, just like me. It annoys me.

She also teaches math and physics, and it's exactly the same.

Apparently his older sisters enjoyed a similar arrangement.

Her eyes glimmered with rage. "How often have I told you not to interrupt the lesson?" She smacked the table in front of me with the ruler. For some reason or other, I'm the only one in the class whom she hasn't had the courage to hit.

"Apologize."

I turned my head to the side without a word and stared out the window.

"Out. This instant."

I went and stood outside the door. To be honest, it was a place I spent a lot of time, and not only during Daw Myint Naing's lessons. Most of the teachers didn't like me. I'm not sure why. They said I was cheeky. I talked too much in class. I distracted the other kids and gave them silly ideas. Of course that was nonsense. The worst I ever did was say the right answers out loud. But as soon as I contradicted the teachers, it just made them angrier. When I was bored I would fold my arms on the desk, put my head down, and try to sleep. They didn't like that, either.

Since first grade my uncle had been giving me instruction in the afternoon and on weekends. He thinks I'm not learning anything at school. As a result I am by far the best student in my grade and the only one who does not take expensive private lessons from the teachers outside of school.

Maybe U Ba is right that that's the reason they don't like me.

Chapter 7

WITHIN TWO DAYS OF U BA'S DEPARTURE my father generally shows up at our door. It'll be in the afternoon if he has taken the train via Thazi. Otherwise, when he takes the bus directly from Yangon, it'll be first thing in the morning. He spends a few weeks with me, and U Ba returns shortly before my father's departure.

Now three days had gone by since my uncle had left, and still there was no sign of my father.

I tried not to wait too much for him, but it's not easy when you're really looking forward to someone's arrival.

Ko Aye Min had invited me to stay with him until my father arrived. That was nice of him, but I wasn't interested.

I was afraid I would miss him. Of course that was silly, because he would be staying longer than just one day. But still. I wanted to be there when my father arrived.

On the fourth day I got up before dawn and rode my bike in the dark to the bus stop on the main road that connects us to the rest of the world.

It was drizzling. By the time I got into town I was cold and wet. I sat down in the only teahouse that was open at that hour. It was diagonally across from the bus stop, and it was packed. Some of the customers were watching a Korean soap opera; others were busy on their phones. The waiter knew me. He was a friend's daughter's boyfriend, and when he saw me soaked to the skin like that he quietly put a cup of warm water and plate of sunflower seeds in front of me.

The bus was late. I got more and more restless with each passing minute.

I looked at the seeds.

One.

Two.

Three.

Seventeen.

Forty-five.

Sixty.

One hundred eleven . . .

The sun was just coming up when the bus came around the corner. With my heart pounding I watched to see who would get off.

Three young monks.

A mother with a sleeping child in her arms.

A fat lady who could barely make it down the steps and who had more luggage than she could carry.

A man who tripped while climbing down because he was looking at his phone.

Two weary tourists with backpacks and dyed hair. They looked around disoriented, as if they'd taken a wrong turn.

A little boy with his father. But not mine.

I walked up and down both sides of the bus. Behind big tinted windows were sleeping travelers, their cheeks pressed against the glass. I couldn't really make out their faces so I slipped onto the bus, but he wasn't there among the sleepers, either.

The way back home felt very long.

Around noon I went to the station. The train had arrived a few minutes early and the platform had already cleared out. Disappointed, I turned to go.

"Bo Bo?"

I knew that voice instantly, even if I hadn't heard it all that often over the course of my life. At least not as often as I would have liked.

It was darker than U Ba's. Stronger, but still soft and inviting.

I turned around. There he stood, looking just as I remembered him. Tall and lean with long, muscular arms and legs. He'd grown out his short hair, though, and put it into a kind of ponytail, a lot of which had turned gray. He wore a green longyi, a red T-shirt, worn-out flip-flops, and a new red bracelet on one of his wrists. I remembered the birthmark under his chin and the missing finger on his right hand. No scar on his cheek, but one on his upper arm.

He had an old brown satchel slung over his shoulder and a guitar on his back. I didn't know he played guitar.

"Hello," he said.

"Hello." What was I supposed to do with all the other things I wanted to say? I felt as if I would explode any minute now.

"How's it going?"

"Good. Very good." In my excitement I forgot to ask him how *he* was doing.

"I've missed you," he said.

We stood there looking at each other without another word. My father is a very quiet person. At least when we're together. I don't really know him in any other context. We can spend a whole day together without talking much. That suits me just fine.

"Thanks for coming to meet me," he said at last. "That's very kind of you."

And then finally he put his arms around me. He picked me up and kissed my cheeks and forehead and gave me a big hug. I buried my face in his hair. I could smell my mother in his hair. Or maybe that was just my imagination. I didn't actually know what she smelled like. Maybe it was just the smell of a long train ride still clinging to him. He took a few steps and put me back down.

"You've changed." He looked me up and down. "You've gotten heavier. And taller. It won't be long before you're taller than I am."

"I don't think so." Try as I might, I couldn't imagine being taller than him.

He grinned.

Sometimes I wasn't sure what to make of the things he said. Probably because we saw so little of each other.

Or maybe because I found his eyes harder to read than anyone else's.

They're dark brown, almost black, and very, very big. They're the biggest I've ever seen. Even so, they reveal nothing to me. When he looks at me I lose myself in his gaze. There is so much peace and breadth in them that I can't manage to focus on anything, no matter how I try. It feels a little bit as if I'm lying in a meadow staring into a deep black night sky full of twinkling stars.

We set off. I took his hand. It was so much bigger and stronger than U Ba's or mine. He squeezed it gently, and I wished I could keep the feel of that single touch with me forever.

I needed to move. I ran a few meters ahead, waited, spun around, and sprinted back to him, jumping over puddles along the way. He watched me and laughed a little wearily. The journey must have been exhausting.

The last time he was here I had wanted to ask him about Mama. I put it off until the day he left, and then at the last minute I had lost my courage. I had sworn to myself that I would ask him this time, but I already suspected that I would chicken out when it came down to it.

Consider carefully which stone you would like to turn, my uncle had always cautioned me.

You may not always find a butterfly.

Chapter 8

MY FATHER has a way with animals. I don't know anyone else who can relate to them the way he does. Especially to chickens. Unbelievable, really. The moment we entered the yard they all came running, big and small, white and brown. As if they all remembered him. He knelt down and reached out toward them. They approached him without fear, pecked at his hand, even let him pet them. He made some strange noises, and some of them started clucking loudly.

I had to laugh. "You speak their language."

"Yes. I'm a chicken whisperer." He smirked. "Aren't you?"

"No." I rolled my eyes. "No one speaks animal languages."

"Are you sure?" He stood up again. "There was a time when my best friends were a dozen chickens."

"How can you be friends with chickens?" I figured he was testing me again. My father told lots of stories while visiting me. Some true, some invented, and he got a kick out of watching me try to figure out which was which.

"You can make friends with a dog. Or a cat. But a chicken?"

"What if you're all alone and have no one else to turn to?"

I knew what it meant to be alone, I thought. There were days when I felt terribly lonely, but never so lonely that I would make friends with a chicken.

My father turned aside. Followed by some of the hens, he walked the length of the yard, looking everything over. He had made a habit of fixing things on the house whenever he visited. Last year he had rebuilt the henhouse. The year before that he had fixed the leaky roof and the porch steps. His gaze settled on the broken gutters that U Ba and I had wired to the roof as a stopgap. From there a rickety conglomeration of blue plastic tubes led to two barrels, where we were trying to collect rainwater. Not very successfully. Even with the heavy rains they were only half full. That was a hardship for us, because the tap water was available only every few days, if at all. We depended on the barrels. At this point they were so leaky that we found ourselves, buckets in hand, relying frequently upon our neighbors' generosity.

We climbed the steps into the house. My father put his bag and his guitar in the bedroom. He looked tired, and maybe also a little worried.

"Are you hungry?" I asked in order to turn his mind to other thoughts.

"Yes."

"Do you want to cook something together?"

"Absolutely."

One of my father's favorite dishes is mohinga, a fish soup, and I had bought the ingredients for it the day after U Ba left. We started with a ready-made paste, but we would spice it up with touches of our own.

I peeled an onion, and when my eyes started to water, my father jumped in for me. He peeled a second onion and some garlic, chopped a stalk of lemongrass into fine pieces, and grated some fresh ginger.

I heated some oil in a pan and tipped in the ingredients. I added a spoonful of chili powder and turmeric and stirred it until the onions were translucent. We mixed the paste and a handful of rice flour with the water, dumped it in the pan, and let it all simmer until the sauce started to thicken. It smelled delicious, and I could hear my father's stomach growling. He tasted it now and then and added more chili. We both liked it hot.

My father put on some rice noodles. Half an hour later we were sitting on the couch eating our soup. His slurping was louder even than mine.

Neither of us had said a word the whole time. Our eyes would meet now and then and he would flash me a smile. That was enough for me.

Like I said, my father is a quiet person. He's not the type to ask a lot of questions, either. As I see it, he often gets his point across without words.

After dinner he lit a cheroot. When he was done with it, he rummaged through his bag until he produced a little cardboard box. "I brought something for you," he said, handing it to me.

My father had brought me some kind of present every year. So far it had always been a secondhand book. In this little box you could barely have fit a little scroll. I opened it, eager to see what it was. A harmonica. I looked it over carefully. It seemed to have been used. I blew into it gingerly. Not a sound.

"Blow harder," my father encouraged me.

I took a deep breath and blew with all my might, but only for a second. It sounded dreadful. Loud, metallic, and scratchy, as if it was broken.

He laughed and took it from me. Holding it between his thumb and forefinger, he put it so far between his lips that it looked as if he wanted to bite it. He closed his eyes and started to play.

With the very first note something magical happened. My father transformed before my eyes. I could barely recognize him. He bounced first one leg, then the other. Soon his whole body was keeping time as he disappeared into the music. He held the harmonica delicately in both hands, and I was blown away by the sounds he got out of that thing. Nothing metallic or scratchy. I couldn't help but move with the rhythm of the music. It was not a song I knew, but I immediately liked the tone and the melody. I would have liked to drum on the table with a stick. The whole house rang with the music.

When he was done he dried it off and handed it back to me. "Try it again. It's really not that hard."

"Where did you learn to play like that?" I wondered.

"I taught myself," he said. "If you like, I can get you started. It won't be long before we're playing together, you on harmonica, me on guitar. What do you think?"

I nodded, too happy for words.

Chapter 9

OVER THE NEXT TWO WEEKS time passed either much too quickly or much too slowly. At school it was as if time stood still. The lessons were more boring than usual, and they seemed to go on forever. By the second class I was already counting the minutes until three-thirty.

I thought about skipping school and forging my uncle's signature on a permission slip. I sometimes did that when U Ba was around. Then I'd go fishing or play around on Ko Aye Min's computer. But the whole point was to spend the day with my father, and he would never have allowed me to stay with him instead of going to school.

It made me miserable as I sat there in class to think about all the things I could have been doing with him. And to think about how each day brought his return to Yangon one day closer. The only thing that helped was counting.

One-two-three-four-five . . .

The minute school was out I would ride home by the fastest route. And so began the part of the day when time would pass too quickly. I would be out of breath by the time I got home. My father would be sitting on the roof fixing the gutters, or he would be digging a trench by the henhouse. He had somehow gotten his hands on a cement mixer, some shovels, bags of cement, and a big pile of bricks. He had decided to build us a water tank. I helped as much as I could. We mixed cement and poured the foundation. I would sort the stones and hand them to him. Two neighbors came by at some point to offer their help. My father thanked them for the offer but said that we would be fine. I'm not sure why he said that. We could have used the help. Maybe he's one of those people who find it difficult to accept generosity.

He worked quickly and skillfully, and we really did make a great team. Within a few days we had finished the first of two tanks.

Early in the evening we would cook together, and after dinner we would play music.

He had brought an odd metal bracket of some kind with him. He could attach the harmonica to it and hang it around his neck so that he could play both guitar and harmonica at the same time.

My father has a beautiful voice. He would always start things off by singing a couple of songs for me. There was one I especially liked. It started with a guitar solo followed by harmonica. I learned the lyrics by heart after hearing it a few times:

"I want to live, I want to give," my father sang. "I've been a miner for a heart of gold ... that keep me searching for a heart of gold ... and I'm getting old ..."

Watching my father sitting on the couch and singing like that, I thought to myself: He's the one with the heart of gold.

Him and U Ba.

And of course my mother, too.

We had expected to spend our weekends hiking and swimming, but nothing ever became of that. We just wanted to make music.

He was right. It was not as hard to learn harmonica as I had originally thought. By the end of the first day I could play scales both in- and exhaling.

I spent every free minute practicing and ended up forging absence notes for school after all. Instead of going to class I would ride out toward the reservoir and spend the morning in the woods with my harmonica. I figured the teachers were just as glad not to see me as I was not to see them.

Some days I would go first to Ko Aye Min's place to watch videos on his computer in which a young man with long hair explained step-by-step how his audience could learn to play harmonica. He was a good teacher.

Two weeks later we played our first father-son duet.

Chapter 10

MY FATHER THOUGHT it was all his fault. I thought both of us ought to have been paying closer attention.

While I was getting bored standing in the corridor at school, he had started excavating the ditch for the second water tank. When it started to rain he covered it with a tarp. When I came home in the afternoon I didn't notice the ditch. I stepped into it and twisted my left ankle. Now it looked as if someone had stuffed a golf ball under my skin. Walking was not an option. That was fine by me. It meant I had more time to play harmonica and I could let my father do the cooking.

The next morning the swelling had gone down and the pain had subsided, but every step was painful and I had quite a limp. I wasn't going to make it to school, even on my bike.

"I'll carry you," said my father.

"How?"

"On my back."

I liked the idea. When it came time to go, he squatted down in front of me. I climbed onto his back, wrapping my legs around his waist and my arms around his shoulders. He put his arms behind him to support me better.

"I'm not too heavy?"

"Not at all. I've got this."

Off we went. Just a few steps later he nearly tripped over a root, but he might have been pretending, just to make me jump. I declared he was my horse, and he galloped down the street. After a hundred meters he had to stop to catch his breath. Even my "Giddyup, old nag!" took a while to get him trotting again.

We were halfway there when, for a laugh, I put my hands over his eyes. "Hey, what are you doing? I can't see," he shouted, and laughed.

"You don't need to," I answered. "You've got me. I'll direct you."

He stopped short.

"What? Why'd you stop?" I wondered aloud.

"Did U Ba tell you anything?"

"What would he have told me?"

"The story of your grandfather."

"No. What about him?"

My father said nothing.

"Am I too heavy after all?"

"No, not at all."

"So what is it?"

"Nothing," he answered, and held me tightly with his arms behind his back. "All set."

Just before we got to the school he took another look at my foot and decided it would be better to have a doctor examine it after all.

On the way there we stopped in at the Mya Myint Moe Teahouse. We sat on the covered terrace. My father ordered tea and a soda for me. The waitress put fresh pastries on the table and came right back with the drinks. My father took two chopsticks and drummed lightly on the table. It sounded good, so I took a pair and chimed in. We used the glass and the bottle and the plate of pastries, and it was as if he was playing a drum kit. "I want to live, I want to give," he sang softly.

Some of the guests looked at us annoyed. Others nodded encouragingly.

Suddenly he winced. From where he was sitting he had a view of the street. He must have seen something strange behind me. He lowered the chopsticks and his eyes went wide. For one brief moment I could recognize something in him. As if a door had opened and then immediately slammed shut.

Was it fear? Anger?

I turned around but I couldn't see anything out of the ordinary. Two women were standing in front of the teahouse chatting while balancing their groceries on their heads. Next to them was a military jeep. Four soldiers had stepped out. They approached us and sat down at the next table. My father was following their every step.

"What's wrong, Papa?"

He hadn't heard my question.

"Papa!?"

He was still staring at the soldiers, who weren't paying any further attention to us. Something was churning inside him. He looked as if he might stand up and walk over to them at any moment. I had the feeling that his whole body was quivering slightly. It was gradually starting to frighten me.

"My foot hurts," I said, hoping to distract him.

No reaction.

"Really, my foot hurts," I repeated, a little louder this time and more defiant.

He turned to me, took out a thousand-kyat note, set it on the table, and stood up with a jolt. His stool fell over. The soldiers scowled at us. We hadn't even touched our drinks yet.

"Let's go," my father commanded.

He strode quickly out of the teahouse. I followed him, limping, into the street. Only then did it occur to him that I couldn't really walk, and he took me on his back again.

"Did you know those soldiers?" I asked once we were out of earshot.

"One of them."

"Where from?"

There's more than one reason to keep silent, I had learned from U Ba.

Fear is one. Or shame. Ignorance. Cowardice. Sometimes you're trying to punish the person you're with. There's also silent happiness. Quiet joy.

I didn't know why my father wouldn't talk now, but I knew one thing: I would not get any answer from him.

The doctor gave us some ointment and a bandage that we were supposed to change twice a day. Unfortunately, the golf ball cleared up in just a few days, and I was able to walk as if nothing had happened.

We never said another word about the soldiers in the teahouse.

Chapter 11

MY FATHER'S VOICE. It was coming from the living room. He was talking softly, almost in a whisper. I figured U Ba had come back early, and I scrambled out of bed to go say hello.

My father was sitting on the couch with his back to me, and he didn't notice me. He had lit a candle and was smoking a cheroot. There was no sign of my uncle.

He was on the phone. His voice sounded strained and breathless. Whatever he was saying was not meant for my ears. For just a minute I couldn't resist the temptation to listen in. All I got was fragments, little pieces of words, but it was enough to tip me off that something must have happened in Yangon. I tiptoed back to bed.

I lay there picturing my mother to myself. I did that often when I couldn't sleep: She is tall and slender and she moves as gracefully as U Ba had claimed. Her hair is black and a little curly and reaches far down her back. Or she has it up in a bun held together by a chopstick. And she's tucked a flower into it, the way many women at the market do. Sometimes it's a white frangipani, sometimes a red hibiscus.

When she calls me, her voice sounds young and bright, as if she were my big sister.

I see her face: Her eyes are radiant like no one else's I've ever seen. And her smile really would warm your heart.

A scar runs across her left cheek, dark red, as wide as a matchstick. It reaches from the corner of her mouth almost to her ear. Even so, I think my mother is beautiful.

We look a lot alike. So much alike that everyone says I'm the spitting image of her when they see us standing side by side.

I like that.

Eventually my father crawled back into bed. His breathing was coming shallow and quick. Like every other evening, I turned toward him and took his hand. He turned toward me, too, so that our noses were nearly touching. The stale smoke of the cheroot still clung to his hair. I could feel his warm breath on my skin, and I had the impression that it smelled differently than it had earlier in the evening. Sourish and sharp, almost a bit bitter.

"Papa?" I asked, as if needing to confirm that he was the one lying next to me.

He didn't answer.

"Papa?" I repeated.

"What is it?"

Were you talking to Mama on the phone? I wanted to ask. Why did your voice sound so strange? Is she not feeling well? Did she ask about me?

I didn't dare. I was too afraid of what he might say. I knew that she wasn't feeling well. Had things gotten worse? Was she not asking about me because she wasn't interested? Or, and this was my greatest fear: He hadn't been talking to her at all, but to someone else. He had a new wife. No one could talk to my mother anymore because she was dead. I was so afraid of that sentence that I couldn't bring myself to ask a single question.

"What is it?" he asked again.

"I . . . I . . . I'm not tired anymore."

"It's the middle of the night. Go back to sleep."

He twisted this way and that and had as much trouble sleeping as I did. Eventually he settled down, and pretty soon he was snoring.

I waited for a while, then got back out of bed and went into the living room. My father had left his phone lying on the table. Before I could think better of it, I took it and looked at the incoming and outgoing calls. Two calls just before midnight, another at 12:37 a.m. All the same number, not one I recognized, but that didn't mean anything, since the only numbers I knew were Ko Aye Min's and my uncle's.

I hesitated only briefly, then pressed the button to return the call. There was crackling on the line, then it started to ring. I felt dizzy and cold. My heart was pounding. I felt it in my whole chest, and I could hardly breathe.

I pressed the phone to my ear and waited. It felt as if the silences between rings were getting longer and longer.

Just as I was about to hang up, a woman's voice, dark and tired, answered: "Hello?"

I stared in disbelief at the device in my hand. Was I really on the line with my mother?

I wanted so badly to say something, but I didn't know what.

"Who's there?" It didn't sound like her. More like a growl.

It took all my courage. "Bo Bo," I whispered. "It's Bo Bo."

Silence.

The woman on the other end was breathing heavily. After an eternity she asked: "Who?"

"Bo Bo."

Silence. My ears started to ring.

"Bo Bo?"

"Yes." I held my breath and didn't dare to move.

"I . . . I . . . I don't know." Her voice trailed off into a question, as if she were trying to remember something.

"From Kalaw," I cried. "Bo Bo and U Ba."

She hung up.

I clenched the phone with both hands. Had she forgotten who I was? Like Daw Hnin Aye's grandmother, who couldn't remember anything anymore? Who poured water into the fire and couldn't find the way back home? Who asked her grandchildren every morning who they were?

No. It wasn't my mother's voice.

It was the voice of an old, sick woman.

The voice of a stranger.

And then the phone rang.

Once.

Twice.

I didn't want my father to wake up, so I turned down the volume.

The vibration in my hand went right through my entire body. It got more intense with each ring.

Eventually it stopped, then started right back up again.

I sat petrified on the couch, not knowing what to do. When it started to vibrate again, I crawled back into bed.

It didn't take long for me to fall asleep.

That afternoon my father was waiting for me in front of the school. I almost didn't notice him. There was always a big rush of people at the end of the school day. A policeman with a whistle was directing traffic. Army jeeps picking up officers' children clogged the street. Other parents on mopeds ducked in between them. Mothers with umbrellas stood waiting for their little ones.

My father was on the other side of the street in the shade of a bougainvillea. He waved to me when our eyes met. I plowed my way past the other children and ran to him.

"What would you say to a fresh sugarcane juice?" He knew it was my favorite. "Or maybe an ice cream?"

We went to the ice cream stand. There were two flavors: green tea and papaya, exactly the two that I didn't like.

My father took my hand and we walked to a wooden shack near the market, where we took a seat beneath a plastic tarp. It was looking like rain.

The juice was delicious, cool and not too sweet. I drank it in tiny sips to make it last as long as possible.

My father lit a cheroot and kept a close eye on me. "I talked with Mama on the phone," he said suddenly.

My stomach flinched, as if one of the boys on the play-ground had rammed an elbow into it. It hurt so badly that I leaned forward and groaned softly.

Had the strange woman on the phone told him that someone had called her from his phone?

I did not want to hear anything about her. Not one word.

"What's wrong?" he asked worriedly.

"I've got a bit of a stomachache," I lied. "Nothing too bad."

"She sends her love."

"Who?"

"Your mother."

I stared at him point-blank and tried to read his eyes. As if I had only to fix my eyes on him long enough in order to see what was going on inside him. That was impudent of me, but I couldn't do anything else. He did not turn away from my gaze. Suddenly his eyes flashed a little. My father raised his eyebrows and furrowed his forehead.

"What's going on with you?" he asked, and I heard the surprise in his voice. Or was it embarrassment? Insecurity, because he was lying?

The thunder crashed so loudly that I flinched, and then came the rain. Just a few drops at first.

"Nothing."

"Why are you looking at me like that?"

"How . . . how am I looking at you?" I asked, lowering my head.

"As if I were some stranger you were afraid of."

I had no idea what to say.

He was waiting for an answer. "Bo Bo," he said at last. He put his hand under my chin and lifted it gently so that our eyes met again.

"Bo Bo," he started again. "The news isn't good. Mama needs me. I've got to catch the bus back to Yangon this evening. I am really truly sorry."

I jerked my head away. He lowered his hand.

I didn't care what was going on inside him. Whether he was truly sorry or not. Whether he was telling the truth or lying. Whether it was difficult for him. I didn't want to know anything about it.

Most of all I just wanted to scream.

To kick my feet.

To punch him.

He hadn't even been here for three weeks. We wanted to finish the second water tank together. We wanted to make more music together. Whittling. Cooking. We still wanted to go hiking and swimming.

"Do you want another juice?" he asked quietly.

"No," I answered loudly and rudely, and it sounded completely different from how I really felt. Or maybe it didn't.

"Can't I come with you?" I had never dared to ask that question.

He looked at me, surprised. "No, it's out of the question."

"Please."

"It's impossible."

"Why can't I?"

"Because it's impossible. It's too soon for that."

"But why—"

"Because I said so," he interrupted bluntly.

"Just for a few days."

"No. Period. That's enough lip. I don't want to hear another word, you understand?"

My father had never spoken to me like that.

The rain was coming down in torrents now. The water was streaming off the tarp, but I didn't care. I stood up and walked along the street toward the train station. Within just a few steps my shirt, longyi, and school bag were completely drenched. My right flip-flop stuck in the mud. I just kept walking.

"Bo Bo, wait," I heard my father calling.

I picked up my pace.

"Wait right there."

A moped approached us. It drove through a puddle right next to me, splashing mud all over my white shirt.

"Wait for me."

I was done waiting. It was time for him just to stay with me.

The tears on my cheeks mingled with the raindrops. I didn't care.

My father had nearly caught up to me. I started to run. I ran as fast as I could. Past the train station. Across the tracks. Up the mountain. I was indifferent to the rain or the pain in my chest or the blood or the scrapes on my feet.

When I finally got home I got the harmonica from my room and put it on the table.

A few minutes later my father stood dripping and panting in the doorway. In one hand he held my shoe.

"You may as well take that harmonica with you," I said pointing to his gift. "I don't want it anymore."

Chapter 12

I SPENT THE NEXT FEW DAYS at Ko Aye Min's place. In the evening we sat in his hut, and I told him about the woman on the phone and my father's hasty departure.

He took it all in without a word. From time to time he would wrinkle his brow, sigh, or bite his lip. When I was done he thought about it long and hard before saying a word.

"He must have had his reasons," he decided in the end.

I scowled at him. That was not what I had been wanting to hear. Not at all. Though when I think about it carefully, I'm not sure what I would have wanted him to say.

Poor Bo Bo?

No. I was not looking for pity.

How rotten of your father to take off like that. How can he leave you here all by yourself?

Not that either. If Ko Aye Min had criticized my father, I would have risen to his defense. I was all twisted up inside, and I had no idea who could sort me out again. I certainly couldn't.

He must have had his reasons.

The longer I thought about that sentence, the more hopeless I felt.

His reasons. Of course he had his reasons. If only someone could explain them to me.

Next morning I forged an excuse for myself and sent it to school with Ko Thu Riya. He was the best friend I had in my class; he wouldn't rat me out.

Ko Aye Min left the house early. He had to meet a group of tourists at the airport in Heho and take them to their hotel on Inle Lake. I spent hours in his office in front of the computer, played a few games of chess with a kid from America, lost every single one, poked around halfheartedly in the bookshelves, watched a YouTube video of all Cristiano Ronaldo's most beautiful goals. When I got bored of that I looked for videos of penguins and parrots, my favorite animals, but they didn't hold my interest long, either.

I sat under the canopy outside the door and waited without having any idea what I was even waiting for. When it started to drizzle I watched the rain raining.

Ko Aye Min returned in the afternoon and gave me a little package wrapped in old newspaper. "I brought something for you."

I could feel right away what it was and had no desire to unwrap it.

"Don't you want to open it?" There was a hint of disappointment in his voice.

"Of course." I tore open the paper. A shiny new harmonica flashed in the light.

I swallowed. It was such a kind thought, but that just made it worse.

"Thanks." For his sake I put it to my lips and blew into it.

It sounded like my father.

It sounded awful.

"It sounds good," he said happily. "Can you play a song for me?"

"Not yet, but soon," I fibbed, and I was ashamed of myself for being such an ingrate.

That evening he invited me to join him and his girlfriend, Ma Ei, at the Red House for dinner. There was pizza and noodles and a jasmine-white cheese called "mozzarella" or something like that, served with raw tomatoes and olive oil. That seemed really odd to me. The only thing I knew about olive oil was that some girls rubbed it into their hair to make it shinier. I always ordered spaghetti with spicy tomato sauce and hoped that it wasn't prepared with olive oil.

I had met Ma Ei once before at Ko Aye Min's office. She was short, hardly taller than me, and she had asked me to teach her chess. She said Ko Aye Min was too strict a teacher. She was from Kalaw, and she worked with her younger sister at their mother's restaurant near the market.

Her hair was so long that it reached nearly to her hips. But the most striking thing about her was her eyes. So round, and not brown, but bluish gray.

Ma Ei was delighted to see us. She was kind of wound up for the first few minutes, but it passed quickly. She asked what my favorite subjects were in school, how my uncle was doing, what it was like living with just him, the chickens, and a pig. She really listened to my answers, and when I told her she had very beautiful eyes she laughed and stroked my hand.

No one had ever done that in quite that way.

"You're sweet."

No one had ever said that to me, either.

It was clear to see that she really liked Ko Aye Min. In her eyes I could see a warm glow, a joy, even admiration. But there was something else lurking there, too. I hadn't noticed it right away because I had let her smile and her questions distract me. The longer we talked, the more time the three of us sat at the table, the more clearly I could see it.

As if a fog were slowly lifting from her eyes. I just needed to be patient.

A lot of people were like that, I thought: they could laugh, I mean really laugh, with their mouth and their cheeks, their whole face, and their eyes would beam, yet still there was some profound heaviness in their heart.

Once I had noticed it with Ma Ei it was plain to see, and it did not go away the whole evening long.

Just before we left, Ko Aye Min had gone to the counter to ask about something and to pay, our eyes met again. I saw in that moment that she understood that I had discovered what was hidden behind her gentle smile.

She didn't say anything.

Instead, for the second time that evening, she gently stroked my hand.

The next day, suddenly, there was U Ba standing in the doorway. I don't think I had ever been happier to see him.

"Here you are! No one at school could tell me where you were. The teachers were astonished. They insisted that I had written a note to excuse your absence..."

For a minute I got scared that he would be mad at me. "I'm sorry, I..." I stammered, embarrassed.

"It required all my powers of imagination to explain plausibly that I nevertheless did not know where you were..."

A smile flashed across his face, and I knew that he was not angry. I ran to him, and he took me in his arms.

"Have you been home long?" I asked.

"No, just since this morning. I took the bus, and I needed to catch up on some sleep."

I hugged him long and tight.

"Will you come home with me?"

"Of course. I was just waiting for you. The house was so big without you or Papa..."

I locked up Ko Aye Min's office and left the key under the mat. We strolled down the road. U Ba linked arms with me. At the market we bought a bunch of flowers for the altar, soft bread, and instant coffee for my uncle's breakfast, and eggs, rice, onions, and vegetables for dinner.

Chapter 13

MY UNCLE HAD CHANGED while he was away. The journey to Yangon had taken a lot out of him. Even when I rubbed his feet, it didn't revive him the way it used to. I could sense it clearly even though he claimed I was mistaken.

He looked as if he had gotten shorter and thinner. He walked more slowly, more stooped, as if each step took a toll on him. If I were as big and strong as my father, I thought, I would take my uncle on my back and carry him across the yard and all over Kalaw. We would go shopping together at the market and then order Shan noodles and an extra-strong tea at his favorite teahouse. And if he wanted, I would even carry him up the two hundred steps to the monastery so that he could enjoy the view of the whole city. But it will be another three or four years before I'm that strong.

It was harder and harder for him to get out of bed in the morning. He didn't even join me for breakfast. When

I got home from school in the afternoons, it seemed to me as if he had just woken up. At night, on the other hand, he was keeping long hours. When I came into the kitchen in the morning the ashes in the fireplace would still be warm. Same with the tea. Why was he staying up so late? What was he doing all that time by himself? It must be awful to sit there alone on the couch at night while everyone else was fast asleep. Not a sound from the neighbors. Not a bird to be heard. Not even a chicken clucking.

He had said that his soul traveled more slowly than a bus or a train, so I imagined that that part of him just hadn't made it home yet. Maybe it got hung up somewhere. I was sure he would be more talkative as soon as he was whole again. But then there was no improvement, and I started to worry again, even though he didn't want me to. I couldn't help it.

I kept hoping the whole time that he would tell me something about his trip. At the same time I was afraid. I certainly did not have the courage to ask. My fear of the answers had only increased since the conversation with the woman on the phone and my father's hasty departure.

A few weeks after his return I was woken in the night by a strange noise. It was too loud and uneven to be the ticking of a clock. It was too weak and soft to be hammer strokes. But it sounded like someone hitting something. It was too close to be coming from a neighbor's house.

The bed beside me was empty. A light was on in the living room. I got out of bed and crept to the curtain, where I peeked through a small opening.

My uncle was sitting at his desk with a pot of tea and the old portable typewriter he had bought a year ago at the market. I had never seen him use it. There was a big pile of paper next to it, and there was one sheet loaded into the machine. Half a dozen candles burned around him. It was just after four in the morning.

U Ba typed with two fingers. He would pause at times, leaning forward, holding up the paper and reading what he had written. Then he would furrow his brow and look very dissatisfied.

From time to time he would pull out a sheet and lay it on a shorter stack on the other side. Or he would write on it with a pencil. Mostly he would crumple them up and drop them in a wastebasket next to him. There was already a big pile in there.

The sight of my uncle like that did nothing to ease my fears. He had a tortured expression. Absorbed. Absent. Alone. He would groan out loud at times, shake his head in frustration, or bury his head in his hands.

The next night I stayed awake. My uncle checked on me several times, and when he thought I was asleep I heard him taking the typewriter and paper out of the drawer.

After a few days my curiosity got the better of me. I woke up early in the morning, got out of bed, lit the fire, and put the water on. I dusted the altar, threw out the wilted flowers, cut fresh ones, and put them in the vases. I filled two bowls rather than one with rice, and I set out an extra-large banana for the Buddha. And two of his favorite candies. I was going to need his indulgence today.

After a quick glance into the bedroom to make sure that my uncle was still asleep, I crept over to the dresser and lifted the lid.

In the drawer was the black typewriter, a package of blank paper, and a smaller stack of typed pages. I hesitated. If my uncle had wanted me to know what he was doing in the night, he would have told me about it. If he had wanted me to see what he was writing, he would have shown it to me himself.

In the end, my curiosity won out.

I took the stack out of the drawer, closed the lid carefully, and sat down on the floor.

My heart was pounding wildly, as if I had just run all the way up the hill from the market. Wildly and recklessly. I wanted to read these pages more than anything, but I already had a guilty conscience. I didn't want to keep such a big secret from U Ba.

I lit a candle so that I could see better. Very slowly I pulled away the empty first page and on the next I found a single line:

For my beloved Bo Bo, the Brave!

If it was dedicated to me, how bad could it be for me to read it, I thought.

Part I

They demanded a courage of themselves beyond the strength of their hearts.

By the time they realized their mistake, it was already too late.

I knew after two sentences that it was the story of my parents.

And so also my story.

Ours.

All the same I was afraid to read on. Or maybe precisely for that reason.

Did I want to know what happened when two hearts demanded a courage of themselves beyond their strength? Did I want to know what that led to?

I lowered the pages and gazed for a long time into the light of the candle. As if I might find some answer in its flickering glow.

I felt utterly alone in the world. U Ba was sleeping in the next room, and yet he was infinitely out of reach.

I didn't even want to think about my parents.

She had no plan. But a dream.

He had neither one nor the other. He was afraid.

And of course fear is the natural enemy of love.

A person who loves has no fear. A person who fears cannot love. Only cling.

Both were prisoners in their own worlds who believed they could free one another if only they loved sufficiently.

Love can accomplish many miracles, but it could not fulfill this hope, a hope as old as love itself.

Their stories could not have been more different.

Julia had only a vague inkling of all this when she stepped out of the ready-for-departure airplane without a word, took her pack on her back, and walked out of the terminal at the Heho airport. Her plan had always been to go back to New York, but she could not. She had to stay in Burma, close to Thar Thar.

In the shade of an acacia a taxi was waiting for her. Her brother was leaning on the back, a wreath of jasmine blossoms in his hand. One hour ago they had said goodbye to each other. He greeted her with a knowing smile.

Without a word they watched as the plane taxied to the runway. After accelerating briefly it rose into the air and swiftly gained altitude. It flew in a semicircle and then set course for Mandalay. In a short time it was little more than a white dot in a deep blue cloudless sky.

Julia closed her eyes. There was more than a promise growing inside her. There was also a new life, the size of a matchstick.

A second chance. How often did one get that?

A gift.

A part of her, and so it would always remain.

This time she would be cautious. No one would ever be able to separate them.

I was too confused to read any more. It must have been me growing inside her. No one was ever supposed to be able to separate us, but I had been living with my uncle for a long time now while she lived in Yangon.

Why?

Out of the corner of my eye I saw two old bare feet on the floorboards, and I looked up: There was U Ba right in front of me. I hadn't heard him coming.

"What on earth are you doing?" he asked in a voice that froze my heart. "Bo Bo, my Bo Bo! You . . . you can't . . ."

Part Two

Chapter 1

FOR SEVEN DAYS U Ba and I did not exchange a single word.

Seven days during which our silence penetrated into every corner of the house.

Seven days during which anger and disappointment trickled into our hearts like poison.

My uncle felt as if I had gone behind his back. Betrayed him. Deceived him. He would never have thought it possible that I would go snooping around his things! I would never have dared to read those pages without his permission! I was too young and inexperienced for that sort of thing.

His disappointment had a profound impact. I felt as if the chickens had ceased to cluck. Even the pig refrained from grunting.

I felt so estranged from him that it hurt.

In my opinion he had no right to be angry with me. I hadn't committed any crime. I hadn't stolen anything, hit anyone, cheated anyone. I just wanted to know what courage it was that was beyond the strength of my parents' hearts.

I wanted to know why I was living with my uncle in Kalaw instead of with them.

Why my father visited me only once a year.

Why I didn't recognize the voice of the woman who called him?

It was *my* story.

U Ba was unwilling to divulge even a single sentence more, and that's why I decided to keep my own silence.

Not to cook for him.

Not to rub his feet.

I acted as if he were not there.

And just like every other time he was not there, our house suddenly felt bigger.

And the nights colder.

The quiet quieter.

The emptiness emptier.

On the third day, my uncle spoke to me a couple of times, but when I didn't react he left me in peace.

On the fourth day he acted as if I were not there.

On the fifth day he declared that he would be ready to tell me more in a few months.

On the sixth day I stopped eating. I refused to get out of bed or to go to school.

On the seventh day U Ba had a realization.

Before noon he came into our bedroom and sat on the edge of the bed. Cleared his throat. Cracked his knuckles.

I turned to face the other way.

"Bo Bo, I have reconsidered the entire matter."

I listened and waited.

"You should know what happened."

I rolled over to face him.

"It is *your* story."

I reached out and took his hand. It was cold. My relief warmed it quickly.

"When?" I asked carefully.

"Today. Tomorrow. The day after tomorrow. It's not a story you can hear all in one sitting. For the past few weeks I have attempted to write it out for you so that you might read it when you are older. I wanted you to know what had happened even if I should not be there to tell you in person. You have seen that I did not get past the first few pages." He paused for a moment. "It is long, and it is complicated. It addresses the most important question of all."

"Which one?" I whispered.

He cleared his throat again. "Shortly before my father, your grandfather, died, he said there was only one force in the world in which he truly believed."

"Which one is that?"

"Love." U Ba paused for a long time before continuing. "Your story addresses the question, whether my father might have been mistaken. Whether there might not be a force in our lives that is stronger than love."

My uncle was sitting on the sofa. He took a few hand-written pages out of an envelope that lay beside him.

"What's that?" I wondered.

"A few pages from your mother's diary and a letter your father wrote to her. She gave both to me for safekeeping a long time ago. I would like to read them to you now."

I stretched out on the couch and lay my head in his lap. We had spent many afternoons and evenings like that. He would read to me or tell me tales. I would nibble on sunflower seeds and listen to him.

He breathed deeply in and out and cleared his throat. I could hear his stomach gurgling and rumbling. He took a sip of tea and started his story.

Chapter 2

WHEN DOES LOVE BEGIN?

In that fleeting moment when two people meet for the first time? When they exchange their first curious glances? A first cautious smile?

Or only much later, when the wishes or needs of the other have superseded one's own.

When the ego needs no longer to assert itself.

When fear, having lost its power, has transformed itself into courage.

In Julia's case it began earlier than either of those.

For her love took root when she heard the story of little Thar Thar's life.

When she understood what it meant to be an unloved child.

When something of his loneliness touched her soul as it had never been touched before.

Thar Thar was no stranger when Julia saw him for the first time. She knew his story and he was as familiar to her as a soul mate. And yet he was also full of mysteries.

And when does the end of love begin? With the first white lie that sows the seed of mistrust, however small it might be? With the first serious quarrel? The second?

When the ego returns with all of its entitlements?

When courage dwindles and fear grows like a vine in the rainy season?

Or only after one's own wishes and needs have once again taken precedence over those of the other?

But those were questions that would occupy the two of them only much later.

Julia was an early guest in the teahouse. Kalaw was barely awake. The first monks and novices were passing in long lines from one house to the next on their daily alms rounds. The patches of fog on the meadows and between the hills were gradually clearing. White columns of smoke rose straight up into the deep blue cloudless sky. Everywhere was the scent of fire and fresh food.

It was cold. She had pulled her woolen cap down low over her ears and forehead. In front of her sat a bowl of hot Shan noodles, a Burmese tea, and her open diary.

The last entry, dated January 2, 2007, consisted only of two words:

THAR THAR!?

For his sake she had stepped off an airplane that was ready to depart.

To stay with a man she hardly knew. With whom she had spent no more than a few days.

And two nights.

Half nights.

A man who, for all she knew, might not even want her to stay.

Be that as it may.

She, of all people, who so dreaded surprises. Who did not like to leave anything to chance. Who found it difficult to cope with the unexpected. She had turned into her own biggest surprise.

Between her real life in New York and a future life in Kalaw or Hsipaw lay two seas, three continents, and eight thousand miles.

And that was merely the distance that could be measured in numbers.

Was it possible to exchange one's own ego for another's from one day to the next?

She was thirty-eight years old. Single. Unattached, as one says. But whatever does that mean? As if there were any people in the world who were unattached to anything or anyone.

Not yet forty. A good age, a bad age, she thought. Young enough to change something in her life. Too old to start again from the beginning. Metamorphoses were for animals. We are not snakes who can shed their old skins. Nor caterpillars who can transform into butterflies.

If only we were.

Julia considered what her future here might look like. What did it have to offer? She was a lawyer by occupation. Specializing in corporate law, international copyright, intellectual property rights. Graduate of Columbia University, summa cum laude. Would-be partner at one of the top firms on Wall Street. Her clients prized her efficiency and her clarity of purpose, her diligence and her discipline. She was ambitious. Decisive. Determined. Conscientious. She expected a lot of herself. Of others, too. Her resume and her references would impress anyone. In New York. In Burma? Not so much.

The man she loved did not even know the word *copyright*. Property, intellectual or otherwise, had played no role in his life.

In his country there was no shortage of laws; that much was clear. But there was precious little legal deliberation. And so no demand for lawyers.

There would have been more demand for her services in Burma if she had been a doctor. Or an engineer. Or a teacher.

She owned stocks and bonds and, were she to sell her apartment in New York, a considerable fortune, at least by Burmese standards. Whether the money would be much use to her here she did not know.

To be honest, she had not the slightest idea what she could do.

Julia sipped at her tea and leafed through the diary entries of the past few weeks.

Nausea and occasional vomiting, usually in the morning. The typical symptoms of my nervous stomach, just like at home in New York.

Slept badly. Insomnia till dawn. The fear that I might be hearing voices again.

U Ba is teaching me Burmese. One hour a day. He tells me there's no expression for self-realization. Nor for self-doubt. They have to paraphrase these ideas.

Argued with my brother. For the first time. I cleaned and straightened up his hut while he was at the market. I just couldn't stand the dust and chaos any longer.

I was just trying to do him a favor. He thought I should have asked him first and had little to say to me the rest of the day.

The dread that Thar Thar won't want to see me again, that he won't want me to stay with him and the children at the monastery.

What then?

Wrote a long letter to Thar Thar and asked him to come to Kalaw at his earliest convenience. We need to talk.

I go out walking just about every day. I'm alone a lot, but still I find no peace. Small wonder, says U Ba. "Where love is concerned, everything is always at stake."

卐

Dreamed of New York. I was riding an elephant through Central Park and down Fifth Avenue. A young Indian man was sitting in front of me, guiding the animal. Cars were honking, some pedestrians stopped dead in their tracks and stared at us, though most people just ignored us. At 57th Street a taxi stopped next to us carrying my mother and my friend Amy. They looked at me and the Indian man, shook their heads, and continued on their way. I wanted to dismount but realized that I couldn't climb off the animal's back without help. I asked the young man to stop. He ignored me. I started to shout for help, but no one heard me. The louder I screamed, the faster the elephant walked. Finally U Ba woke me. I had cried out in my sleep.

卐

Burned a letter to Thar Thar. Too afraid what his answer might be.

卐

I'm sleeping too little at night, and so I'm tired all day. Oversensitive. Grouchy. Restless. Uneasy.

卐

I've left U Ba's place and am staying again at the Kalaw Hotel. I was hoping that might improve my situation. Needed a proper bed instead of a pallet.

*Running water. A hot shower in the morning. A flush
toilet in the bathroom instead of a latrine in the yard.*

*My brother says he's not upset about my leaving. But
he doesn't believe that I'll feel any better at the hotel.*

*Living in a bubble. There are hardly any televisions
or radios, no newspapers, no cell phones, no Internet in
Kalaw.*

*Whatever is going on in the rest of the world is
irrelevant. A place without diversion, with its own time
zone, with its own rhythm.*

But is it my rhythm? And if not: Could it ever be?

*U Ba is giving me space. He's busy restoring his old
books, and he asks and expects very little of me. That's his
way, but it doesn't make anything easier.*

I'm used to dealing with demanding people.

*How long should I stay in Kalaw? I've got to go see
Thar Thar in Hsipaw. But when? Should I let him know
I'm coming, explain what's going on? Or should I surprise
him? I just don't know.*

*Asked U Ba what he thought about it. His advice: I
should take my time. Some things in life cannot be hastened.
Love has its own tempo, its own pace, and so also with*

important decisions. Not every choice is the result of a thorough analysis of facts and figures, a balance sheet, a painstaking calculation of the so-called pros and cons. "Answers sometimes come to us of their own accord," he says. "Our only responsibility is to make sure they find us."

So how do I do that?

And how do I know it's the right answer?

Sleeping even more poorly in the hotel. The nausea is increasing. Likewise my inner turmoil. My heart races. Sometimes I can hardly breathe, and I feel like I'm going to explode.

Thinking a lot about my dad. How torn he must have felt all those years living in New York.

If only he were still here. Even just for one day.

Maybe he could hear my heart beating.

Maybe he could tell me what I should do.

Julia quickly closed her diary. Wisps of fog still clung to the valley. She paid and left, then walked down the main street to the market without really knowing where she was going.

Chapter 3

THE OLD MAN SAT watching the street, lounging with his feet up in a bamboo chair. At his back a gorgeous house roofed with wooden shingles. On the porch on the second floor longyis and shirts were hung out to dry. On the first floor was a little shop.

Julia had already noticed him several times in the past few days while walking from the hotel into the city. He had a slender frame, always wore the same longyi, with a green and white pattern, and a pink cardigan, much too large. He had a strikingly long nose and a narrow head, on which he wore a faded baseball cap. His bare, thin feet were red with the cold.

He greeted her with a nod, and she returned the greeting.

"Mingalabar," he called in a way that suggested she was an old friend.

"Mingalabar."

"Where are you from?"

Julia stopped. "New York," she answered. "America."

"I know where New York is," he replied in English with a strong British accent. He regarded her with small, inquiring eyes set below bushy white eyebrows. "I thought you were Burmese, from Yangon."

"What made you think that?" she asked.

"You have such a long, fast stride. As people there do." He grinned briefly and tipped his head to one side. "They don't walk there; they rush."

Julia laughed. "I live in Manhattan. People there walk the same way. They're always in a hurry."

"Why?"

"I guess because they have so much to do and so little time."

"For me it's just the opposite," he replied with a smile that revealed teeth reddened by betel nuts. "Manhattan? Hm. You look Burmese."

"I'm half Burmese, actually. My father was from Kalaw. His name was Tin Win. Maybe you've heard of him?"

"No. I'm from Loikaw. I'm just visiting my sister here." He pointed to an older woman waiting on customers behind a glass display case full of longyis and bolts of fabric. She looked astonishingly like her brother. She gave a friendly wink.

"Do you want to know what the future holds?" the man asked. "If you allow me, I could read the stars for you."

"No, thanks," answered Julia.

"Why not?"

"I don't believe in astrology or fortune-telling."

The woman said something to her brother, and they both laughed.

"My sister says that you are probably more like three-quarters American."

"Or four-fifths, more likely."

"But," the man continued, "I am no fortune-teller. I am a scientist."

Julia wrinkled her brow, uncertain whether he really meant what he was saying. When she did not respond, he added: "You do not believe that the stars influence our lives?"

"No."

"The moon robs people of their sleep. It moves entire seas, every day..."

"That's a different matter."

"Are you sure?" He took off his baseball cap and scratched his bald head. "You could sample my art and then later confirm whether I was correct."

Julia hesitated. She was enjoying the light, unusual musicality of the man's voice. His alert gaze, his welcoming smile. "It's a deal. But I don't want any bad news," she declared with a jocular severity.

"Why not?" There was surprise in his voice and a tinge of disappointment.

His question made no sense to her. "Well, who would?"

The old man raised his eyebrows as he pondered. "But bad news is part of it."

"Part of your predictions?"

"Part of life. Of course I wish you only the best, but I can hardly guarantee you only good news," he stated. "People do not come to me because I promise them good luck. On the contrary. They come because they want to know what misfortunes lie ahead."

"What good does it do them to know in advance?"

"I can advise them on things they should do or avoid. I recommend offerings they can make to avert a calamity. I can warn them."

"About what?"

"A journey, for instance."

An uneasy feeling stole over Julia. The conversation was becoming serious in a way that was little to her liking. She was not a superstitious person, but she could not help thinking of her father. His life had taken a sad, unfortunate turn in accordance with an astrologer's predictions. "I'll give it some thought, then," she said evasively. "Maybe tomorrow."

The man's sister gestured welcomingly. Julia took a step closer and examined the fabrics in the display case. They were extraordinarily beautiful, quite beyond the offerings at the market.

The woman held out a blue, red, and white checkered sarong, the kind worn by nearly all Burmese women, regardless of age. When Julia did not react, she pulled another fabric out of the stack. It was a longyi with a matching top. Julia stroked the cloth with her hand. It shone a warm golden yellow in the morning sun. It was embroidered in little elephants and patterns, handwoven silk. She had seldom seen a more beautiful longyi. "Magical," she said. "How much does it cost?"

The woman flashed her two times ten fingers. Her brother mumbled something, and she added another five fingers.

Julia took five five-thousand-kyat bills out of her purse and handed them to her.

In the hotel she spread the outfit on the bed. She took off her jeans and blouse and for the first time in her life tried on a longyi. It reached from her navel to her ankles. She held it up with both hands, wondering how to tie it correctly. With some effort she wrapped it around her hips. When it did not stay up, she tied a knot that hung like a thick sausage in front of her. It took some time before it finally looked as it did on other women.

She went to the mirror and gazed at herself. Turned to the left, then to the right, ran her fingers through her brown, shoulder-length hair. Hesitantly she pulled on the top. It fit as if it had been custom-made for her. She contemplated her otherwise familiar reflection. Who was that person looking back her? A sister? A friend? A stranger?

The fabric looked splendid on her. The close fit flattered her slender figure, her waist, her breasts. They gave her movements a grace that she had not seen in herself for a long time.

Half Burmese.

Julia wondered whether she had ever identified herself in that particular way before. Probably not. She was an American.

In the private schools on Manhattan's Upper East Side, the only things that distinguished her from her classmates were her dark eyes and her light brown skin. Some of her friends' parents had taken her for a southern European, others for a diplomat's daughter from Mexico or Brazil. Hardly ever had anyone asked her directly about her ancestry. Whenever anyone did, she would explain that her father came from Burma without ever having the feeling that it had anything to do with her. The country in which he had been born had never played a role in the Win family's life. Nothing was ever said about his youth or childhood, as if he had come into the world twenty years old and in New York. When Julia asked about grandparents, aunts, or uncles he would answer her evasively or not at all. If she persisted, her mother would press her to leave it alone. His origins remained a mystery in which Julia eventually lost interest. In all those years she had never heard her father speak a single sentence in Burmese. He had no Burmese friends, and he did not seek out the companionship of his compatriots.

The only indications of his past were the Burmese stories and tales that he told her every night at bedtime. A realm of monasteries and pagodas populated her imagination, where princesses or princes were devoured by crocodiles. A land teeming with dragons. Where life never ended, because a person who died would be reincarnated.

A land of fairy tales.

What must he have been thinking when he took her with him on those nightly journeys into his childhood?

On one occasion she had found her father, pale and tearful, reading the *New York Times* at the kitchen table. On the front page was a story with a photograph from Yangon. Students and monks in the capital had protested against the military regime. There was unrest throughout the country. Soldiers had fired on the demonstrators, killing hundreds, probably thousands. The sight of her father so agitated, her father who was otherwise so unshakable, that sight had so disturbed her that she had left the kitchen as quickly as she had entered, as if she had not noticed a thing.

Ten years ago she had traveled to Burma for the first time. She was tracking down her father, who had disappeared without a trace. It was not her roots that she was looking for.

During that trip she had not thought of herself as half Burmese.

What would that even mean? Which half of her was supposed to be Burmese? Which half American? The designation was little more than a banal description of her ethnic heritage, a heritage that had never shaped her life.

The longer she pondered her reflection, the more she thought of her father—and the more ridiculous she felt. He would have shaken his head and laughed at her, if he could have seen her. He had always dressed elegantly. He wore tailored suits. On his head a Borsalino, a different one for each season. She could not imagine that he had ever worn one of these Burmese wrap-arounds that nearly all the men also wore.

The longyi may well have emphasized her figure, and it may have been a gorgeous fabric, but it suited her as little as it would have suited him. It was foreign to her. She felt as if she were participating in some shabby masquerade. She did not possess the innate elegance of the women she had seen on the street and at the market. Comparing herself with them made her feel dumpy, clumsy, heavy.

The old man by the road had been right. She did not walk; she rushed.

She spent her life running breathlessly from one place to the next.

A longyi would only slow her down.

Chapter 4

WHEN JULIA WOKE she did not immediately know where she was. For one brief, delicious moment she imagined herself in her childhood bedroom back in New York. The sound of her mother's voice came drifting in from the hall. In the kitchen the clatter of dishes. The irresistible fragrances of cinnamon rolls and fresh-brewed coffee.

Through her half-slumber she heard her father speaking Burmese and lurched upright. In the darkness she could make out the contours of a large cabinet, a second bed, her backpack on it. The sight brought her back to the Kalaw Hotel.

She groped around for the lamp switch and listened intently. Not even the chirping of insects. It was as quiet as if she were utterly alone in the world. The clock read 2:30. Julia was wide awake.

On the table beside her bed was the letter Thar Thar had left for her in the monastery.

A farewell letter. She had opened it and refolded it so many times that the lines in the creases had become illegible. No matter; she knew most of the passages by heart.

Dearest Julia,

Never before have I written lines as difficult as these ...

Please forgive me.

These past weeks have brought great joy into my life. A joy that means more to me than I can put into words. I had never imagined I would encounter anything like it again. And I am all the more grateful for knowing how fragile it is. A fleeting visitor in our hearts. No steadfast friend. No one we can count on. No joy. Anywhere.

I must leave because I fear that my heart would fall further and further out of step if we were to spend more time together ...

A person, once abandoned, bears that loss forever.

A person never loved bears an unquenchable longing for love.

And a person who has been loved and lost that love bears not only that love, but also the fear of losing it again.

I carry a bit of all of those inside myself.

Together they are a like a poison slowly working their way through my body. Penetrating to the remotest corners of my soul. Seizing control of all my senses. Not killing, but paralyzing.

Not killing, but making me distrustful.

Fostering jealousy. Resentment.

How much loss can one person bear?

How much pain?

How much loneliness?

You did not come alone. You brought your brother with you, and my memories of me as a young boy.

A boy who would never have existed, had his mother had her way.

A child's soul knows everything.

Lonelier than anyone should ever be. On his hands the blood of chickens that were so much more than chickens. Years would pass before he could look at them again without revulsion. His own hands!

A child's soul forgets nothing.

But it grows, and it learns. It learns to mistrust. It learns to hate. It learns to defend itself. Or to love and to forgive. You had a young boy with you whom I never expected to encounter again.

When you leave he will stay with me, and I will look after him. I will console him when he is sad. I will protect him when he is fearful. I will be there for him when he is lonely . . .

You have shown me that some part of my soul lives still in captivity and will always do so.

Perhaps this is the moment when I must admit to myself that I am not as free as I thought.

Forgive me that error. Forgive me for this letter, if my behavior causes you pain. Nothing could be further from my intention than to hurt you. Yet I must leave. I see no other way out.

I thank you for everything.
Take good care of yourself.

Thar Thar

Julia felt her eyes welling up with tears. She refolded the paper and set it back on the nightstand.

She had initially reacted to this letter with blind rage.

She had cursed Thar Thar. She had wanted to protect herself. No one should get away with treating her like that.

That same morning she had packed her things and gone off without leaving so much as a note for him.

Since then her anger and disappointment had subsided a little with each reading.

Several weeks later she had started to understand why he had left the monastery like that, all at once, in the middle of the night, as if he were fleeing.

Thar Thar had not willingly written these lines; he had had no other choice. Fear had dictated the letter, word for word, line for line. He was a prisoner of the fear that every person suffers who has ever been cast aside.

And who among lovers has never been?

A fear that she could help him overcome—of that she had no doubt. A fear that would diminish and weaken with each day and night they spent together, until it dissipated like fog in the morning, until nothing was left of it but a vague memory.

Before that, however, she would have to overcome her own fear.

Chapter 5

WE MET that afternoon, as we did most days, at the Mya Myint Moe Teahouse.

I was sitting in my usual spot by the door on the terrace, eating fried rice and chatting with the proprietor.

Julia was struggling with her first fragments of Burmese. She ordered a coffee and a soup and joined me. "*Bon appétit.*"

"Thank you."

She took a deep breath and cleared her throat. "I've come to a decision," she declared. "I'm going to Hsipaw to see Thar Thar and the children."

"When?"

"Tomorrow."

My encouraging nod delighted her. "Shall I arrange for a car and driver?"

"No thanks. I think I'll take the train. Will you join me?"

"Is that a question or a request?"

"A question."

"In that case, my answer is no."

She winced. "What?"

"No," I said. "I will stay here."

"Why?" she asked in surprise. There was no mistaking the irritation in her voice.

"Because I believe that the two of you need some time together. I would not like to be in the way."

"But you wouldn't!" she objected. "Moe Moe, Ei Ei, and the ten other kids will all be there, too. We wouldn't be alone anyway."

"Exactly. The last thing you need on top of all that is your older brother getting in the way."

"Nonsense."

I finished off the last of my rice, pushed my plate to the middle of the table, and wiped my mouth with the back of my hand. "Why do you want me to go with you?"

"Because...because..." She did not wish to say out loud what she was thinking.

I waited patiently.

"Because I feel safer when you are with me."

"Safer about being in the country or about being by yourself?"

"About being by myself."

"Are you really so frightened?"

"Yes."

"Of what?"

"That Thar Thar won't be happy to see me. That he'll send me away again."

This was not a fear that I could remove for her.

"And what if it's a request?" she asked.

"To do what?"

"To come with me."

I sighed deeply. "That would be another story, then."

Our car rolled almost silently into the courtyard, where we were greeted by two barking dogs. The monastery, a heavy wooden building on pilings, must once have been an imposing structure. Now it was only partially habitable. Planks had broken away from the walls in many places. Brown rust was eating away the tin roof. One wing had partially collapsed. A broad staircase with crooked railings led up to the entrance.

At the back of the yard a novice stood beside a pile of chopped wood that he was stacking against the wall of a shed. Two boys were playing soccer on a field in front of a bamboo grove.

We stepped out of the car and asked the driver to wait.

Moe Moe was the first to recognize us. She came around the corner with a basket full of laundry and stopped dead in her tracks, as if she did not dare to believe her eyes. Then she let out a long, shrill cry.

"You're back!" she shouted from the other side of the yard. "You came back!"

The novice by the woodpile straightened up, and the two boys let the soccer ball roll into the bushes.

Soon nearly all of the monastery's inhabitants were clamoring in a semicircle around us: Moe Moe, with one arm, hopping with delight from one foot to the other; the blind boy Ko Aung with his milky white eyes; Ei Ei, who had limped across the yard with her rigid leg; the deaf boy Ko Maung, who seemed always to understand what mattered; Soe Soe, who had lost one of her feet but none of her shy smile. Ko Lwin, the hunch in his back shaking with excitement as if he had the hiccups. They looked at their guests and then called quietly in chorus and in English, as if someone had issued a silent command: "You are very welcome."

Julia smiled hesitantly.

Seconds later Thar Thar appeared at the top of the stairs. Their eyes met. His gaze locked on her; he opened his mouth as if to say something, then turned away without a word and disappeared back into the prayer hall.

Julia reached for my hand. Her entire body was quivering.

Chapter 6

THAR THAR looked desperately around the hall, as if somewhere among all the statues of the Buddha, among all the altars and bowls full of offerings, there must be someplace to hide.

She had come back. There was nothing he desired more. And nothing he so dreaded.

He had run off in the middle of the night in order to protect himself. He had walked high into the mountains toward Namhsan, or rather he had run, and he would have liked to have kept running on and on into the foothills of the Himalayas, just to make certain that he would never see her again. He had crossed tea plantations and hidden poppy fields. He had spent a week meditating in an abandoned monastery and trying not to think of her.

To calm his heart that had somehow lost its rhythm.

To close the doors she had reopened.

But how can a person guard against his own memories?

How can he guard against his desire for another once it has been awakened?

Against vulnerability?

Against need?

How can a person guard against love?

He heard voices drifting in from the courtyard.

Voices of the children and of the visitors. Voices of longing and of expectation.

And he heard the unmistakable voice of fear.

As a child he had seen his father die. The experience had taught him that love knew no justice. It followed its own laws. Even a mother's love. His mother had never felt close to him, the way she felt close to his brother.

Later he was abducted by soldiers and betrayed by his mother. They had held him prisoner in a camp, where they tortured him. They had compelled him, along with many others, to work as minesweepers. During military actions they had to march ahead of the soldiers to trigger the mines with their footsteps. Several hundred young men and children had been torn to pieces right before his eyes.

Thar Thar had survived and believed there was nothing else in the world he would ever be afraid of.

He was wrong.

For just a moment he thought once more of fleeing. He could climb out a back window, creep over to the bamboo grove, and disappear unnoticed into the forest. From there he could follow the river up into the mountains. Julia would wait two, maybe three days for him. Then she would leave again, and he could not imagine that she would ever return after that.

He quickly discarded that idea. No place was safe for him. He carried the threat within himself. It would follow him wherever he went.

Thar Thar closed his eyes and breathed deeply. In. Out.

He stepped out onto the veranda and with slow, deliberate steps and one hand firmly on the railing he descended the stairs.

He stood before Julia, his eyes shining in a way they had no right to, given all they had witnessed.

The children's eyes were all on him.

"You must be exhausted from your long journey," he said. "Can we offer you some tea and something to eat? I hope you are not in a hurry and can stay awhile."

"That would be lovely," Julia replied. "We're in no hurry."

"I'm glad to hear it," Thar Thar answered.

We fetched our luggage from the car and paid our driver. To his question about whether he should pick us up again, we answered no.

As we mounted the steps Moe Moe walked beside Julia and kept whispering: "You back. He happy. So very happy."

"Sure?"

"So very sure."

We stepped into the meditation hall filled with the fragrance of incense and fresh flowers. Statues of the Buddha glinted in the light of bare bulbs. Some were draped with strings of lights or with chains of jasmine. In front of them stood vases of red gladiolas and hibiscus. Smoke from the incense drifted among them. On two columns there were crucifixes, and close at hand was a gilded poster of the Virgin Mary.

In the kitchen we could hear someone putting on a kettle. Moments later Ei Ei hobbled out with a tray. A thermos and three cups. Moe Moe set a plate of dry pastries beside it.

The quivering Toe Toe insisted on pouring our drinks. With great effort she managed to fill each mug halfway. They stood in a sea of warm tea that lapped from side to side with each movement of the tray.

The eyes of all three girls were riveted on our movements.

Julia wanted to start a conversation. She wished to express her gratitude for the warm reception, the tea and the pastries, to inquire after everyone's health, to explain how delighted she was to be there. But she had the feeling that none of it was quite fitting. Everything that came into her head struck her as loud and chatty.

Instead, she said nothing. Her eyes wandered aimlessly through the hall. Beside her an agitated Thar Thar rocked his torso back and forth.

It was Moe Moe who broke the silence. "You. Stay. How long?" she asked.

Julia did not know how to answer. She looked to me for help, but it was not a question I could resolve for her.

Moe Moe's eyes wandered from her to me and back.

"Until...until...you throw us out," said Julia with a nervous laugh.

Thar Thar and the girls stared at her, perplexed.

"We would never throw you out," he declared, as confused as he was earnest.

"Oh God, that's not what I meant. That . . . it was just a joke. It's just something people say."

"Really?"

"I know, a stupid expression. It just means that we don't have any concrete plans."

Thar Thar whispered something in Burmese, and the girls nodded thoughtfully.

"What did he say?" Julia immediately wanted to know.

"That it might be better not to take everything you say literally."

Chapter 7

IT WAS THE CHILDREN who gave Julia the feeling that she had hardly ever left. The familiarity with which they approached her. Their carefree and candid joy. Their desire to share everything with her.

Moe Moe led her to her own personal corner of the meditation hall, where she kept her few belongings in a plastic bag, and she proudly showed her the tattered English-Burmese dictionary she had bought in Hsipaw. She took her vocabulary notebook out of the bag. Here, in a delicate penciled hand, she entered each new English word she had learned in Thar Thar's lessons. Beside each, equally neatly, was a Burmese translation, sometimes accompanied by a small illustration, sometimes by a question mark.

Ei Ei took Julia impatiently by the hand and led her limping down the stairs into the courtyard. In the shadow of the woodshed were two piles of bamboo baskets that she and Ko Aung had woven during the previous weeks.

Ko Lwin sat down in front of her and waited until everyone else was quiet. On her first visit, she had tried in vain to teach him more than a single English sentence. "My name is Ko Lwin," he murmured softly now. "How are you? I am very fine." He thought for a moment. "I am from Burma. Where are you from?"

The delight in his eyes.

They cooked together. Julia and Ei Ei were always in charge of peeling the potatoes. During the meal, as she had frequently done during her first visit, she would feed the quivering Toe Toe, on whose spoon no rice would stay.

Thar Thar kept his distance without being aloof.

That evening he saw personally to the sleeping arrangements. He swept the floor, then he and Moe Moe hauled mats, blankets, and sleeping bags out of a cupboard and laid them on the floor in one corner of the hall. Across that corner he hung a curtain. For Julia he piled the mats three deep and then knelt on them to test whether they were soft enough. From one of the altars he fetched a bowl of rose blossoms. Their scent would help her sleep peacefully and keep bad dreams away, he said. When she went to bed Julia found a red hibiscus on her pillow.

"U Ba, are you still awake?" she whispered after a while.

"Yes," I replied.

"Thank you," she said.

"For being awake?"

"No. Thank you for coming with me. Thank you for not leaving me alone. For being there for me."

"I am your brother. It goes without saying."

"No, it doesn't," she contradicted. "I can't imagine what I would do without you."

In the morning we woke to the sound of barking dogs. On the other side of the curtain the children were walking lightly and quickly and whispering to one another. There was the scent of fire, fried eggs, garlic, and coriander.

A moped rode into the courtyard.

Julia was about to get up when someone pushed the curtain aside. Moe Moe brought her hot water on a tray with a packet of instant coffee and a tube of sweetened condensed milk. Breakfast in bed. On the saucer she had put one of the dry pastries. For me she had brought tea.

"Thank you so much."

"You is welcome."

"You *are* welcome," Julia corrected her.

Moe Moe faltered, thought hard for a moment, then nodded, embarrassed. "Oh, sorry. So sorry."

"Where are the other kids?"

Moe Moe searched hard for the right word. "Working."

"And Thar Thar?"

She smiled. "Working. And waiting."

Julia prepared her coffee and sampled the pastry. "Very good. So nice of you."

Moe Moe beamed.

We rose, rolled up our sleeping mats, and went into the courtyard.

Thar Thar was balancing two heavy sacks of potatoes on a motorcycle. The driver tied them to the back of the seat with some twine, paid for them, and zoomed away.

He walked over to us, still somewhat out of breath from the exertion. "Good morning. Have you eaten yet?"

"Moe Moe served us some coffee and tea. Many thanks."

His left eye twitched repeatedly from excitement. "I have to take care of something in Hsipaw," he said, turning to Julia. "Would you care to join me, if you have time?"

"On foot?"

"No." Thar Thar went to the shed and returned with a moped. It looked rather old. The rearview mirror was missing. Likewise the front mudguard. Loose cables hung from the headlamp. But it started on the first try. He handed her a helmet—much too small—climbed on, and invited her to sit behind him.

With ease and grace he dodged the many potholes, tree roots, and sand pits along the dirt path that led from the monastery to the main road. She did not feel confident enough to put her arms around his hips and braced herself instead with both hands on the luggage rack.

It had been years since she had sat on a motorbike. Her hair flowed in the wind. As she smelled the flowers and freshly cut wood, she found herself hoping he would take a long detour.

In Hsipaw they stopped before a teak villa with an expansive overhanging veranda where a cluster of people stood waiting. Through the open windows she could see men and women sitting at large desks with mountains of tightly packed folders and binders. From inside the building she could hear the sound of typewriters.

Thar Thar asked her to stay with the moped while he went to the veranda. The waiting people respectfully cleared a path for him and he disappeared into the house.

A man called out to Julia in Burmese, but she did not understand what he said; nor could she interpret his tone.

"American," she answered, hoping that he had been asking where she was from.

Everyone started talking at once, and the mad swirl of voices rose until two police officers stepped out of the villa. Immediately it was quiet.

Moments later Thar Thar returned.

"I had to register you as visitors with the authorities," he explained. "Otherwise they'll think we're harboring spies."

"Spies?" she wondered. "For whom?"

He shrugged. "For the American secret services. Or by the order of Her Majesty the Queen. It doesn't matter. Do you want to get something to eat?"

"No. Or maybe? Something small."

They drove to a teahouse on the banks of the Myitnge. Thar Thar parked the moped and led her to a quiet table on the patio. Nearly all eyes were on them as they walked through the place. Conversations were suddenly hushed; some faltered entirely. In a few faces she recognized a friendly curiosity; in others, the ugly, dark shadow of disapproval. Julia turned her back on them and sat down on a stool.

In front of them lay a broad, lazy river on whose banks houseboats gently rocked. Children were playing on one.

On another a man sat mending a fishing net. Beside the boats two women stood knee-deep in water, doing their laundry.

Julia turned around. Even now many of the other guests were still watching her.

She leaned over to Thar Thar and whispered: "I get the feeling we're not exactly welcome here."

"It's my mistake. Don't worry about it," he said.

"Why are they all staring at us like that?"

"Because we're not following the rules."

"What rules?"

"A monk going around with a beautiful young woman. They've never seen anything like that. It's not supposed to happen."

"But you're not even officially a monk."

"Most of them wouldn't know that. They see my red robe and my shaven head. That's enough."

He called for a waitress. A young woman scuffled over, and she, too, stared at them unabashedly. Thar Thar ordered two bowls of noodle soup.

When she had gone again, he took several deep breaths. "Can I ask you something?"

"Anything you like."

"Please don't answer with some American expression that I can't understand."

"I won't. I promise."

"How long will you stay?"

Julia let a few seconds go by before she answered. "As long as you like."

"I mean, when are you going back to New York?"

"Never. Not without you," she declared quietly and assertively. "I understood your question perfectly."

His disbelieving expression, his penetrating look, as if he hoped to find some indication in her eyes, in the shape of her mouth, in the tilt of her head, whether she really meant what she was saying.

"Of course, only if it's what you want," she added hastily when she saw his earnest face.

A waiter brought the steaming soups. He put them on the table too quickly. They splashed and the hot broth dripped through slats in the table onto Julia's legs. She did not move.

"You . . . you . . . want to stay?"

Julia nodded.

"With me?"

He looked puzzled at the prospect.

Chapter 8

"HOW DO YOU KNOW ALL THIS?" I interrupted my uncle. "When Mama and Papa were in the teahouse you weren't even there."

"I witnessed many things firsthand," he said, "and your parents told me the rest."

U Ba leaned forward and handed me a bowl of sunflower seeds. I thought about my mother.

"So why wasn't my father happy that my mother had returned?"

"He was."

"But not that she wanted to stay with him."

"No, no, he was. Very, very much so."

"It doesn't sound that way from what you're telling me."

"He was not able to show it right away. At least not so that she could understand it. It's complicated. Even when two people say the same thing, they might not mean the same thing.

"Even when they hear the same thing, they might not understand it the same way.

"And even when they want to do the same thing, one cannot assume that they will therefore do it.

"Joy left Thar Thar speechless, whereas for Julia it was fear or anger that had that effect. Of course that is another matter altogether, and it can take a long time before we understand another person's language. Some people are more adept at it than others."

"And my mother couldn't manage it?"

"Let us say that it was not easy for her initially."

"Why not?"

"Ah, Bo Bo, you are asking very intelligent questions. Perhaps she was too wrapped up in herself." U Ba scratched his head and wheezed a little. His stomach had been growling and gurgling the whole time he was talking and now he let out a long, loud fart. I could see how worn out he was.

"Are you tired? Would you like to take a break?"

"That might not be a bad idea."

"How about something to eat?"

"A little something would be lovely."

I brought him some toast and an instant coffee. He loved to dip the bread. Afterward he stretched out on the couch. I brought the dishes into the kitchen and quickly washed up. When I came back, his eyes were already closed.

While U Ba was sleeping I hopped on my bike and pedaled as fast as I could to Ko Aye Min's place. I was dying to tell him the story of my parents. But he wasn't there, and his office was closed.

I went to the market to see whether he was maybe having some noodle soup at Ma Ei's stand. There wasn't much going on there. Ma Ei was sitting behind the counter, playing on her cell phone and swatting flies. She was happy to see me.

"Do you know where Ko Aye Min is?"

"He's off with two French tourists, hiking to Inle Lake. He'll be back tomorrow."

She must have seen the disappointment on my face. "Is there anything I can do for you?"

I shook my head.

"Are you hungry? Do you want some soup?"

"No, thanks." I said good-bye and wandered around the market and along the main street. It was too crowded there for me. I was looking for somewhere to be alone with myself, so I climbed the 272 steps to the Thein Taung monastery above the city. It was quiet up there, and I liked the wide view of our little valley, the market, my school, the soccer fields, all the way down to the Kalaw Hotel.

I was met at the top by two sleepy cats. Some of the novices were playing soccer behind the prayer hall. Freshly laundered robes hung on a line to dry in the sun.

I sat down in the shadow of the pagoda, looked out over the city, and pondered. A child's soul knows everything and forgets nothing, my father had written. But if it has such a good memory, then how come I knew so little about my mother? Why was it that I remembered almost nothing about the time we spent together?

My uncle once told me that before moving to Kalaw I had lived several years with my parents in a monastery. I had completely forgotten it.

A young dog approached warily. He nudged me with his nose, looking for some affection. As I sat there scratching him and listening to the voices of the soccer players behind me, visions appeared before my eyes.

A young woman with a bright voice helping me into a tree. She was a skilled climber and made her way clear to the top, though she had only one arm.

A young man who could not stand up straight but who still played soccer with me until I was tired.

My father splitting logs with a hefty ax.

A dog who never left my side.

I guess memories were like other kinds of answers: they appeared of their own accord and in their own time. We just needed to make sure they could find us.

Or we could hide from them.

Two older novices sat down a few yards away from me and nodded in greeting. I nodded back.

Gradually I started to remember the monastery grounds, too. They did not look exactly as U Ba had described them. I thought of the great hall and the strings of lights on the Buddhas. Of the soccer field. The crooked goals. But in the yard beside the shed there was a stone building. Inside was a shower and bathtub with hot water. There was a proper flush toilet. I could see my mother sitting on it.

A car in which we would drive to the city.

I heard strange voices. Shouting. Saw bright flames blazing into the night sky. Thick smoke, gray and black. Someone grabbed me by the arm and ran.

The smell of burning wood.

Where were my mother and father?

The memories broke off as suddenly as they had begun. The end. No more. Someone had drawn a black curtain over my mind. I waited in vain for it to reopen. My memory was empty. No more images. No smells. No voices.

As if I were demanding recollections beyond its strength.

U Ba was standing on the porch when I got home. He yawned and stretched so that his joints creaked. "That was refreshing. Will you please make me another coffee? Extra strong." He came down the steps into the yard. While I made the coffee I could hear him spluttering outside, repeatedly pouring cold water over his head.

Back in the house he looked more alert, refreshed, and lighthearted than I had seen him for a long time. On the table stood his steaming coffee. Next to it I had set two pieces of toast.

"Thank you. Would you like me to carry on with our story?"

"Of course. But first I have a question."

My uncle dipped a piece of bread in his coffee.

"We used to live all together in the monastery, right?"

"Yes."

"For how long?"

He did some math. "More than four years."

"That long? How come I don't remember anything about it?"

"You were still quite little."

"How little?"

"You were about five when we left. The memories are stored in your heart."

"My heart has a memory?" I asked skeptically.

"Naturally. The heart remembers more accurately than the mind. And it is incorruptible. All the important things have a place there. Often, though, we find it difficult to put those memories into words."

"But they're there all the same?"

"Certainly."

"Was there ever a fire at the monastery?"

"Why would you say that?" he replied in a strict tone, as if the subject were off limits.

"I don't know," I said, startled. "I just had a feeling."

"Hm. Yes."

"Did . . ." I hesitated. "Did anyone die?"

"No."

"Why didn't we put the fire out?"

"No one could put that fire out. It was much too big. There was nothing left of the monastery but charred beams, a pile of ashes, and the tin roof."

"How did it catch fire?"

"It just happens sometimes."

"But not without a cause," I contradicted.

"Maybe a candle tipped over. Maybe someone was

careless in the kitchen. The monastery was built of old, dry wood. We never found the cause."

I did not need to look into his eyes to know that he was not telling the truth. A lie, he had once told me, is always born out of some difficult situation. What necessity drove him at that moment to tell that lie?

Before I could ask another question he quickly took a big mouthful of coffee. "Evening will be here soon. Shall I continue our story or not?"

Chapter 9

THE NEXT FEW DAYS were as difficult as they were exciting for Julia. Thar Thar treated her with the utmost respect and kindness. The way he looked and smiled at her would give her goose bumps; his gentle voice made her heart jump. When their eyes met she could barely control her desire. She wanted nothing more than to be alone with him, but some of the kids were always around, even late at night.

Just when she started to wonder whether Thar Thar shared her desire, he surprised her with an invitation for an outing.

The children prepared a picnic. Ei Ei had made pancakes and a fresh vegetable curry with rice and eggs. Moe Moe and Ko Maung had risen early and gone into the city to buy fresh crackers and pastries, bananas and bottled water. The provisions were packed neatly in a bamboo basket alongside some dishes and a tablecloth. Everything had been strapped to the back of the moped. All the children stood in the yard and waved, as if the two were setting off on a trip around the world.

Just beyond Hsipaw Thar Thar turned off the main road. They drove along dry, dusty lanes, increasingly narrow, past banana plantations and rice paddies farmed by isolated families. At one point they had to dismount and push the moped together across a nearly dried-up streambed.

Eventually the brush swallowed the path altogether, and there was no way to go farther. He put the moped aside, hoisted the basket onto his shoulders, and led her up a steep slope.

After a short hike they found themselves standing beside a small lake, fed by a waterfall, or at least what was left of one. In place of a rushing stream, thin rivulets trickled down the rough gray face of the rock. The lake was only half full and surrounded by trees and dense brush. Its smooth surface reflected the blue sky and the occasional white cloud.

Thar Thar looked around, surprised. "Last year at this time things were not nearly so dry."

"It's beautiful all the same," said Julia.

She scrambled down to the water. It was so clear that she could easily see the bottom. "Shall we take a dip?"

Thar Thar shook his head. "I'm not much of a swimmer."

"Come on."

"No, really."

Without a second thought she stripped down to her undergarments and slipped into the water. It was marvelously soft and refreshing. After a few strokes she could feel the cold prickling her skin. She swam a crawl stroke and quickly reached the opposite shore.

Thar Thar looked across at her, waved, and started unpacking the basket.

Julia warmed herself in the sun and looked on as he carefully laid out their picnic on a flat stone. She could not help but think of her father. Thar Thar radiated the same sense of calm, the same serenity. He, too, was a loner, and he had the same remote, absent manner. Her father had been strict with himself, but not with others. He would have smiled if someone cut in front of him in line or snatched a taxi out from under his nose. Whenever anyone treated him rudely, he felt it was that person's problem, not his own. Thar Thar felt the same way, and Julia realized that she was starting to understand the particular way of thinking, the particular view of the world, that fostered that attitude.

Physically, too, they were not dissimilar. About the same height, muscular, striking lips, the same white, flawless teeth she had always envied in her father. Their movements conveyed a similar dignity, a quiet elegance.

She was suddenly overcome with longing for Thar Thar, as if he were on the other side of the world rather than the other side of the lake. She felt a chill now and needed to go to him, at once. She dove into the water, and three dozen quick strokes later she was back on the other shore. She dried herself quickly with her blouse, and, pulling on her T-shirt, she scrambled up the bank.

"You're a good swimmer! Aren't you cold?"

"No." She looked lovingly at the picnic he had laid out. "You remind me of my father."

He laughed a little shyly. "Was he also a bad swimmer?"

Julia considered. "I don't recall that I ever once saw him swimming. But that's not what I meant."

"What then?"

"You have a lot in common. He would have liked you."

She took him in her arms.

"You're shivering," he remarked, surprised. "Was the water so cold?" He opened his robe, wrapped it around her, and held her tightly. His warmth felt good.

She could sense how her body aroused him. How his heart began to beat faster.

How a desire swelled in her so that she felt as if she would burst.

She closed her eyes.

He caressed her lips. Kissed her neck. His warm breath on her skin. His hands, everywhere.

He lifted her up and carried her behind a jutting rock. His powerful arms. His scent, which had so excited her that first time.

She began to lose herself—and to find herself.

Never before had a man touched her like that. Never before had she felt so desired, so at one with another person.

And with herself.

Later they sat amid the empty bowls and plates. With his fingers he brushed her hair out of her face while he fed her Ei Ei's pancakes. She stretched out and lay with her head in his lap.

"Did you always want to have so many children?"

He laughed. "No, certainly not."

"What is their legal status, anyway?"

"What do you mean by that?"

"Who is responsible for them?"

"They are, of course. Who else?"

"But most of them are under age, aren't they?"

"I guess so. Not all, but some."

"So who has custody?"

"Custody?"

"Who is legally responsible?"

He thought about it. "I don't know. Probably I am."

"Have you adopted them?"

"We are a family, if that's what you mean." He kissed her tenderly on the forehead, on the tip of her nose.

"Is there anything in writing?"

"From whom?"

"Certificates from the authorities, waivers from the parents, that sort of thing."

"No. Is that so important?" Thar Thar was genuinely flummoxed by her questions.

Julia sat back up. "Of course."

"Why?"

"What if something happened? Someone needs to be responsible."

"What would happen?"

"How should I know? Something can always happen."

"Hm."

"On top of that, the parents could always come and take them back unless you have some kind of documentation."

He furrowed his brow. "It was their parents who brought them to me in the first place. And the children are happy to be there. Isn't that enough?"

"Oh, Thar Thar." Julia let out a deep sigh.

And suddenly he started to sing, so softly that she leaned in very close.

"Someday she will come to love me."

She smiled, embarrassed. No man had ever sung for her before, apart from her father, at bedtime.

"Someday she will come to love me," he continued, unabashed and now somewhat louder.

I want to change places with the red roses she is wearing in her hair.
Trying my best to make my loved one even prettier.
Someday she will come to love me.

Chapter 10

THOSE WHO FEEL LOVED AND DESIRED radiate a special beauty and inner peace. They are generous. They want to share their joy. They like to help others. No task is too big for them. Their happiness is palpable. It speaks out of their eyes, in their laughter, in their every movement. Their feet hardly touch the ground.

And their joy is contagious. Julia, Thar Thar, and the children were filled in the following weeks with an almost uncanny lightness.

Julia patiently instructed the children in English. She became an ambitious student of Burmese. She was determined to master the language as quickly as possible.

Nearly every afternoon Julia and Thar Thar would disappear for a few hours, making excursions in the vicinity. Generally on the moped, though sometimes they would just start hiking. They always returned a bit more chipper and exhilarated.

Julia greeted each new day with anticipation. She had never felt that way in America, not even on vacation.

She marveled at the way Thar Thar interacted with the children. The patience he exhibited when Ei Ei with her stiff leg or Moe Moe with her missing arm needed more time in the field than he would have. The calm and discretion with which he resolved the occasional spat without ever casting blame. "You would be a good father," she told him.

"I don't think so," he replied, embarrassed.

"Why not?"

"I'm still a child myself."

"You?" she contradicted. "After everything you've been through? I'm not sure I know anyone more grown-up than you."

Ei Ei had promised to let Julia in on the secret of her pancakes.

The two were squatting in the kitchen. Ei Ei heated some milk for the batter, frothed six eggs, added flour, a teaspoon of sugar, and a pinch of salt.

"Do you cook for your parents every day?" she wanted to know.

Julia chuckled at the thought. "No. I live alone."

"Alone? You live completely alone?"

Julia did not recall ever having evoked as much pity as she did from Ei Ei at that moment.

"That's how it is for us. If you're not married and don't have a partner or any kids, you live alone."

"Is that a rule?"

"No, of course not."

Ei Ei looked at her, dumbfounded. "Then why do you do it?"

"Because," Julia considered, "because it gives us a lot of freedom."

"What kind of freedom?"

"We can do what we want. If you live alone, you don't have to worry about anyone else." Julia could see that every sentence was creating greater confusion. "It's difficult to explain. Life in New York is very different from life here. People work all day, so they're happy to have some peace and quiet in the evening."

"What do you cook for yourself, then?"

"At home I only cook on the weekend. Otherwise I go out to eat or have something delivered."

"By the neighbors?"

"By the neighbors? No. By a restaurant. Lots of people do that. We rarely have time to cook."

"No time to cook?" Ei Ei shook her head, baffled, while she melted butter in a hot pan. When it was ready she poured in a scoop of batter and spread it around so deftly that it covered the bottom of the pan in a very thin layer. "It must be no thicker than the leaf of a eucalyptus tree," she explained. With quick movements of the pan she flipped it several times in the air. As soon as it was golden on both sides, she drizzled a little condensed milk over it and rolled it up.

It was the most delicious pancake Julia had ever eaten.

The next day, to show her gratitude, she bought a colonial-era music box at the market in Hsipaw. It was shaped like a Scottish castle and played an English march. From then on Ei Ei took it with her wherever she went.

One morning Julia wanted to show me a particular pagoda she and Thar Thar had visited several times on foot. It stood on the crest of a nearby hill. Its crown gleamed with gold, and one whitewashed side was intact while the other was bare stonework in which many deep cracks were visible. Small trees and grasses were growing out of the crevices. The stupa listed so to one side that it ought long ago to have collapsed. It looked as if it were defying gravity.

"Have you ever seen anything like it?" Julia asked me.

I walked around the building, examining it carefully. "I have not. Indeed it is quite puzzling."

Thar Thar explained that according to legend, the pagoda had been destroyed by earthquakes many times over the centuries, and that it had always been rebuilt. Some time ago there had been a violent tremor that had damaged it so badly that it ought to have fallen over. People attributed the fact that it had not to some protective power. It was to this power that all of the altars standing about were dedicated. People made offerings, hoping that the same spirit would also protect them.

Julia took three pastries out of her backpack and set them carefully on one of the altars. She nodded to me. "One for each of us."

She was ready to return home, but it was a warm day, and I was weary from the hike. I suggested we rest for a while and crouched in the shade of the stupa. Thar Thar handed me a bottle of water. In silence we gazed out over the valley. I noticed that Julia was growing restless, and I gestured to a spot beside me. "Do sit down."

The two of them squatted next to me.

After a while Julia stood back up. She walked nervously to and fro before us. "I have some ideas about what we can do with our spare time in the monastery."

"What do you have in mind?" asked Thar Thar.

"We can make better use of it."

"Is time a tool that a person uses?"

"That's how we talk about it at home," replied Julia.

"What should we use it for?"

"We could fix the roof. We could expand the English instruction for the kids. We could plant more vegetables. We could try different varieties to find out which ones are the most productive, and then we could sell them at the market. We could even open a little café or restaurant in Hsipaw."

"Hm." Thar Thar leaned back and considered. "So it's not a good use of our time to sit here with your brother in the shade of the pagoda?" he asked with some concern.

"No, it is."

"So?"

"It's not a good use if we're trying to accomplish anything."

"What do you want to accomplish?"

"Do you really not understand?"

"I do, but..."

"There's a lot I want to accomplish," she interrupted. "Providing a better life for the children, for instance."

He furrowed his brow in thought. "Do you feel that they are not living well with us?"

"That's not what I mean," she answered. She was starting to get impatient.

"What then?"

"If we plant more vegetables, or a different kind, we can use the money that we earn at the market to build a reasonable toilet and shower in the courtyard. We could have an electrical connection to the power from the street put in, or we could buy a generator and use it to power a water heater. Then we would have hot water, and we wouldn't have to take icy showers in the freezing cold every morning. Wouldn't that be an improvement?"

"No."

She looked at each of us in turn, flabbergasted. "No? Why not?"

"The children have never lived any other way. Not one of them has ever taken a hot shower."

"Ever?"

"Never."

"Well, I can promise you that after a week they would love it and would never want to go back. You can bank on it."

"That may be so, but as it is they don't miss it. And we would have less time to sit together in the shade of a pagoda. I would miss that..." he said with a cautious, expectant smile.

"Me, too, but one thing does not exclude the other."

"Doesn't it?"

"No!"

Thar Thar did not look convinced, but they left it at that.

Shortly thereafter we set out for home, and we spoke very little on the way back.

Chapter 11

A CHILD.

It was a simple test that even the hospital in Hsipaw was equipped to perform. Positive. The doctor's broken English was adequate enough to convey that much.

The nausea in the mornings, the occasional twinges in her abdomen, the gentle pressure in her breasts had all been pointing in that direction. Now she knew for certain.

New life was stirring inside her, the size of a matchstick.

A second chance, she thought. Not something everyone gets.

A child.

His child.

It took a while before Thar Thar understood what she was saying.

A gift of such proportions that he hardly knew how to accept it. He had been many things already in his life: Brother. Pest. Unloved son. Orphan. Unwilling soldier. Monk. Refugee. Substitute family. Lover.

The thought of being a father had never entered his mind. Neither as something he desired, nor as something to be avoided or feared. It had simply never occurred to him. At first he had the feeling that Julia was not talking about the two of them, but about some other woman and man.

Could he provide what a child needed? He thought about his parents. He did not have many memories of them. He could not even quite picture how his father had looked. He must have been big and strong. As a day laborer and lumberjack, he had been away most of the year, away from the rest of the family. His visits seldom lasted more than a few days, during which there was not much time for his children. Thar Thar had no recollection of ever playing or doing anything with his father. It was more a feeling than a face or a voice that he associated with him. Loneliness. Unfulfilled longing.

The only clear memories Thar Thar had of his father were of the final few seconds of his life. He had stood in the crown of a tree and waved to him. The cracking of a branch. The dark, terrifying noise that leaves make when something heavy falls through them. A dull thud. The faces of the adults that revealed more than he wanted to know.

His father had left him at a very young age.

It was the thoughts of his own childhood that helped him appreciate the import of Julia's words.

A child.

Regardless of anything else that might happen, he was determined to be a different kind of father to his own child.

Moe Moe and Ei Ei rejoiced in their quiet way, as if they were about to acquire a much-craved sibling. They did not let Julia out of their sight.

In the evening, in place of a flower on her pillow she would now find two—one large and one small.

She would open her eyes in the morning to find one of the girls sitting beside her bed, inquiring how she felt and whether she needed anything.

Whenever she worked in the field or did laundry in the courtyard, they would stay close to her and eye her nervously, until Julia would point out that she was not sick but merely pregnant.

"Are people here always so protective of pregnant women?" she asked Thar Thar.

He had to laugh at the thought. "No, on the contrary. I suspect they imagine that that's how it would be for you in America, and that they just want you to feel at home. To make sure you have everything you need."

Julia did not want anyone at the monastery to be making special allowances for her. She asked Ko Lwin and Ko Aung to show her how to weave baskets, so that she would be able to continue contributing even when physical labor started to be too much. They showed her which bamboo stalks were best suited for the job, how to cut them with a knife into very thin strips without cutting oneself, and how then to weave those into baskets large and small. Without a word, but with infinite patience, the blind Ko Aung would guide her hands. When she threw down her knife, discouraged by her own sense of clumsiness, he would encourage her.

"How long does it take you to make a basket?" she wanted to know.

Neither of them knew for certain. They guessed they could make two or three large baskets, but only one small one per day. They sold the large baskets for six thousand kyat, the small ones for four thousand.

Julia was confused. "Why are they less expensive if it takes you three times as long to make one?"

"The customers are not willing to pay more than that for them," Thar Thar explained.

"So then why don't you make only large baskets?"

"Because the customers also want small ones."

"Then they should pay for them."

"They do."

"Not enough."

"Four thousand kyat is a tidy sum," he contradicted.

"Maybe so, but selling the small ones for less than the big ones makes no financial sense."

"Why not?"

Thar Thar did not understand the logic of production costs or supply and demand, not even after Julia explained it a second time.

All three of them lauded her first attempt, even though it fell apart as soon as she tried to carry something in it. Compared with those of the children, her fingers were sluggish, cumbersome, and awkward.

Julia did not give up. She spent entire afternoons alone in front of a pile of bamboo strips, cursing from time to time and practicing until she had mastered the pattern and the technique and her baskets no longer fell apart on first use.

Within weeks of learning she was pregnant she started to make plans for life with a baby in the monastery. She wanted to use some of her money from America to build a bathroom with several showers and a tub. To get electricity, to fix the roof, to buy a used jeep. She was thinking about a well with an electric pump. The road from the monastery to the street was in desperate need of repair. During the rainy season, with its countless potholes, it was all but impassible to cars.

Thar Thar had no objections, or if he did, he never expressed them. He was even more affectionate and attentive than otherwise. If Julia craved fish, he would go to town, buy a fish, and prepare it for her. If she wanted fresh milk at breakfast, he made sure she had some. If she had trouble sleeping, he would rub her feet, and if that did not help, he would tell her and the children stories until they dozed off.

Physically, though, he was somewhat distant. That was new. Julia's attempts to seduce him on their various excursions ended in caresses and tender hugs, nothing more. He did not want to disturb the child growing inside her.

A child. Her child.

Chapter 12

FAMILY. For Julia, as a child, it had meant father, mother, and brother.

A father she had loved above all else in the world, but who was rarely there, and almost never when she needed him.

A mother whose moods she feared, who had no idea what to do with her daughter, and who would spend days on end sequestered in her darkened bedroom.

An estranged big brother whom she admired but who showed little interest in her, who regarded her with disdain for reasons she never understood.

She remembered dinners that dragged on forever, where the only sound was the clinking of the flatware. Glances exchanged between mother and son, hints at a world full of secrets, a world to which she would never have access. A big house on the Upper East Side where laughter seldom rang.

There are families, she thought to herself, where happiness never resides. Or it is at most an infrequent visitor.

Families where everyone contributes as much love as they can, but still it is not enough. Where everyone shares according to their ability, but still the hearts go hungry. No one to blame. No bad intentions. Where wounds are inflicted that even a lifetime cannot heal.

The place where it all begins. Love. The longing for love. The fear thereof.

The place we can never escape. Where the hearts are too big or too small. Too voracious or too satiated.

Where we are more vulnerable and defenseless than anywhere else.

Because love knows no justice.

The family of her childhood no longer existed. Her father was dead. Her mother lived with her brother in San Francisco. Her contact with both was limited to the brief phone calls that courtesy demanded on birthdays and Thanksgiving.

Now she would be starting a family of her own, a family with its own rules: mother—father—child.

And twelve siblings.

And an uncle.

Living in a monastery in the mountains in Shan State.

A place where there was enough for everyone. Where everyone was interested in everyone else. Where no one regarded anyone with disdain. Where no one ever sequestered herself in a darkened room.

She needed only to bide her time, to be patient. With Thar Thar's and U Ba's help everything would turn out fine. She had no doubt.

Chapter 13

THEN TRAGEDY STRUCK.

Ei Ei was one of the first girls whom Thar Thar had taken in. She was shy and at first so quiet that he sometimes wondered whether she was actually capable of speaking more than two sentences at a time.

Her parents had dropped her off one day. An eight-year-old girl, a victim of polio, she was small and deformed with an inflexible leg and twig-thin limbs.

They had heard of a peculiar monk who would look after children when no one else would.

They were farmers who could neither read nor write and who had many other children to care for. Their harvests were insufficient to feed a child who could not work.

In the beginning she would follow Thar Thar's every step, as if she worried that he, too, might one day abandon her. Even when he needed to relieve himself, she would wait patiently by the wooden shack in the courtyard. He grew accustomed to her and slowed his pace so that she could keep up with him. If he was in a hurry he would hoist her onto his back or his shoulders or carry her around in his arms.

She was able to sleep only when he lay beside her.

In time she learned trust. She could let him out of her sight without panicking. She started learning to cook, became increasingly independent, and grew into a fine big sister and one of Thar Thar's most important helpers.

No one was shocked one morning when Ei Ei was too exhausted to work in the fields. The disease had left deep marks on her body, not only the frozen leg.

At first Julia and Thar Thar suspected she had caught a cold. The coughing and fever were no cause for alarm. Many children experienced minor illnesses in the winter and spring. There were reliable remedies for such things.

But the herbal tincture had no effect.

The cold poultice that Julia applied proved as ineffectual as the pain pills from her first-aid kit.

Ei Ei's fever rose.

A sliver in her foot.

An infected wound.

Perhaps they would have gone sooner to the hospital if Ei Ei had confessed how badly she was feeling, but she was not one to complain.

There was no medicine in Hsipaw to counteract the toxins in her blood. Julia enlisted a taxi driver to fetch some in Mandalay. The round trip was twelve to sixteen hours under the best of circumstances. She hired a second man so that they could take it in shifts to drive around the clock.

In the meantime she never strayed from Ei Ei's side. She wound the music box and refreshed the poultice several times in the night. She spoke encouragingly to her, as if words alone could lower the fever.

Ei Ei clenched Julia's hand as if it had been her mother's.

Early in the morning the drivers returned, weary from the road. They had not taken a single break. Julia poured the medicine into the enfeebled Ei Ei, waited, told the others to take heart. But it was too late.

Ei Ei had a big heart, but not a strong one.

The tinkling of the music box was the last sound she ever heard.

Ei Ei's passing changed many things.

She had become very dear to Julia. The friendship that had developed between them was rivaled only by her friendship with Moe Moe. She admired the equanimity with which Ei Ei bore her physical afflictions. Her courage. Her cooperative spirit.

Now her pale, lifeless body lay there on a dirty straw mat. Julia had never seen or touched a corpse before. She felt as if a part of her had died with Ei Ei.

Thar Thar tried to console her. Ei Ei would soon return in a new incarnation. In her next life she would not need to hobble across the yard or the fields with a crippled leg. She would garner the rewards that—for whatever reason—had eluded her in this life. For Thar Thar this was a reassuring thought. For Julia it was not.

Until that day she had hoped, initially with considerable doubt, that she would be able bring her child into the world in Hsipaw or Mandalay. In spite of the miscarriage she had suffered two years earlier. A hematoma on the uterine wall.

Destiny. Fate. Bad luck. Call it what you will.

From a medical perspective it was nothing that would in any way complicate or threaten a second pregnancy. Several doctors had independently assured her of that much. And after all, she told herself, healthy children were born to healthy mothers every day in Burma. The first three months of the pregnancy had proceeded without complication, and she had even found a woman gynecologist in Mandalay who had been trained in England and whom she trusted no less than her gynecologist in New York.

No more. If a simple sliver in the foot was enough to kill a child, imagine the dangers that lay in wait for a newborn baby.

And for the mother.

From one day to the next she was once again ridden with doubt. She did not want to leave, but now each mosquito seemed a threat. Each dirty mug. Each unboiled drop of water. There were germs everywhere. Viruses. Bacteria.

A simple pregnancy became suddenly a complicated one. A fearless woman was suddenly terrified. Confidence turned suddenly to dread.

Her gynecologist saw no reason for her not to fly to New York. The most important thing was for her to feel safe and well cared for during the birth, which was going to be taxing enough, especially at her age.

Julia knew one thing for certain after Ei Ei's death: her child would come into the world in a hospital in Manhattan. Nowhere else. Not even Bangkok, Hong Kong, or Singapore.

The scents and sounds of her new environment, the faces and voices, now seemed strange and sinister to her. What had fascinated her only a day earlier, she now found distressing. She longed more than anything for the familiarity of New York. A language she understood. Faces that she could read, when necessary. Habits and customs that she understood and that promised her security.

And whatever was good for her would also be good for her child.

Chapter 14

THAR THAR found it difficult to appreciate how she felt. He could not understand how her attitude had so drastically altered.

She wanted desperately to get out of there. With each passing day she pressed for an earlier departure. As if she were on the run. She even kept the children at arm's length for fear they might be contagious, though no one was showing any signs of illness.

He wanted to reassure her, but he had no idea how. He, too, was grieving Ei Ei's sudden death, but the reality was that people died sometimes. Even children. It was sad, but there was nothing to be done about it. To fear death was to fear life, for that is where life always led. He could not understand the connection between Ei Ei's death and Julia's pregnancy.

"What do they have to do with one another?" he asked cautiously. "Blood poisoning is not contagious."

"Don't you think I know that?" she answered gruffly.

"I'm sorry. I didn't mean to anger you." This was not the Julia he knew.

Neither of them spoke. He had previously enjoyed their shared silences, but this was making him uneasy. "Do you think"—he made another attempt—"that you and your child are at greater risk since Ei Ei's death?"

"No, of course not," she declared, only to contradict herself a moment later: "Yes."

"Why?"

"Because I'm afraid. Because I don't feel safe anymore." Ei Ei's passing had reminded her how frequent a guest Death was in Burma. How he would appear unannounced. How little anyone could do to stop him when he suddenly showed up at the door. How they had learned to live with the inevitable and how little able she was to do the same. Unable and unwilling.

"Less safe than before?"

"Yes."

"Why?"

"Because I saw how our Ei Ei was taken from us by a silly sliver in her foot. Is that so difficult to understand?"

"No," he replied, aggrieved.

"I was naive. I had forgotten how dangerous it could be to get sick in Burma."

"More dangerous than elsewhere?"

"Seriously, Thar Thar!? In America seven children or mothers out of a thousand die in childbirth. I asked the doctor in Mandalay about the mortality rate in Burma. Do you know what it is?"

He shook his head.

"Seventy. Ten times as high!"

Statistics meant as little to him as probabilities. He knew that seventy was too many, just as seven in America was also too many.

"And just imagine if there's any kind of complication. I'm not twenty anymore."

Thar Thar was silent. Her fear, like most fears, was not to be allayed by good arguments. It was for her to choose. It was for her to bring the child into the world, not for him. He would go along with whatever she decided.

"Is there any chance you would reconsider?"

"No."

Thar Thar could not bring himself to tell the children that he would have to leave them alone for a while. He skirted around it for several days, promising Julia each morning that he would do it that evening. But after the meditation he would just bid the children good night and withdraw.

They were his family. They gave him what he had craved for so many years: a sense that he belonged.

His parents were dead; his brother, lost. After escaping from the military camp, he had lived for eight years with a Catholic priest. He had kept house for him, cleaning, shopping, cooking, doing the laundry. When the priest died Thar Thar was alone again.

As a mendicant monk he had wandered from village to village, from monastery to monastery. Sometimes he would stay for a few weeks, sometimes only a few days. Thar Thar told himself he was seeking enlightenment, but all he really wanted was to arrive somewhere.

When he discovered the abandoned monastery near Hsipaw he knew that he had found a home. He spent the first weeks there entirely alone. He started to repair the dilapidated meditation hall. Then he met Moe Moe begging at the market, and her parents implored him to take her in.

Soon thereafter Ko Maung was standing in the courtyard. A few days later Ei Ei. Then Ko Aung. Soon "his children," as he called them, were an even dozen. He had been living with them for years. Under his care they were growing into young adults. From them he learned one of life's most important lessons: that we can transform our weaknesses into strengths; that within every sorrowful spirit there is a joyful one, within every fearful spirit a brave one.

When he had trouble sleeping, when in the dead of night the mine blasts and the cries of the prisoners still rang in his mind, he would get up and pace back and forth in the meditation hall. He would listen to the children's quiet breathing and marvel at his own good fortune.

"It's just as difficult for me as it is for you," Julia said, consoling him. "It's only for a few months."

"I know."

"If all goes well we'll be back by the end of the year at the latest."

"And if all does not go well?"

She had no answer for that. "Would you rather stay here?"

The thought had crossed his mind, but he had dismissed it out of hand.

"I wouldn't blame you," she reassured him, and laid his hand on her belly. It was easy to feel the bulge now.

"I'm staying with you."

"Or you could come just a few weeks before the birth. My brother will come with me. He'll be a great help to me, and I have friends in New York."

He shook his head without a word and took solace in the fact that the children at the monastery would be in good hands. U Ko Tun, a widower from Hsipaw, had volunteered to stay with them for the duration of the trip. He had been a frequent guest at the monastery, staying sometimes for weeks or even months at a stretch.

In the end it was Julia who summoned all the children into the meditation hall. They crouched in a semicircle around her. Thar Thar sat next to her.

She straightened her back and shoulders, drew a deep breath, and made a face as if a chicken bone were caught in her throat. She turned from one to the other of them, looking for help.

When she finally started to speak it was in terse sentences. She spoke English. Thar Thar translated, his head lowered, his eyes on the floor.

Julia told them about the life growing inside her and how it had to be protected. That it was her job to protect it. How she had had a miscarriage, and how that compelled her to exercise additional caution. About hygienic standards. The health risks of pregnancy. The possible complications that one needed to account for, especially at her age. The best possible medical care.

How there really was no alternative.

It took some time for Thar Thar to find a suitable Burmese translation for that sentence.

The children listened intently. Sometimes someone would cough or sniffle. And when she was finished talking, there was a long silence. Ko Maung, robbed of his hearing by an explosion at ten years old, was sitting in the first row, and one could see from his sorrowful expression that he had, in his own way, understood every word. Moe Moe tried in vain to suppress her tears. Others nodded. As if they had seen it all coming: Julia's decision to bring the child into the world not here, but in a distant country. Now they did what life and their parents had taught them to do from they day they were born. They accepted it. They acquiesced. It would not have occurred to any of them to moan about it, or to beg Julia to reconsider, much less to question the wisdom of her decision.

It was what it was.

Julia explained that she and Thar Thar wanted to spend the first few months after the birth in New York, and that they would return after that with the baby. It might be as soon as Christmas. At the latest the Burmese New Year in April. The time would all pass more quickly than they expected.

There was no Internet in Hsipaw at that time. No cell phones or even land lines over which one could make a call to New York. All the same Julia left her telephone number and email address with them. In an emergency they might try to contact her from a hotel in Mandalay.

To a casual observer we appeared to be traveling light. Thar Thar carried Julia's backpack to the train station. He had just a satchel, and it was not even full. I had a small suitcase that we had bought at the market.

But how much baggage a traveler is really carrying often becomes apparent only during the journey.

Chapter 15

THE SPEED OF AIR TRAVEL was beyond Thar Thar's comprehension. He lost all sense of time and place during the flight. He ate whenever someone put food in front of him, whether he was hungry or not. Though the sun was high in the sky he slept. In the dark of night when the stars shone he was wide awake.

"Are you excited?" Julia asked.

"No."

"You're going to New York for the first time and you're not excited?"

"Should I be?"

"It doesn't matter to me, but I thought . . . I mean . . . *New York*!!!"

Not wanting to disappoint her, Thar Thar thought hard. He did not know much about the place he would be spending the next few months. In a teahouse in Mandalay he had once seen a poster of a city skyline at dusk. The owner had boasted that it was Manhattan, though he always told the soldiers who frequently drank their tea in front of it that it was Bangkok. Thar Thar remembered lots of skyscrapers, a bridge, and two impressive towers that looked as if they might truly scrape the sky. They made him think of massive, branchless tree trunks towering over a dark forest.

When he lived with Father Angelo he had read a couple of novels that were set in New York. Apparently none of them had made an impression, because he didn't remember much about them.

"I have no idea what awaits me there," he said. "How can I feel excited?"

"You might be afraid to be disappointed."

"But I have no expectations."

"None at all?"

"Not of the city."

"You might be nervous that you'll feel uncomfortable there."

"That seems unlikely, as long as I'm with you."

She stroked his head, pondering. He was not sure whether she understood him.

Julia thought about her departure from New York five months earlier. She had left the city a sick woman. Full of fear. Haunted. Trapped. Drained by sixty-hour weeks and a job she did not even want. Single. Unhappy for years without having admitted it to herself. Thinking that she was hearing voices. She had stood up one day in the middle of an important meeting and left. Without a word of explanation. She had gone to her office and packed her things, left the firm never to set foot there again. She of all people, the ambitious, assiduous Julia Win.

That voice had been asking her questions she did not care to entertain and to which she had no answers:

Who are you?

Why are you so alone?

Why don't you have any children?

A psychiatrist had told her it might be an early indication of schizophrenia.

A reaction to a life from which she felt estranged, her friend Amy had thought.

A life that she no longer wanted, even if she had no idea what a different life might look like.

Now she was returning pregnant, having spent months in a monastery taking care of children who had taught her so many things she never knew. A man at her side whom she loved above all others. The father of her child.

She was no longer alone.

Thanks to him she had started down the path toward finding out who she was.

Maybe she had been wrong. Perhaps the ability to metamorphose was, after all, not limited to certain kinds of animals.

Outside the terminal a cool wind was blowing. It gave her the feeling that she could smell New York. A salty tang from the nearby Atlantic hung in the air, and with it so many memories. Like it or not, she would be forever connected to this city.

She was exhausted from the long journey, but she was wide awake.

Thar Thar, by contrast, became very quiet once they had arrived. She supposed it was because he was tired. Or because the many impressions were leaving him speechless. Or because in his mind he was back at the monastery. She could sympathize with all of these possibilities. It would take time for him to arrive.

During the ride from the airport he said hardly a word. She, on the other hand, could scarcely sit still for excitement. She chattered on without thinking much about what she was saying. The sentences just bubbled out of her mouth. It was quite out of character for her.

She explained that all the taxis in the city are yellow, and that a person can simply hail one from the side of the street. That there are three airports, five boroughs, and more than a dozen subway lines. That New York was the largest and most important city in America, with the most inhabitants, the most theaters, the most museums, and the most restaurants and that some of them were certainly Burmese. She went on and on while the taxi was stuck in a never-ending line of cars. Thar Thar understood very little of anything she said.

Her apartment was just as she had left it, except that a thick layer of dust covered the bookcases, tables, and floor. The two potted plants on the kitchen counter had completely dried up.

Julia demonstrated how the showers worked and showed us where to find the towels.

"Are you hungry? I could order something."

"No," replied Thar Thar.

"I'll get something anyway." Seconds later she was gone; she came back fifteen minutes later with two bags of groceries. She wanted to unpack and to start a load of laundry, but she could feel a heaviness working its way through all of her limbs as exhaustion gradually crept over her.

"Are you sure you don't want anything to eat?"

"Yes," he said. "I just want to sleep. How late is it in Burma?"

"Just before five, I think. But we shouldn't go to bed too early," she cautioned, "or we'll wake up at three in the morning and we won't be able to go back to sleep. We should stay on our feet for another two or three hours."

Within half an hour we were all in bed and sound asleep.

Chapter 16

"DID MAMA REALLY HEAR A VOICE, or did she just make that up?"

U Ba poured himself another tea and drained half the cup. "Why would she make up something like that?"

"Maybe she was tired of sitting in her office all the time. I often feel that way about school."

"And then you make something up?" My uncle's voice sounded stern, but his heart was smiling. "No, I am afraid that she truly heard the voice. Things were not going well for her before she met your father," he said gravely.

"Why not?"

"There were many reasons."

He didn't say anything else, and I got the point that he didn't want to talk about it. "Do all adults hear voices?"

"No."

"How about you?"

"No, fortunately not."

"I'm happy to hear it." It was dark out now, and the air was full of the voices of evening: the rattle of dishes, children shouting, dogs barking. Next door someone was playing guitar and singing. U Ba's stomach growled. "It's getting late. Should I make us something to eat?"

He nodded. I got up and went into the kitchen. There was some leftover rice from the day before. I diced peppers, onions, and tomatoes, fried them briefly in a wok, added the rice and two eggs, seasoned it all with soy sauce, chili peppers, and a few coriander leaves. U Ba wanted to help, but I told him that he should rest.

We ate in silence, each of us lost in our own thoughts, I guess.

After the meal my uncle was too exhausted to carry on with the story. It came as no surprise to me, and maybe it was even a relief. My head was spinning from all I'd heard.

My uncle lay in the bed beside me, just about outsnoring the pig below us. I couldn't stop thinking about my mother and the voice in her head. Maybe it had come back, and that's why she was having a difficult time. Maybe it was a voice telling her that she should not see her son. Maybe *never* see her son. Was there anything I could do about it, if that was the case? Was there any kind of medicine for a problem like that?

I finally fell asleep but was jolted awake in the night by a bad dream. I lay there in my bed, quiet as a mouse, listening and fearing that I, too, was hearing a voice. But the only sounds I could make out were U Ba's snoring, the cicadas, and a handful of frogs.

In the morning the rooster woke me. I was dead tired, and I briefly considered skipping school, but my uncle would certainly not have approved, and I worried that he might withhold the story for a few days as punishment.

I got up, went into the yard, and dunked my head in the barrel of cold water. That always helped.

I let my uncle sleep. I grabbed two hard-boiled eggs and two pieces of dry toast, then headed off to school.

School was even more boring than usual, but today it didn't bother me. I sat at the window, looking out and wondering whether I knew anyone else who heard voices. The aunt of one of my classmates, Su Myat Phyu, had tried to kill her husband with rat poison last year. She had mixed it into the food, but apparently he didn't like the taste of the tainted curry. At any rate, he had given it to the dogs. Su Myat Phyu says that it didn't agree with them. Afterward people said that the aunt had lost her mind and that she was possessed by a spirit. Was that just a way of saying that she heard voices?

I wondered if you could tell by looking that a person was hearing voices. I could imagine that they would make faces or that they would cover their ears. Maybe it made their noses tickle. Maybe our teachers heard voices telling them to beat us and to treat the soldiers' children differently from the rest of us. That would be a good explanation for their behavior. In fact, it would be a good explanation for loads of things I didn't understand.

But it probably wasn't so easy.

On the way home Su Myat Phyu walked with me as far as the train station. I asked casually how her aunt was doing, and she told me that she had killed herself a few weeks ago. That was a frightening thought.

When I got home, U Ba said that he didn't want to go on with the story today, that he was too tired, that I would have to wait until tomorrow.

At first I was disappointed. I wanted to know how it was for my parents in New York. At the same time I had to admit that it was making me uneasy. Something awful must have happened. Otherwise they wouldn't be living in Yangon while I stayed with my uncle in Kalaw. So far, it seemed to me that they hadn't demanded any courage of themselves that their hearts were not able to handle.

The next day U Ba was waiting for me outside the school at the end of the day. He had gone to the market, and he had made my favorite meal, something he had not done for a long time. Yellow curry with peas and fried shrimp from Inlay Lake.

When we were done eating he settled onto the couch and lit a cheroot. "Would you like to hear more?"

"Definitely." I lay down next to him, my head resting in his lap. He tickled my neck.

U Ba started right in, but I interrupted him. "Can I please ask a question?"

"Of course."

"Is hearing voices hereditary?"

He smiled. "No, don't worry."

"Are you sure?"

"Completely sure."

That reassured me, even though I wasn't completely convinced he was telling the truth.

Chapter 17

THAR THAR awoke in the middle of the night. Out in the street he heard first one siren, then another, then a third, as if there were an echo. A few seconds passed before he recalled where he was. A floor lamp cast a shadow on the white wall beside him. The silhouette resembled a gallows. Julia lay sleeping on the other side of the bed. He wanted to snuggle up to her, as she had done to him before falling asleep. But he was afraid to wake her and decided against it. Very cautiously he shifted a little closer to her. He wanted at least to smell her.

Thar Thar felt wide awake and uncharacteristically restless. He could hardly lie still. After a while he sat up quietly, folded his legs, closed his eyes, and attempted to meditate. His breath was flat and rapid. He felt the cool air entering his nose and then escaping again warmer. A flood of images streamed through his mind: Buildings taller than trees. Ei Ei crouching in the kitchen and blowing into the fire. Cars. The monastery at dusk. Clouds from above. A narrow footpath through the jungle. Moist earth and dry branches flying through the air. Voices. Cries. Gunfire. A severed foot. Thar Thar opened his eyes in fright. He had not had a flashback like that in a very long time. He tried once more to meditate, but the images would not go away.

He rose without a sound, wandered into the living room, and gazed about. On a shelf on the wall he discovered some mementos of Julia's first trip to Burma: half hidden by books and vases was a Buddha carved in wood; beside it, a dusty lacquer box and a photograph of her in front of a pagoda. Her unusual smile suggested that she was lost in reverie. On the opposite wall hung an original painting, a red skull of some kind, in bold brushstrokes, with bulging eyes and swollen lips. The image had disturbed him from the moment he spotted it the day before. Feeling alienated, he turned to the window and looked out over the city.

Light still shone from some of the windows. There were still cars on the road. He gazed down into a canyon of traffic lights, dozens of them alternating to a rhythm of their own from red to green to yellow and back.

After a while he heard steps behind him; seconds later he felt Julia's warm breath on his neck. She stood right behind him. "Can't you sleep anymore?"

"No. I never imagined there really were buildings as tall as this," he whispered. "And that people lived in them, no less."

"No?"

"No. That there were sooo many of them. And so many cars, so much..."

"So much what?"

"So much of . . . of everything."

Julia put her arms around his waist and laid her head on his shoulder. Another siren howled into the night. A police car sped through the intersection against the light.

"You must be happy to be back home," he said quietly.

"Yes, I guess."

"You guess?"

"I don't know. Everything here is familiar, of course, but at the same time it feels"—she was searching for the right word—"strange to be back. Weird. I don't know. Maybe I am just exhausted."

He turned around. Julia did look tired. Her cheeks seemed a little swollen; her eyes were small and reddish, as if she had been crying.

"Are you okay?"

"Yes, I just woke up from a bad dream."

"What kind of dream?"

"Very peculiar. I was pregnant and all of a sudden my belly started to grow bigger and bigger. It wouldn't stop. You weren't there; nor was U Ba. I was by myself and panicked. For some reason I was at my parents' house on Sixty-Fourth, and I ran out to the street. Someone called 911. The ambulance took me to a hospital, and they put me straight into the intensive care unit. Half a dozen doctors stood around my bed in their white lab coats. They didn't know what to do, whispered to each other, and looked very concerned. No one dared to talk to me. I pleaded for help; my belly was already twice as big as a basketball, and I could feel it was about to burst any second—at that moment I woke up."

Thar Thar took her in his arms and held her tight. All of a sudden her whole body was shivering. "It was just a dream."

"I know. Still . . . it's been a long time since I woke up so terrified."

He gently stroked her head.

"Sometimes I am scared," she said after a long pause.

"Of what?"

She shrugged. "I wish I knew."

"I am sorry."

A deep-drawn sigh escaped her. "Do you think I am ungrateful?"

"Why would I think that?"

"Because you came all the way to New York with me, you left the kids behind for me. I am with my doctor now, I am safe and well taken care of. What right do I have to feel anxious?"

Thar Thar paused for a moment. "Do you know the story of the Mouse and the Elephant?"

"I don't think so, what is it?"

"A Burmese tale."

"No, tell me."

"Once there was a Mouse and an Elephant living in the jungle, and they became close friends. One day, as they clambered over the roots of the mighty trees and beat their way through the thick undergrowth, the Elephant said: 'Earlier today I was walking along, minding my own business, when I suddenly heard a heavy stomping. I caught sight of a vicious elephant I know. Hoping to avoid him, I turned and ran behind a dense stand of trees. As I did so, one of the lower branches gouged a cut in my back. You can see that it is more than two feet long.'

The Mouse looked at his friend. 'I am sure that hurts. But with all due respect, please recall that you were never in mortal danger—neither the elephant nor the branch could have killed you—whereas I was hunted by a wildcat today. She nearly caught me, too! One of her claws left a large wound in my side. You will see that it is at least two feet long.'

The Elephant smiled. 'As much as it pains me to accuse you of lying, I can't help but observe that your whole body, from the tip of your nose to the tip of your tail, is not even one foot long. How can you have a two-foot scratch, then?'

'Mark these words, my large friend,' the Mouse replied. 'To each his own foot! You may measure your scrapes with your large feet, but then you must in turn allow me to measure my injuries with my own little paws.'"

Julia smiled. "Who am I? The Mouse or the Elephant?"

"It doesn't matter. That is the point. Pain. Fear. Happiness. All these emotions are subjective. There is no right or wrong."

Julia looked at him for a long time and then nodded. "Thank you." She put her hands on his cheeks and gave him a kiss. "Are you hungry?" she asked.

"Yes, I am. And thirsty." He walked to the sink and opened the tap. He sniffed the water and ran some into a glass. He held it up and eyed it critically. "Is it safe to drink?"

"Of course."

After hesitating briefly, he took a large gulp.

Julia went to the fridge, took a couple of croissants out of the freezer, and put them into the microwave. She set the kitchen counter with two plates, mugs, knives, and the butter, cheese, and jam she had bought the previous night at a shop around the corner.

"No rice and no curries, I'm afraid," she said, attempting a smile without looking at him.

"That's okay."

"Would you like a coffee?"

"Do you have tea as well?"

"Yes."

She poured water into an electric kettle and turned it on, fetched two bags of green tea out of the kitchen cabinet, cleaned a dusty plate, and threw two withered plants in the garbage bin.

He watched her move. She looked different than in Burma, he thought. Fretful and fragile. Vulnerable. Much more so than she ever did in Hsipaw with the kids. Perhaps she was just worn out from the long trip and the lack of sleep.

Perhaps not.

Chapter 18

AMY CAME BOUNDING down the stairs. Julia flung her arms around her neck, and it seemed their embrace would never end. They washed the tears of joy from each other's eyes. Then Amy turned to face Thar Thar and took a good look at him.

"So you're the love of her life."

Thar Thar smiled nervously. He had no idea how to answer her.

"That counts for a lot. My friend is very choosy." Amy laughed. "Welcome. It's nice to meet you." She gave him a big, long hug. He felt his entire body involuntarily tense up. He cast Julia a questioning look. It was the first time an unfamiliar woman had ever embraced him.

Amy had two small adjoining apartments on the top floor of a building on Rivington Street. She used one as a living space and the other as a studio. Between the apartment doors hung a little altar where several sticks of incense were burning. She had invited some of her and Julia's mutual friends and acquaintances to a welcome-home dinner. You could smell the fried garlic, coriander, and chili even out in the stairwell.

Thar Thar looked around. In every room there were figures of the Buddha, large and small. On the shelves, on the nightstand, even in the kitchen. A miniature brass Buddha presided over the spices on the stove. There were hardly fewer than back home in the monastery. He looked at the paintings on the wall. A wild tumult of garish colors and shapes. They disconcerted him, just as the one in Julia's apartment had.

"Do you like them?" asked Amy, who was suddenly standing next to him.

"Hm, they . . . they are very different," answered Thar Thar uncertainly.

"That sounds like a polite Asian no."

He laughed, embarrassed.

"What don't you like about them?"

"I'm sure it's my own fault, but I can't recognize anything in them."

"You just need to look long enough, then you'll see whatever you like," she said with a grin, and turned back to the other guests.

Both apartments were lit only with candles. In one room a long table was set. More and more people arrived. They all knew one another, and they all hugged Thar Thar as if he were part of the group.

A young woman introduced herself. "Hi, I'm Charlotte." She had curly red hair and a face full of freckles. "And you?"

"Thar Thar."

"Amy tells me you're from Burma."

He nodded.

"I work at a Free Burma coalition," she explained.

"Free Burma? What is that?"

"We're fighting for a free Burma with democratic elections and a free press!"

"That's good," he said, because he had no idea what else to say.

"A few months ago I was in a refugee camp on the Burmese-Thai border. You can't imagine what's going on there. Thousands of people are living in tents without running water or electricity. No doctors. No schools. Even so, no one wants to go back. They're all afraid. It's dreadful."

Thar Thar followed her every word, as if he had never heard anything about it. Once in a while he nodded politely.

"You wouldn't believe the stories they are telling us. The soldiers rape women and murder children. I guess most Burmese people know nothing about it, right?"

Without waiting for an answer, she kept right on talking. After her return she had gathered donations from friends and colleagues. She and her friends had participated in several charity races, 5K's and 10K's, and they had collected enough money to finance a school in one of the camps. She talked and talked. Thar Thar nodded and nodded. Sometimes he would close his eyes.

Amy called everyone to find a place at the table. Julia sat across from him. Next to her sat a lean man with round glasses, a long nose, and a goatee. He introduced himself as

Bob and leaned over the table to Thar Thar. "What did you do in Burma?"

"I lived in a monastery."

"You were a monk?"

"No."

"But you lived in a monastery anyway?" he asked in surprise.

"Yes."

"I see, a kind of retreat. You were meditating there."

Thar Thar nodded. "Among other things. Yes."

"I've been doing the same for the last few years. Half an hour, twice a day, morning and evening. It saved my marriage." He laughed. "Which school do you follow?"

The question confused Thar Thar. He wished Julia would intercede, but she was engrossed in a conversation with Amy. "I'm not sure I understand your question."

"I mean which form of meditation. Zazen? Vipassana? Metta?"

Thar Thar thought long about it. "My own form."

The man leaned back and regarded him skeptically. "Your own form?"

The other conversations at the table suddenly subsided. Everyone was looking at him. This interest flustered Thar Thar even more.

"Yes," he answered in a near whisper.

"Does your form have a name?"

"What kind of name?"

"Every meditational tradition has a name."

"Hm. No, I'm afraid mine doesn't."

"Thar Thar lived with twelve handicapped children in an old, abandoned monastery," Julia said, coming to his rescue. "Naturally they also meditated together."

For a moment there was utter silence at the table. All eyes were on him. The situation was making him increasingly uneasy. He did not wish to be the center of attention, never mind their admiring gazes. He pressed his lips together, swallowed, and looked at Julia.

"He taught them to read and write, and he cared for them," she explained. "Their parents had brought them to him when they were little."

"What do you mean by handicapped?" Charlotte wanted to know.

"One was blind, another deaf. Moe Moe was missing a hand, another girl was missing a foot. One of the boys stuttered."

"And you lived there with them?" asked one woman incredulously.

"Yes."

"How did you ever cope with that?"

Julia smiled and nodded toward Thar Thar. Then she told them of her time in the monastery. She told them about helping with the harvest, about shared cooking, their hikes, Ei Ei's pancakes, and Ei Ei's death.

Thar Thar listened. He saw her eyes beaming; even her voice sounded different than minutes before, it was filled with such warmth that he had the feeling she could get up any moment to go back to the monastery.

And he was glad that she was such a good storyteller. He would have found it difficult to share these stories with strangers. For all he knew, they were not even interested in them.

Eventually, to Thar Thar's considerable relief, the conversation turned to other matters: whether George W. Bush was a war criminal and whether he ought to stand trial. It was about the wars in Iraq and Afghanistan and about the upcoming presidential election and which Republican was going to lose to Hillary Clinton. Everyone spoke loudly and all at once. To Thar Thar's ear it sounded like an argument, but if he was understanding them correctly, they were all of one mind.

"Did you have a good time?" Julia asked on the way home.

"Yes," Thar Thar answered wearily.

"For real?" She laughed. "It might take a while to turn you into a New Yorker."

"What do you mean?"

"How could you stand it?"

"Stand what?"

"The way Charlotte was talking to you. Why didn't you tell her about everything you've been through?"

"Why should I have? She never asked."

"So? You've just got to speak up for yourself if you want to be heard." She shifted over toward him and laid her head on his shoulder.

Thar Thar said nothing.

"If it had been me I would have interrupted her after a few sentences."

"Why? That would have been impolite."

"Sometimes you have to be impolite. Wasn't she getting on your nerves?"

He shook his head. "No."

"Really not? Amy was mortified by the way she was talking to you."

"There's no need."

Chapter 19

JULIA HAD WRITTEN "For You" in Burmese on an envelope and laid it on Thar Thar's pillow.

"What's this?" he inquired.

"A surprise."

He pulled a picture the size of a postcard out of the envelope. On it he saw nothing but little white dots on a black background. They reminded him of stars twinkling in a night sky. He examined the image carefully. "What is it? I can't make any sense of it."

She indicated a few dots in the middle that reminded him vaguely of a tiny ant. "It's a picture of our baby," she explained.

He scrutinized it more closely, holding it very near his face, as if he were nearsighted.

Julia pointed out four tiny lines and a couple of dots. "Those are the arms, the legs, the head, the belly."

He looked at the photograph incredulously and then handed it back to her.

"Aren't you happy?"

"About our baby? Of course. But I can't see a child in that picture. Only dots."

Disappointed, Julia tucked the photograph back into the envelope.

"Did I do something wrong?"

"No. I thought you would be happy about the picture. I can see our child clearly in it."

"I didn't mean to upset you."

"You haven't. It's just..." Julia took his hand. "You've been very quiet since we got to New York. I have no idea how you're doing. Whether you're happy. Whether you miss the children. Whether you need anything. Is it all too much for you here? Maybe you're even regretting the decision to come? I can't tell."

Thar Thar sat awhile in thought. "In my entire life no one has ever asked whether I was happy. Whether I was missing anything. Whether it was all too much for me."

"No one?"

"No."

"Not even your par—"

"No," he said, cutting her short.

"I'm sorry."

"We come from different worlds."

"I know. That's why we have to talk about it."

It got very quiet. To Julia it seemed that even the din of traffic on Second Avenue subsided. Thar Thar sank back onto the bed. He found it difficult to look at her.

"What would you like to talk about?" he asked.

"Everything. How you're doing. How I'm doing. What we're feeling, the two of us, the three of us, soon to be the four of us."

He groaned. "That's difficult."

"Why?"

"I'm not accustomed to it. Those . . . those are questions that I seldom ask myself. Things are the way they are."

"How they are can be good or bad."

Thar Thar took a long time with his answer. "How they were," he finally stated, "they were often bad. Should I have asked my mother why she preferred my brother to me? Should I have asked myself as a human mine detector how I was doing? You know my story. I've spent most of my life just worried about survival. Then I had twelve children to look after. There wasn't much spare time for these kinds of questions."

"But still they are important."

He rocked his head from side to side, wondering whether he should just agree with her. "For you."

"For us, don't you think?"

"I'm not sure . . . At some point, maybe."

"No. Now. We have time now, and I would like to know how you are feeling about us, about my ever-expanding belly. Whether you are feeling okay about being here in New York with me."

"Yes."

"Are you missing anything? Aside from the kids, of course."

"No." After a while he added: "People at home just don't ask so many questions."

"Why not?"

"It's considered impolite. Or even disrespectful. A person either offers information or does not."

"Maybe they are afraid of the answers?"

"Sometimes, sure. But not only that. The wrong questions can be dangerous."

"What do you mean?"

"Should I ask the police chief of Hsipaw how he managed to build such a grand house on his meager salary? Should I ask the judge how he can afford a car?"

Julia shook her head. "No. But you can ask me anything."

"I'll make an effort."

"Just ask." She waited.

He thought about it. "Are you happy?"

"Yes."

"Do you need anything?"

"No."

"Are you feeling good about being with me?"

"Hey, are you asking these questions because you want to know the answer, or because you think that's what I want to be asked?"

"Both."

Julia caressed his face gently. She stood up right in front of him, held his head against her swelling torso, and stroked his neck. He wrapped his arms around her hips and held her tight. They stayed that way for a long time.

He heard her voice at his ear.

"I love you," she whispered. "I need you. More than anything."

"I love you, too."

Happiness, he thought, has no meaning until it is shared.

Chapter 20

HOW WELL MUST WE KNOW another person in order to love them? How much must we know about them and their history in order to trust them?

Thar Thar had no answers to these questions, but he had decided to explore Julia's world. He wanted to grasp how this strange life in New York worked. What rules and conventions applied? What were the penalties for breaking them? And the rewards for abiding by them? What made the people in this city tick? What gods did they believe in? What mattered to them, and what did not? How did they show their respect or contempt for one another? What did a smile mean?

Thar Thar went out often and almost always alone. Julia had frequent appointments with doctors and lawyers, and for me his brisk pace quickly became too taxing. He, on the other hand, was fixated on the idea of covering Manhattan entirely on foot. He kept track on a map with a red marker of every street he had been to. He hiked down the avenues from Sixty-Fourth Street to the southern tip of the island. He crisscrossed the Financial District, roamed Chinatown, Little Italy, then SoHo, the East Village, and Greenwich Village, and marched in wide arcs back up past 125th Street.

Initially it was small things that would catch his attention.

At a coffee shop he let so many other customers go ahead of him in the line that the barista warned him that the café was not a rain shelter.

At a subway entrance, he politely held the door open and an endless stream of people passed right by without even looking at him. He stood there for several minutes. Not impatient, merely astonished.

He was baffled by the T-shirt merchants on Canal Street. The messages printed on their garments puzzled him, all the more so the longer he thought about them:

"Life is good"

"It's your life—enjoy it"

"Just do it"

"Happiness for sale"

"Kiss me"

At an intersection in Midtown he noticed a woman approaching who, at first glance, resembled Julia. She was about the same age, had a similar complexion, Asian facial features. She wore spiked heels, a tight black skirt, a white blouse, a gold bracelet. She held a phone to her ear into which she poured an unrelenting stream of words, loudly, but so quickly that he could not understand a single one. She was walking so fast that she nearly barreled right into him.

It occurred to him that that might have been Julia. He suspected that a year ago she might have been similarly dressed and similarly stressed, rushing about the streets of Manhattan from one appointment to the next. Thar Thar turned and watched how, heedless of the honking cars, the woman crossed against the light and disappeared into the throng on Fifth Avenue.

He tried to imagine Julia sitting in one of the skyscrapers, leading negotiations about things he did not comprehend. Meeting one of the suit-men bustling by for lunch. Treating herself to a little break at a coffee shop, sitting there momentarily lost in thought or maybe on her phone again before scurrying off to the next important appointment.

Simultaneously he saw her crouching in the kitchen in Hsipaw and making pancakes with Ei Ei. Saw her and Moe Moe on their knees in the field, drenched in perspiration, rooting for potatoes with their bare hands. He saw her playing soccer with the children and throwing her arms around a limping Ko Aung after, with the help of all the other children, he had finally scored the first goal of his life.

She had had a very long journey.

Of course he had understood from the very beginning that they came from different worlds. In Hsipaw, though, he had largely been able to ignore that fact. She had come to him. She had adapted, integrated herself into life at the monastery. Without complaint or demand. Without any great fuss. Now and then he had been caught off guard by her impatience. Her urge to plan things, and then actually to carry out those plans. How difficult she found it to cope with reticence or, worse yet, silence. How irritated she could become when something did not go quickly enough for her, or when she had to wait a long time for anything. He had not imagined it was very important.

He had been naive.

Only on his long hikes around Manhattan did he begin to appreciate how different their worlds were. How little they had in common on the face of it. How long the bridges were that they must cross.

And while he considered that thought, a shadow of doubt slowly crept in, doubt that she would ever be able to settle down with him and the children in Hsipaw. Not just for three months, or six, but for years. With a baby. A life that lacked so much of what was familiar to her. A life of so little comfort, of so many imponderables. Surrounded by so much dirt. A woman who would not tolerate even a few harmless spiders or cockroaches in her apartment.

Would she subject herself to all of that for his sake? Was she even capable of doing so, never mind whether she was willing?

Or would she ask him to stay in New York with her? He could not imagine it. She had given her word to him and the children that they would be back by the Water Festival. At the latest. Julia was not one to break a promise.

Even if her world was foreign to him, thought Thar Thar, still he knew everything about her that mattered. He had seen her teaching the children English. Making cold compresses for the feverish Ei Ei in the middle of the night. She had never left her side in the hours before her death.

That was enough for him.

He stood in the rain on Lexington Avenue, filled with such a longing for Julia that it constricted his heart.

How well can we know another person, after all? Perhaps everyone will always have some secrets. Some little, some big. And maybe those are just a part of the story. Of every person. Of every relationship.

Chapter 21

THAR THAR WANTED to be an unbiased observer. He was in New York to understand, not to pass judgment. He would learn that it was not always so easy to remain impartial.

Julia had taken him out to the Boathouse, one of her favorite bars. It was in Central Park. They sat on the patio by a little lake and Julia was telling him about her first trip to Burma. Thar Thar was having trouble paying attention. His eye was repeatedly drawn to a married couple at the next table.

At some point Julia, too, looked casually over at them. "Why are you so interested in those people?"

"The woman looks disfigured," he explained in a whisper.

"What do you mean, 'disfigured'? I think she looks pretty good for her age."

"Her face and her hands don't go together."

"How so?"

"She has the withered hands of an old woman and the smooth face of a young one."

"Maybe she didn't like how she looked. She probably got a face lift."

"Got a what?"

"A face lift. They pull your skin back behind your ears so that the wrinkles disappear."

Thar Thar shook his head, appalled. "How can a person not like her own face?"

"She probably thought she had too many wrinkles. Or droopy eyelids that made her eyes look small. Or she thought her lips were too narrow. There's lots of reasons."

"And then?"

"Then you can get it corrected."

Thar Thar was in for quite a shock when he saw the total on the bill.

"Two hundred dollars for two people? Why would you spend so much on a dinner?"

"It's really not so much," she countered. "There are loads of places more expensive than this one."

"We could live nearly a whole month on two hundred dollars in Hsipaw."

"But we're not in Hsipaw," she answered a bit testily. "You're comparing apples to oranges."

Thar Thar was about to reply but thought better of it.

Julia did not want any conflict. "I'm sorry. I just wanted to spoil you a little," she said amicably.

"Why?"

"Because it's fun. Is that so bad?"

"No, but you really don't need to."

"I like to."

"I don't deserve this kind of luxury."

"People don't always get what they deserve. You should know that better than anyone."

"What do you mean?"

"Did you or any of your fellow prisoners in the jungle deserve to suffer?"

"No."

"Did Ei Ei deserve to die so young?"

"Of course not." He considered this for a while. "But still."

"What does 'But still' mean?"

"That I don't feel good about it."

"I'm sorry to hear that. It's not easy to spoil you," she sighed. "You're very low-maintenance."

He was not sure what she was trying to say. "Is that a good thing or a bad?"

She stroked his hand gently. "Take it how you like..."

"What do you mean by 'low maintenance'?"

"You're not very demanding."

"You mean I'm humble?"

"You could call it that."

"Frugal?"

"Sure, that, too."

"And you? Are you very demanding?"

"Absolutely."

"Why?"

"Because...because..." She thought about her answer.

He waited patiently.

"Because you have to be demanding in order to get by in this city."

"Why?"

"Because modesty doesn't count for much here. New York was built by people who were never happy just to settle for what they had, people who didn't know the meaning of the word *moderation*. People who demanded a lot. Of themselves. Of others. Of life."

That evening she had trouble falling asleep. "Tell me a story," she asked him. "I love to hear your voice."

"What kind of story?"

"Anything."

"A Burmese fairy tale?"

"That would be lovely."

"Do you know the one about the Clever Monkey and the Crocodile?"

Julia searched her memories. "I don't think so."

"Your father never told it to you?" Thar Thar was surprised.

She laid her head on his chest and listened to his heart beating. "Maybe by some other name. What's it about? Tell it to me."

"Once there was a Crocodile who lived with his wife on the banks of a broad river. One day the wife fell ill and believed that her only hope of recovery was to eat a Monkey heart. The Crocodile, who loved his wife very much, set out immediately in search of a Monkey. He floated patiently up and down the river, keeping a sharp eye on the trees. When he finally spotted a Monkey, he paddled over to the shore and asked if the Monkey had ever visited the other side of the river. The bananas there were bigger and sweeter, he said, and the papayas juicier. If he was interested, the Crocodile would gladly carry him across.

"At first the Monkey was skeptical. 'I don't believe a word you're saying,' he declared. 'You just want to eat me.'

"'Not at all,' the Crocodile insisted, 'whatever gave you that idea?' And that's how things went for a few days, until the Monkey's curiosity got the better of him. While the Crocodile swore he intended no harm, the Monkey climbed onto his back.

"In the middle of the river the Crocodile slowly began to descend.

"'What are you doing,' the Monkey cried in horror, 'I'll drown!'

"Now the Crocodile admitted that he had lied because his sick wife needed a Monkey's heart.

"The Monkey laughed and explained that the Crocodile could eat him if he liked, but he wouldn't get his heart.

"'Why not?' the Crocodile wanted to know.

"'Do you really think that we Monkeys carry our hearts around with us?' the amused Monkey asked. 'How on earth could we frolic through the jungle, springing from treetop to treetop, while carrying our heavy hearts the whole time?

"'No, we hide our hearts in hollow trees and fetch them only when we really need them. If you'll take me back to shore, I'll see to it that you get not just one but two monkey hearts for your sick wife. I know all the hiding places.'

"That made sense to the Crocodile, who brought the Monkey back to shore.

"The little Monkey leapt to dry land and quickly returned with two big, ripe figs dripping with red juice. He claimed they were two especially nutritious Monkey hearts. The Crocodile should give them to his wife and she would surely recover.

"The Crocodile did as instructed, and in a short time his wife felt much better."

Thar Thar stroked Julia's hair and listened to hear whether she had fallen asleep.

"No," she said. "I've never heard that one."

"I'm surprised. It's very popular in Burma."

"So why did you pick that particular one?"

"I was thinking of it earlier in the day while I was out walking and watching all the people rushing about."

Julia lifted her head sleepily.

"The Crocodile would probably think that they, too, must be hiding their hearts somewhere. How else would they be able to run so quickly from one place to the next...?"

She kissed his hands, kissed his arms. "Will you sing to me? Please?"

Someday she will come to love me, someday...
I want to change places with the umbrella in her hand
To protect her from the sun...
Someday she will come to love me...

A short time later she had fallen asleep.

Thar Thar, on the other hand, lay there awake. The fairy tale and the song had carried him back to the children in Hsipaw, and he could not stop thinking about them.

He missed them more with each passing day. The worst part was not knowing how they were doing. Whether they were healthy. Whether U Ko Tun was looking after them, as he had promised. He had written a long letter to them months ago, and he was waiting with increasing impatience for their reply.

They were separated by more than the two days of air travel. Much more. He was going to find it difficult to explain to them where he had been. To find the right words for all that he had seen and experienced. He had not traveled merely from one place to another, from one country to another; he had traveled from one time to another, and now he understood how dangerous that could be. The longer he stayed in New York, the more he worried that it would be impossible to go back. One can return to a place easily enough, but to a time?

How much of the unfamiliar could a person tolerate?

Chapter 22

"JULIA! JULIA!" A booming voice rang out. A man waved from the opposite side of Prince Street, then strode quickly across to them. He was about Julia's age, and he had squeezed his heavyset frame into a shirt and pants that were much too small for him. Clearly he was quite delighted to see Julia.

"Marc. What a coincidence."

"How are you?" he asked, taking no notice of Thar Thar.

"Fine, thanks, and you?"

"I'm good, thanks. Long time no see."

"An eternity . . . You've lost weight."

"Not really." He shook his head. "There's no one left in the office who will hide the muffins and doughnuts from me. What about you? Are you feeling better now? I mean health-wise . . . You disappeared from one day to the next, and Mulligan made some strange insinuations—"

"Yeah," she said, interrupting him. "I'm doing much better now."

"I'm glad to hear it," he said with a sigh of relief. "I was worried about you." Only now did he notice Thar Thar standing half a step behind Julia. He looked him over, surprised, as if this dark-skinned man with his big eyes and shaved head could not possibly have anything to do with Julia. "Mulligan said you resigned."

"It's true. I did."

"I suppose you found something better."

Julia nodded.

"Lucky you. Are you allowed to say where yet?"

"Where?"

"I mean, which firm?" He gave her a sidelong glance. "Don't tell me Wellington and Partners..."

"No."

"Mulligan would never forgive you for that."

"I'm going to get married. We're expecting a child in the fall, and I'm taking some time off."

"Time off? You?" It took a few seconds to sink in. "Wow. I mean...that's...that's big news...And you're pregnant? My God...Congratulations. So who...if I might ask...who's the lucky guy?"

Julia smiled and gestured elegantly toward Thar Thar.

The man looked from her to him and back again. His eyes revealed that he was not sure whether to take her seriously. When Julia offered no further explanation, he reached out his hand. "Marc Fisher."

"Thar Thar."

"Nice to meet you. How are you?"

Having no idea how to respond, Thar Thar said nothing.

"You . . . you're from New York?"

"No. From Burma."

"But I suppose you live in the city."

"No."

"We just came here to have the baby. After that we'll be going back to Burma."

"I see. Are you a lawyer, too, then?"

"No. A monk."

Marc Fisher chuckled, thinking it was a joke. When neither Julia nor Thar Thar joined in, he fell silent and had no idea what else to say. He cleared his throat and ran his fingers through his thick hair. Thar Thar could see how confused he was, and how uncomfortable the situation was becoming for him. He would have liked to ask him a question out of courtesy, but he was afraid it might be inappropriate, just like his first questions to Julia. Better to say nothing, he thought.

"Well, I've got to get going," said Marc Fisher, breaking the awkward silence. "Maybe we can get together for a coffee sometime?"

"I'd love to."

"You've got my number. Take care. Good luck."

"You too. See you later."

Moments later he had disappeared into the tumult of people on Broadway.

Julia took Thar Thar's hand and squeezed it firmly. For a while they walked along together in silence.

"We're getting married?"

Julia nodded.

"Women make the proposals in America?"

"Yeah," she said with a laugh. "Only the women."

"Hm. I didn't know that. Have we set a date?"

"Any time you like."

"Tomorrow?"

She stopped in her tracks and turned to him. "Tomorrow?"

"Why not?"

She took his face in her hands and pulled him toward her. Julia felt him hesitate. He was not accustomed to public displays of affection, and she knew he still felt uncomfortable about them. But she could not do otherwise. She could not wait until they got back home. She had to feel him, right now, right here. Julia felt how he tensed his lips and opened his mouth only a little, how he kept his arms at a distance rather than wrapping them around her. After a few seconds he began to relax and to kiss her with a passion that coursed through her entire body.

"I love you," she whispered.

"I love you, too."

"Please don't leave me."

Chapter 23

JULIA WANTED TO SHOW him the view from the Empire State Building, but when Thar Thar heard that he would have to take an elevator eighty-six floors up, they decided it was not such a good idea after all.

Instead they took the subway to the Brooklyn Bridge. It was a warm, cloudless summer day. Julia linked arms with him and they strolled to the middle of the bridge. They stopped there, and she told him about her occasional excursions to the bridge with her father. But Thar Thar was not really listening. His gaze was fixed on the downtown skyscrapers.

"There's a hole in the sky," he said at last.

"What kind of hole?"

"Two huge buildings are missing. I saw a picture of the New York skyline once in a teahouse in Mandalay, and I remember it well. I'm quite certain that it looked different."

Julia understood right away that his ignorance was not feigned. She told him about that cloudless late summer day in September. About two airplanes piloted by Hatred.

About men and women, about mothers and unborn children whom Hatred had sent to their deaths.

About people who jumped from the roofs of those burning towers because Hatred had left them no other way out.

He listened quietly to all of it without taking his eyes off the hole in the sky. He knew what she was talking about. She did not need to explain to him the possible extent of human cruelties. So Hatred had found a foothold here as well. Apparently it sprouted up between the high-rises, shops, cars, and people, just as it ran riot in the deepest jungle. It knew no bounds.

It had that in common with Love.

They stood for a long time on the bridge, arm in arm, exchanging neither word nor glance.

After that he was not ready to go right back to the thirty-fifth floor of a skyscraper, so they headed to Central Park.

Young men on the Sheep Meadow were tossing a football. Everywhere children were playing; couples were lying in the sun on the grass. Thar Thar was tired. They sat down in the shade of a beech tree. Thar Thar lay back and soon nodded off.

Julia watched him sleep. His chest slowly rising and falling, his face relaxed. What a dramatic difference a single person can make, she thought.

One single person.

The strength and conviction that he could inspire. How his smile could change the world. How nothing would ever be the same without him.

She felt that Thar Thar had transformed her world during the few short weeks she had spent with him in New York. He had calmed her inner tempest, reined in restlessness.

He had transformed her from someone who was always searching into someone who had found what she wanted.

In the past the intimacy would have been too intense for her. More than once she had packed up and cleared out as soon as things started to get serious. She had found ways to blame the men she left even when she sensed that she should be looking at herself.

She had not meant to be that way.

She did not know why Thar Thar succeeded where others had failed. What gift he possessed to allay her fears. And when she thought about it, she did not really care.

The only thing now was that nothing upset the balance.

She was working without a net.

We are born defenseless. At some point we learn that we must protect ourselves. From other people. From ourselves. Love begins at the moment when we no longer need, or want, to protect ourselves.

An oppressive fear stole over her out of the void. She had made herself vulnerable. Defenseless. She had surrendered herself. Perhaps for the first time in her life.

Things were going well for her. She no longer heard voices, though the memory of that experience was still quite vivid.

She had let herself be terrorized by it for weeks, and she was shocked at how little able she had been to resist it.

Her life had gone off the rails, and she had noticed it only when it was already too late. She was forced to watch her own power dwindle. To see herself losing control. Abandoning herself.

She would never let that happen again.

Julia laid both hands on her belly. She thought she could feel the first movements. A gentle flutter. Like the irregular heartbeat that afflicted her from time to time.

She wanted so badly to know what kind of person was growing there inside her. Someone who would come into the world with a big heart or a small one. Someone who would look like her or like Thar Thar.

Would her love suffice? Would she be a good mother? A better mother than her own had been?

She wanted to shelter her child from all this world's pain and suffering. The recognition that that was impossible brought tears to her eyes.

Julia could feel the cracks opening in her confidence. What would happen if she was not up to the task? If her strength again waned and the voice reappeared in her head?

Second by second she felt weaker, more fragile.

She could not manage it without Thar Thar. She draped her arm across his chest and nuzzled up close to his warm body. The scent of him calmed her a little.

"Everything okay?" he mumbled, half asleep, and squeezed her hand.

"Yes," she whispered. "Everything's okay. Sleep. Rest."

Did she have any other choice?

In love, everything was always at stake.

Chapter 24

THEY SAT IN A CAB, stuck in traffic on First Avenue. Several streets were closed. A helicopter circled overhead; there were police on every corner. It would have been faster to walk, but Julia's legs hurt, and on top of that, it was raining. The traffic lights and brake lights reflected off the puddles in the street. Thar Thar gazed out the window and held Julia's hand.

"If someone asked you where you belonged, what would you tell them?" he suddenly wanted to know.

"What made you think of that?" she wondered.

"You were born in New York. You grew up here. It's your language, so this is where you belong, right?"

"What are you getting at?"

"Nothing. It was just going through my mind."

"I spent the first thirty-eight years of my life in New York, and I'm an American; that's true. Does that mean I belong here?" She shrugged. "I suppose so."

Julia hesitated briefly before posing the question that had been nagging at her for days: "Could you imagine staying here for a longer time?"

"What do you mean by longer?"

"A year? Maybe two?"

It was the moment he had been dreading. "I don't know how to answer that."

"Tell me what you think."

"That's not so simple," he objected.

"More yes or more no?"

"More no."

"What if you knew that the children in Hsipaw were fine?"

Thar Thar thought about that for a long time. "Still no."

"Why not?"

"I feel like I don't fit in here."

"Why do you say that?" she asked in a raised voice.

"Because it's true."

"And what makes you think you don't fit in here?"

Thar Thar was surprised by her sudden agitation. He paused for a while. "The world I come from is so different."

"Why should that matter?" Julia nodded toward the turbaned taxi driver. "Where do you come from?" she asked him.

"From Gujarat in western India, madam," he replied politely while nodding his head gently.

"Is life there anything like here in Manhattan?"

"No, madam," he said, smiling and looking in the rear-view mirror. "Most certainly not."

"What exactly is different there?"

"Everything, madam."

"Would you like to go back?"

"No, madam. Most certainly not."

She turned back to Thar Thar. "See? And maybe our next driver will be from Bangladesh. Or Algeria. Or Liberia. And there, too, life is completely different. Do you see what I mean?" With every word she sounded more anxious. "New York is full of people who come from different worlds. They all manage to find a place here. Why would it be any different for you? Tell me: Why?"

"But didn't you yourself say that you have to be demanding in order to live here? That modesty counts for nothing here?"

"I did." She thought about it. "Of course we wouldn't have to stay in Manhattan."

"Where else would we go?"

"We could move to the countryside. Upstate New York, for instance, or Vermont, or Maine." She took his hand and laid it on her swelling abdomen.

"I lack for nothing," he said. "But still I'm missing something."

"What?"

"I wish I knew how to put it into words. I'm sorry. I know that I'm being ungrateful." After a pause he continued: "Perhaps I might even succeed in becoming a good citizen of this city or this country. Perhaps I would eventually learn to understand the rules, the written and the unwritten. But I don't want to."

"Why not?"

"If I were to assimilate, then I would be a different person, no longer the one you love. Do you see what I mean?"

"I'm also a different person here than in Burma. Do you love me any less for that?"

"No," replied Thar Thar. "Of course not."

Julia would later replay this conversation over and over in her mind. *Where do you belong?* She could not get Thar Thar's question out of her head. Did she belong in New York, or more precisely, on the Upper East Side, just because she was born there? Because she spoke the language and was familiar with all the customs, rituals, and rules of the place? She felt no sense of belonging in spite of all that.

Do we belong to a country, a tribe, a village? Or rather to a family or even a particular person?

To you, she ought to have answered. To you.

Thar Thar sat on the floor in front of the bed, intending to meditate. He tried to focus, but his thoughts were a tumult. Peace eluded him.

To meditate means to come back home, he had learned from an old monk. He had the feeling that everything in New York was twisting and wrenching him away from himself. The never-ceasing din, even at night. The throngs of people with their unfamiliar voices and faces. The lights, the smells, the sounds. All of it was strange to him. Everything demanded his attention. It was as if the children at the monastery had hidden themselves and were calling out from every corner: "Here, here, here."

For him New York was a city of many gods dominated by the muddled roar of the world.

Chapter 25

THE FIRST REPORTS came trickling in around the middle of August. Thar Thar often listened in the morning to the news from Southeast Asia on the BBC World Service, where he started to hear stories of isolated protests in Myanmar sparked by governmentally imposed increases in fuel costs, which had precipitated a drastic spike in food prices. Many well-known critics of the government had been incarcerated.

A few days later there were reports that hundreds of people had gathered at a demonstration in Yangon. An uneasy quiet lay over parts of the city.

The following week the BBC reported on a demonstration by more than five hundred monks in the city of Pakokku. Thousands of citizens had lined the streets in support of the monks. Soldiers had fired warning shots and used considerable violence against the onlookers. According to unconfirmed sources, three monks were among the wounded.

From that point on Thar Thar spent nearly every free minute in front of the radio or television. Every day brought fresh reports of demonstrations and disturbances. Pictures unlike anything he had seen before. People standing in the middle of intersections blocking traffic. Chanting crowds demanding greater freedom and calling the name Aung San Suu Kyi, of whom one previously spoke only in whispers, if at all. Police and soldiers stood by without taking any action.

While Thar Thar watched these things on television, tears would stream down his cheeks without his even realizing it.

As a sixteen-year-old, after he had been taken by the military, he had often wondered how it would feel to be able to defend himself, not to have to put up with all of the atrocities. How it would feel if the question of whether he should live or die were not left up to any random individual in a uniform.

How it would feel to be free.

As he lay in the death house, beaten half to death for refusing to flog a fellow prisoner, he had imagined the day when the soldiers would have to account for what they had done. In a fevered dream he had seen them disarmed and stripped to their undergarments. In columns they walked, heads bowed, along dusty streets all throughout the country, falling to their knees and begging the people's forgiveness. A long march of repentance. This thought had helped keep him alive even when he felt he would never see the light of another day.

One morning Julia set the *New York Times* in front of him on the table. An article on the front page described the growing resistance in Burma and the increasing number of protest marches. It painted a picture of a country on the brink of upheaval, whose citizens were daring for the first time in twenty years to rebel against military rule.

When he finished reading the article, he stood up and took her in his arms. "I have to go back," he whispered.

"Back? Where?"

"To Burma."

"When?"

"Tomorrow. The day after tomorrow. As soon as possible."

Julia twisted out of his embrace. "But why?"

"Because ... because ..." Thar Thar faltered. How could he explain to her what for him required no explanation? How could she understand what it would mean to him to stand up and defend himself? To reclaim his dignity? She, who lacked for nothing. She, who had no need to fear the police. She, who need never worry that soldiers would come in the night to take her away. It had something to do with courage. With self-respect. The military had tried to strip the people of his country of both those things. And now it turned out that they had failed. Courage and Dignity had merely gone into hiding, and now they were feeling confident enough once again to show their faces.

"Didn't you read the article?"

"Of course I did."

"Haven't you seen the images on television?"

"I have."

"Do you know how long we've been waiting for this moment?"

"A long time."

"A long time? A long time?" He looked at her with an almost unbearable intensity. "Our whole lives, my love. Our whole lives!"

Julia said nothing.

"We have been ruled by criminals for fifty years. By murderers. It's not like here."

"I know," she said almost inaudibly.

"We can't just vote them out of office. For decades they've been robbing us of our land. Torturing us. Attacking our villages. Hauling us off and murdering us." Thar Thar had to stop and take a few deep breaths before he could go on. "You know my story, and it is only one of so, so very many. We had to put up with it because they had weapons and we didn't. Because we were crippled by fear. And now that's over with!" He wanted to take her in his arms again, but she retreated from him.

"I understand all that, but I'm afraid for your safety. In two months we'll be bringing a child into the world."

He lowered his head. When at last he looked at her again, his eyes were red. "I'll be back by then. You have my word."

Thar Thar paced up and down in the living room. Stood at the window and gazed out. Heavy raindrops splattered against the glass. Julia had never seen him so agitated. He turned to her again. "In Yangon and Mandalay people are risking their lives while I sit here in Manhattan doing nothing. A kept man. Dining in posh restaurants."

What could she possibly say to that?

"I can't do it any longer. My country needs me."

"I need you, too."

"I know. Please try to understand me."

"What are you going to do in Yangon?"

"Be a part of it."

"The city is full of protesting monks. One more or fewer is not going to make a difference."

"If everyone says that, no one will march."

Julia let out a deep sigh. She was at once disappointed and furious. "I don't understand you," she said, and she was surprised at the edge in her voice.

"It's only for a couple of weeks," he said, attempting to reassure her. "Then I'll come back."

"When? When the protests are over and the government has collapsed? Maybe they'll appoint you as some kind of minister. Then your country will really need you."

He said nothing.

"Or when they've shot everyone? The military is not going to stand idly by for much longer."

"They won't dare to fire on monks."

"You don't really believe that."

"It's a line they won't cross. You know how important the monks are in our society. There are more than half a million of them, and they are honored above all others. The more of us on the street, the smaller the danger."

Julia walked over to him at the window and took his head in both her hands. "I'm asking you not to go."

But there are things we should not ask of someone we love. We either get them or we do not. When Julia saw how Thar Thar was wrestling with himself, she added: "Will you at least reconsider it?"

Thar Thar flew to Yangon the next day via Frankfurt and Bangkok. The return flight was scheduled for fourteen days later. They had booked a ticket that could not be changed. Julia could rest assured that he would keep his promise and be back in New York in two weeks.

He intended to spend the first six or seven days in Yangon. During the second week he thought he might go to Hsipaw to make sure that all was well with the children at the monastery.

They agreed that he would call at least once a day from Yangon. Hopefully it would not be difficult to arrange a call to New York from the Strand Hotel or from the Traders.

The following day the connection was as clear as if he were calling from the next room. Thar Thar sounded euphoric. He had marched through the streets of Yangon with several thousand monks accompanied by men, women, and children. True, the atmosphere was tense, but it was also more filled with hope than anything he had ever experienced. No sign of soldiers, and even the police were holding back. Julia had nothing to worry about. He missed her terribly.

On the second day he told her about more than twenty thousand monks, singing as they marched through the city while more and more onlookers joined the throng. People had lined the streets. They filled balconies, windows, and rooftops. People on all sides were waving or offering them food and water. The atmosphere was much more relaxed than on the previous day. More like a fair. On every corner one could feel that a big change was in the works. He wished she could be there with him to share in the experience.

On the third day he was breathless. More than a hundred thousand people had filled the streets of Yangon. He had heard of similar demonstrations in a number of other cities. In Mandalay a parade miles long had wound its way through town. Yangon was full of rumors. Supposedly soldiers had begun to desert and were joining the monks in their protests. In Mandalay an entire company had left their posts. The officers were reluctant to give any order to move against the monks. General Than Shwe was apparently about to resign. Others claimed that the opposition leader Aung San Suu Kyi was soon to be released. If things continued like this there would soon be a million people on the streets. If only she could be there to share it all with him. He could not express how much he was missing her, how much he loved her.

The following day Thar Thar was pressed for time. His voice sounded gloomy, and he was in a hurry. She could hear chaos and shouting in the background. There was continuous interference on the line.

"Where are you?"

"At a shop near the Sule Pagoda."

"Why?"

"___!?"

"Thar Thar, I can hardly understand you. Why aren't you calling from the hotel?"

"___!"

"Dammit, I can't hear you! What's happened?"

"The streets . . . Hotel . . . sealed off."

"What are you saying?" The static on the line was unbearably loud.

". . . never . . ."

"Hello? Thar Thar?"

". . . not worry . . . not . . . Hsipaw . . ."

"Thar Thar," she shouted into the phone. "Why? What's wrong? For God's sake, Thar Thar?"

"I . . . you."

She heard an unfamiliar voice, urgent shouts, a busy signal, and then lost the connection.

"Thar Thar?" she whispered, knowing she would get no response. "Thar Thar?"

I . . . you.

A short while later she heard on the radio that military trucks had been posted around the Shwedagon Pagoda. Soldiers were patrolling all the streets. According to reports, the monks were not backing down. Again there were thousands in the streets.

She heard nothing from Thar Thar the next day. Nor the next.

Julia followed the news on television and radio around the clock. The BBC reported that the military had imposed a curfew. In spite of everything, tens of thousands led by monks and nuns had again taken to the streets in Yangon. Without any kind of warning, the military had opened fire on the demonstrators. Even on the monks. There were many dead and wounded. No one could give an accurate count. The military reported eight dead; the opposition in exile claimed the number was in the hundreds. Radio Free Burma said it was thousands. The crematoria in the city were reportedly working around the clock.

Soldiers throughout the country were now raiding monasteries and taking monks prisoner. Thousands were loaded onto military trucks and carted off. Only the army knew where they were being taken or what was happening to them.

Where was Thar Thar?

Julia tried to reach him at the last number he had called from, but the line was dead. It was the only number she had. Who could tell her anything of his whereabouts? The American embassy in Yangon said they were not responsible for him because he was not an American citizen. She got the same answer from the State Department in Washington.

No one was answering the phone at the Burmese consulate in the United States. The delegation to the United Nations refused to make any comment.

There was no phone at the monastery.

She could only hope that he had gone underground and found a safe hiding place and would call when he could.

I . . . you.

I . . . you.

I . . . you.

Chapter 26

JULIA WAITED. She stayed close to the phone, ate little, and tried to sleep during the morning and afternoon so that she could stay awake during the night, when it was daytime in Burma. But that was not easy; the child inside her was becoming restless. It kicked and elbowed so boisterously that it continually woke her. As if it sensed precisely what was going on out there in the world.

She started to have terrible backaches that reached right down into her thighs. Light bleeding. The doctor was worried. She was in the thirty-fourth week of the pregnancy. The baby, from all they could see on the ultrasound, was developing normally. It would survive a premature birth, but that was always fraught with risks.

Was anything bothering her? Stress can be a significant factor for premature deliveries. Julia shook her head.

The doctor ordered bed rest. She needed to watch herself, to avoid all excitement. He assumed there was someone who could look after her for the next few weeks. She nodded. The baby's father was on his way back to New York. He would be landing at Newark in three days.

In two.

In one.

Today.

Despite the gynecologist's warning, she drove to the airport. She left plenty of time to spare in case the flight from Frankfurt should arrive early.

All around her people were falling into one another's arms. Two little children ran toward their mother. An older couple kissed intimately. He wiped the tears from her eyes. Beside her a young man was holding a heart-shaped balloon and chewing nervously on his fingernails. Julia held a long-stem rose.

The first passengers from Frankfurt came walking down the long corridor into the concourse. She could tell by their luggage. FRA-EWR.

She was nauseous with worry. She had to sit down. Her child was kicking ferociously. Nothing got past him.

Maybe he was having troubles at Immigration. On bad days it could take two or even three hours for a foreigner. Or maybe his baggage had not arrived.

She waited until the flight had disappeared from the arrivals board and she had not seen an FRA-EWR sticker for a long time.

She waited until it got dark.

He's dead.

It was not a voice talking to her, more an inner conversation. A suspicion, an intuition. A thought on an infinite loop replaying itself in her mind.

He's dead. He's dead. He's dead.

A woman asked with concern whether she was feeling ill. Did she need any help?

Yes, thought Julia. "No," she replied. "Thanks, it's just poor circulation." She pointed to her rounded midriff. "I'll be fine in a minute." The woman led her to a chair and brought her a cup of water.

She did not know how long she had been sitting there. Eventually she drove back home and went to bed. Her body felt as if someone had poured lead over it, or pulled out a fuse. Every ounce of energy was gone. She had not even enough strength to cry.

He's dead.

She had no idea how she would get through the next weeks and months. How she would be able to care properly for her child.

How thin is the wall that shields us from insanity? No one knows how much strain it can bear. How much pressure it can handle. Before it yields.

He's dead.

We all live on the edge, she thought. Some of us realize it. Others do not.

It was just one step away. One small step.

Chapter 27

"I DON'T BELIEVE IT," I said, interrupting my uncle.

"What do you not believe?"

"That soldiers shot at monks."

"But it is true."

"Why would they have done that?" I asked, still skeptical.

"Because someone ordered them to. In the military a command is a command. You must follow it."

"And if you don't?"

"Then you get thrown into prison or you get shot yourself. It's not like at school!"

"Will I have to join the military?" The idea had never crossed my mind, and I found the prospect so frightening that I soon started counting. Onetwothreefourfivesixseveneightnineten...

"No. Military service is non-compulsory. No one is forced to join."

"Really not?" There was a flicker in his eye that revealed to me that he was not telling the truth, or at least not all of it.

"Even if it were compulsory, I am watching out for you. Do not worry."

I was reassured only for a moment. What could my old uncle do if the soldiers came to take me away? Stand in their way? Threaten them? Better for me not to count on his protection, I thought. It would be smarter to find someplace to hide or to ask Ko Aye Min for help. As far as I knew, he had never been a soldier. The thought that they certainly never took twelve-year-olds offered some relief. I still had a few years to figure something out.

"Anyone who shoots at a monk is bound to be reborn without arms or legs. Or blind and deaf. Don't you think?"

U Ba nodded. "Surely."

"Weren't they afraid of that?"

"If they had disobeyed the order, then they would have suffered severe penalties already in this life."

I nodded as if I had understood, but that of course was nonsense. Soldiers shooting at monks! As if anyone could understand that.

I thought of my mother lying there alone in her bed, missing my father. I knew what it meant to miss someone. I felt sorry for her. Even now, almost thirteen years later, I felt a strong desire to be there for her. I would have lain down next to her, taken her in my arms, and never let her go. I'm certain that would have helped her.

"Couldn't you do anything for her?" I asked U Ba.

"I did try. It was not easy. She lay in bed for days, and yet never slept. I went shopping and cooked for her, but she wanted neither food nor drink. I could see her withering away before my eyes, but there was little more I could do for her than to sit by her bed and hold her hand. I was very worried about her. And about you."

My uncle's voice was quivering at these last words.

"Why about me?"

"You were a part of her. Everything she was doing to herself, she was also doing to you. I urged her to see the doctor, but she would not."

"So what happened?"

"She grew weaker every day. One morning in a delirium she mistook me for Thar Thar. In desperation I rang at the neighbor's door. He called an ambulance immediately." U Ba was quiet for a moment. "We were lucky. Your mother was not sick. She was drinking too little water and had become dehydrated. After two days in the hospital she was feeling much better. At least physically."

He got up and lit some candles.

My heart felt heavy listening to this story. It was nearly dark outside. In the kitchen we still had some leftovers from lunch, but I had no appetite, not even for yellow curry with fried shrimp from Inle Lake. "Are you hungry?" I asked my uncle.

"No."

"Should I make you some tea?"

He shook his head. In the light of the candles he looked old and fragile.

We spent the rest of the evening together on the couch. I was in no mood for talking and neither was he. Sometimes it felt good just to sit by him in silence. He was leafing through a book, but I didn't get the impression he was reading it.

The next morning I could hardly move; that's how heavy and exhausted I felt. As if I had spent the whole night pulling weeds or doing laundry. I tugged softly at U Ba's shoulder and asked if I could stay home sick from school. He mumbled a yes and fell right back to sleep.

After breakfast my uncle asked whether I was feeling well enough to make a brief excursion with him. I couldn't believe my ears. "An excursion? Where to?"

"To Sharbin. There is a lovely spot for a picnic there."

I couldn't hide my disappointment. During the last dry season I had been there with Ko Aye Min. It was a good hour's march from here, and with U Ba at my side probably two. There was nothing to do there and nothing in particular to see, just a view down into the valley and across the mountains. Tourists loved it, Ko Aye Min had told me. They always took lots of pictures. I thought it was boring.

"What are we going to do there?"

"I'll tell you that when we get there. We'll need some food for the road." He packed a bag with hard-boiled eggs, toast, pastries, two bottles of water, and two bananas, then slung it across my shoulder. I was mystified. We hardly needed so much food for a hike to Sharbin.

He took the walking stick I had carved out of bamboo for him, and off we went. We walked awhile beside the road and then turned off onto a narrow cart track that climbed gently past the Hsay Win Gabar Monastery on the way out of Kalaw. I was still feeling lousy, and every step was an effort. U Ba was a different story. On some days almost every movement pained him, but today he was skipping along beside me with a light bounce in his step. It had been a long time since I'd seen him walk like that.

"Memories, Bo Bo," he said with a grin and by way of explanation. "Memories can put wings on one's feet."

I thought about that for a long time. I did not have so many memories and none that would put wings on my feet.

He must have guessed what I was thinking. "Not all of them, of course," he added. "Some memories can paralyze you. Or weigh like stones upon your heart."

"And then?"

"Then you must see to it that you put them aside."

"How?"

"By not clinging to them. Most of them will vanish of their own accord. It requires only a bit of practice."

"What kind of practice?"

"Letting go."

As if anyone would cling to bad memories. If I got angry at a teacher at school and thought about it the next day, that was the memory clinging to me, not the other way around.

We walked past the monastery. The incline got steeper, but U Ba slowed his pace only a little.

"So what memories are putting wings on your feet today?" I asked.

He stopped and leaned on his walking stick. I could hear how out of breath he was, wings or not. His forehead was covered with little beads of sweat.

"I used to come this way with my mother from time to time."

"I thought she couldn't walk?" I asked in surprise.

"I would carry her up on my back."

"The whole way?"

He nodded. "I was young once, myself. The last time we came here was a few weeks before she died. She had her heart set on making the trip one last time. Unless I carried her—and she let no one else carry her—she could move only by crawling. That's why she loved hilltops. It meant a lot to her to be able to look out over the world."

"Doesn't that memory make you feel sad?"

"Not at all. It was a lovely day. We took breaks and laughed a lot. I set her down on a big rock, where she had the best view. Her gaze and her thoughts wondered off into the distance. She was quiet. Tin Win will come back soon, she suddenly announced.

" 'What makes you think so?' I asked.

" 'I can see it. Over there. On the horizon.'

"I worried she was losing touch with reality.

"He lived in New York. She had not seen him for more than fifty years, and now she was suddenly certain she would see him again. She claimed he was busy taking care of the final arrangements for the journey.

"In the weeks that followed she began to prepare for his arrival. She crawled into the remotest corners of the house in order to get it properly clean. Every morning I had to bring in fresh hibiscus, chrysanthemums, or frangipanis from the garden that she would use to decorate the room. She wore a blossom in her hair, and with each passing day she grew younger and more beautiful. A few weeks later I was sitting across from my father in a teahouse. He had returned, just as she had foretold. The following night they died together in each other's arms."

U Ba looked down into the valley and then at me. "We know," he said in a whisper, as if to himself, "so much more than we think we do." He wiped the sweat off his face with his sleeve, and then he was off. I was right behind him.

"Didn't you miss your papa when you were little?"

"I did not know him. Is it possible for me to miss someone I don't know?"

"Yes," I answered without hesitation. "Of course."

"Perhaps. But I lacked for nothing, my little Bo Bo."

"I'm not little anymore."

"Forgive me, that is not how I meant it. I know that you are no longer little. You are quite grown, in fact." He stopped, turned to me, and put his arms around me, just as he used to do so often but hadn't done in a long time. I felt his hands on my back, his soft cheek against my scarred one. He held me tightly. I felt his heart beating strongly against my chest, and suddenly I started to cry. Tears ran down my cheeks like raindrops on a windowpane. I didn't want to cry like that, but I couldn't help it. I wept bitterly.

That did not happen often.

Actually, never.

U Ba held me firmly and said nothing.

When I was quiet again, I felt much better.

We walked through a Danu village, went past a *nat* altar festooned with flowers, climbed down into a little valley, and then sped up the other side. The memories had given U Ba a second pair of wings on his feet.

We rested in the shade of a banyan tree. He asked me for a banana and some water.

"And now we are nearly at the end of the story," he said, taking several gulps of water. Far from being eager to hear it, I would have preferred that he not go on. It was on the brink of becoming my story.

Would I find my own heart incapable of the bravery demanded of it?

I started counting.

One.

Two.

Three.

Four.

Five.

Then I heard my uncle's voice and I let it carry me away. Back to New York.

To my mother.

To memories that caused no wings to sprout.

Chapter 28

STATIC ON THE TELEPHONE LINE. It crackled and clicked, then the line went dead. The clock by her bed read 4:44 a.m. A few moments later it rang a second time.

"Hello?" she said again. Her voice quivered with emotion. "Thar Thar?"

"—?"

"Hello? Hello?"

"—?"

"Who is this?"

"Julia?"

"Thar Thar? Thar Thar! Finally. Where are you?" Her words rang out into the hallway.

"In . . ."

"Where, my love? I can hardly understand you."

"I'm . . ."

"Where? . . . Shit. This connection is awful."

". . . Mandalay. In a hotel. I . . . use the phone."

"Oh, God, I'm so grateful you called. I was so scared. Are you okay?"

"__."

"Where have you been the last few weeks?"

"A . . . story." He said something in Burmese. Someone else answered gruffly. "We don't have much time," Thar Thar whispered. All at once the static and crackling ceased, and she could understand him clearly.

"When are you coming back? Should I book a flight for you?"

"I can't come back."

"Please don't say that."

"The police seized my passport."

"Why?"

He did not answer.

"Who? I mean . . . how can they do that? They can't just—"

"They can do whatever they want," he said, interrupting.

"When will you get it back?"

"They won't say. Maybe tomorrow. Maybe in a year. Maybe never."

Julia's voice was brittle. "I . . . I'm so happy to hear from you. I thought you were dead. Oh, Thar Thar, if only you knew . . ."

"Don't cry. I'm all right."

She tried to suppress her sobs. "Are you sure?"

"Yes. The most importing thing is how you are doing."

Should she tell him of the many sleepless nights? Of

her fear? How she often struggled for breath because the child was pressing against her diaphragm? How she found even the slightest movement difficult and how she could hardly wait until the birth? Thar Thar was far away, and he could not help her, so why trouble him? "I'm all right, too," she lied.

"Really?"

"Yes, quite all right, in fact. And our son, too."

"Is . . . has he already been born?" he asked cautiously.

"No. The doctors say it'll be another two weeks, but it could also happen anytime."

Again there was shouting in the background. "I'm so sorry that I'm not there," said Thar Thar. "Forgive me. I should have listened to you . . ."

"Stop. The most important thing is that you're alive. Where can I reach you?"

"You can't. I'll call again."

"I can't?" Her voice was breaking up again. "But I have to . . ."

"___?"

"Hello? Thar Thar, please, it's so hard to understand you."

". . . Everything here is so difficult . . ."

"What do you mean?"

"Fear has returned. The military is everywhere. People are disappearing . . ."

"Have you seen the children?"

"Not yet. I'm going there tomorrow."

"Isn't there any way I can reach . . ."

A man's voice, shouting. Thar Thar answered something. It was turning into a dispute, more heated with each exchange.

"Hang on a moment, my love. Don't hang up," he told her. A few seconds later she lost the connection.

"Thar Thar. Sweetheart. Hello???" she cried, as if to be heard in Burma she had only to shout loudly enough.

The line was dead.

This call was what she had been waiting for, what she had craved above all else. To hear his voice. To feel his presence, be it only for a few minutes. To know he was alive and healthy. She had hoped that this knowledge would reassure her, calm her nerves. Quite the contrary. As soon as the initial relief had ebbed away she found herself feeling worse than ever. More alone. More helpless. More abandoned. She wanted to talk to him, to help him, yet there was again nothing she could do but wait, and this powerlessness did not sit well with her.

The apartment felt to her like a prison. She had to get out, to move about, but with the child in her belly she could not manage more than a block before she was short of breath. She set out with Amy to go for a walk in Central Park, but they turned back at the corner of Madison Avenue. The crowds of people, the crush, the din. It was worse for her than the solitude of the apartment.

She sat by the phone, biting her nails till they bled, a habit she had broken as a child. Her heart skipped a beat every time the phone rang.

When Thar Thar called she could again hear him as clearly as if he were sitting beside her.

"I got my passport back," he said, but still he did not sound relieved.

"Oh God, that's wonderful! When are you coming? Can I book a flight for you?"

"I can't come."

"Why not?"

"I'm worried they won't let me back in."

"Why wouldn't they let you back into your own country?"

"That's what's happening to lots of the people who fled to Thailand. The government just says their passports are invalid."

"I can't believe it. Is there any kind of charge against you?" Julia asked.

"No."

"Those people were probably wanted for something. We don't know the circumstances. I can't imagine that they wouldn't let you back into the country."

"But it's happening."

"We could file a complaint."

"What are you talking about? The government can do whatever it wants."

"I know. I just mean that the risk is very low." She paused briefly. "Please, Thar Thar. We need you here."

"I know. We've got to say good-bye now, my love. I've got to go."

"Why? Where?"

"I'll explain it all later. I can't talk now."

"Please wait."

"I'll be in touch," he said, and hung up quickly.

In the days that followed the news from Burma was spotty and grim. Mass incarcerations. Monks disappearing without a trace. Refugees to Thailand on the BBC with reports of torture and summary executions.

Thar Thar did not call back.

A week later she got a letter in the mail, postmarked in Los Angeles. Julia recognized his handwriting on the envelope. He must have given it to someone. On the back of an old calendar page he had written a few hasty lines.

October 2007, Hsipaw

Dear Julia,

 I'm doing well. I'm with the children.
 They are still taking monks and even
 nuns prisoner, so it's best that
 I lie low for a while.
 Please don't worry about me.
 I'll call as soon as I can.
 Forgive me.
 Take care of yourself.
 I miss you.
 With love,

 Thar Thar

Chapter 29

YOU WERE BORN twenty-four hours later. A few days short of full term. You could not wait. As if you could no longer stand being inside your mother's anxiety-ridden body.

According to the gynecologist it was a smooth delivery, but he was concerned only for Julia's body, not her soul.

I had never held such a small person in my arms. The weight of the world. I will never forget the expression in your big brown eyes.

Julia was too exhausted to take care of herself or even to exhibit any joy. She lay pale and drained in her bed and barely reacted when a nurse brought you to her, freshly bathed and changed. According to the nurse her behavior was not unusual during the first few hours after childbirth; no reason at all to be concerned. Many women needed a few days to recover from the exertions before starting to bond with their child. It was a myth that every mother is immediately in love with her baby.

Who was I to contradict her? What did I know of the relationships between mothers and newborns?

I was worried all the same.

You were hungry, and she could not give you what you needed. Or not enough. She found it difficult to hold you, and she was visibly relieved anytime a nurse came by to take you off her hands. Gone was her heartwarming laugh. She no longer had even a smile.

I had hoped in vain that you might bring the light back into your mother's eyes, that you might distract her from her fears about Thar Thar. She asked me every few hours about the latest news from Burma. Whether Thar Thar had called. Whether a second letter from him had arrived in the mail.

The doctor suspected that she would feel better back at home in a familiar environment, and he honored her request to be released from the clinic.

The first few days were very trying—and things were only getting more difficult.

All of the strength and energy seemed to have passed with you out of her body. She had given life and gotten nothing in return, or at least not what she would have needed.

She found it difficult to concentrate on anything. She did not care even to leaf through the magazines I bought for her.

She complained of dizziness and headaches. I massaged her feet and shoulders, both of which were tense and hard.

Some evenings she would suddenly be chatty. She wanted to discuss our impending return to Hsipaw. She made sketches of the renovations and additions she was planning for the monastery. Other evenings she would sit for hours in silence across from me on the couch.

Your sister needs one thing above all else: attention. That is what the doctor told me, and I did the best I could to look after her. I did the shopping, prepared her favorite dishes, read out loud to her from books or the *New York Times*, told her all the Burmese fairy tales I knew. I came to understand that living with an unhappy person is a demanding art. I was constantly haunted by feelings of inadequacy.

Fortunately you required very little of her during those first few weeks. You spent most of your time asleep in your cradle. We had to feed you with a bottle, and we planned to take turns at night. Already during the second night she woke me. She stood there holding you. You had been crying, and she, too, had tears in her eyes.

"He won't eat," she said fretfully while pacing back and forth. "I don't know what to do for him."

We sat on the couch. She held the lukewarm bottle, and you would suck a few times, but then the milk would just run out of your mouth. "He's been doing this the whole time. He spits everything right back out."

"Maybe he's not hungry?"

"He didn't drink much the last time, either." She was becoming impatient. She held you tighter. "Bo Bo, my love, come on now, please." You just turned your head from side to side. It was as if her own disquiet was infecting you.

I saw how she gradually became angry, and she was very near to shoving the nipple into your mouth. You started to cry again.

I took you on my lap, hummed a little melody, rocked you back and forth. It took a long time for you to settle down. Eventually you started to drink. By that time Julia was already asleep on the couch next to me.

One morning we got a second message from Thar Thar. This time with a postmark from Thailand. Julia wanted me to open the letter and read it out loud.

My love,

I hope these lines find their way to you. A secret courier promised to mail it off in Bangkok, but over the past few days a number of them have been discovered at the border and taken into custody. So I can't be sure whether this letter will ever make it to New York.

Has our child been born? What does it look like? Does it have your wonderful lips? Your shining eyes?

Please forgive me for not being there with you. I think of you and long to be with you every day, every hour. I hope that you are well.

I have been asking myself for weeks whether I should maybe have listened to you. Was it a mistake for me to come back here? I could have spared you considerable sorrow. It breaks my heart to think that I have caused you such distress.

But I will never forget those days in Yangon during the uprising.

I had the privilege of watching people get the better of their fears. Of seeing their eyes aglow with pride and joy, of seeing them stand up for themselves for the first time in their lives as they joined us marching in the streets. Every step, no matter how large or small, was a victory. In the pouring rain, people lined the street and wept.

After decades of dictatorship fear had become flesh and blood. It had become a part of us. Very few among us had any real awareness of the power it held over us.

I was reminded repeatedly of my time in the jungle. You know what I suffered there. Fear had devoured our souls. Everyone seemed to think that I had somehow overcome it, but the only reason I felt no fear was that I had shut down inside. I had become completely numb. That's not the same thing.

And I firmly believe that there's no going back. Having once put our fears behind us, we now have the taste of freedom. We may again be cautious. We may retreat. If necessary we may go into hiding or disguise ourselves, and our fear may even return, but we will never again allow it to hold us captive.

I have taken refuge in a hideout on the border to Thailand. I can flee the country at any time, if it comes to that.

The children are at the monastery. U Ko Tun is taking good care of them, and they are in no danger. I will return to them in a few weeks when things have settled down.

My sincerest wish is to see you again soon. It is of course up to you when you are ready to travel, and

I understand completely if you prefer to wait and see what happens here in the next few months. That would probably be the best choice for all of us, given that no one knows what to expect. Life here has not gotten any easier.

I can hardly wait to hold you in my arms. If it were up to me, we would be reunited tomorrow.

Don't forget me.

With love to both of you,

Thar Thar

Julia took the letter out of my hands and read it a second and third time. She wanted to answer it immediately. She fetched some stationery and wrote his address on an envelope:

Thar Thar
The Monastery for Special Children
Hsipaw, Shan State
BURMA (Myanmar)

She sat at the table, staring at the white empty sheet, not knowing where to begin. With Bo Bo's birth? Her fear? The question of when and where they would meet again?

Her head was overflowing. Her thoughts were reeling so wildly that she could not catch one to put into words.

Eventually she pushed the pen and paper across the table to me. "Can you answer him?" she asked me.

"Me? What should I write?"

"That I love him."

"What else?"

"That's all."

Chapter 30

FOR CHRISTMAS we went with Amy to an old farmhouse and remodeled barn that she had recently bought in upstate New York. We were planning to ring in the new year there, too.

Amy was convinced that the peace and seclusion would do Julia good, and she had promised to spoil us. She took care of everything. She did all the shopping, organized a Christmas tree and presents for everyone. She decorated the tree, baked cookies, cooked. For the first few days Julia felt better than she had in a very long time. She was sleeping well and taking walks. She pitched in with the cooking, and she was more talkative. From time to time she warmed the kitchen with her laughter.

Outside the first snows were falling. We spent the afternoons and evenings by the fire.

"I've been thinking that we should open a kind of wellness center in Hsipaw," Julia said one evening, half to me, half to Amy. "We could have a variety of massages, treatments, and yoga classes alongside a little café or restaurant where visitors could learn Burmese cooking." She looked at us, full of enthusiasm: "What do you think?"

"Whatever made you think of that?" Amy wondered.

"The children need to learn something, and blind people supposedly make good masseurs. We could fly a massage instructor in from Thailand to give lessons. I'm thinking tourists would love it. And I imagine it would be the first of its kind for Hsipaw, wouldn't you think so, U Ba?"

"I suppose so." I nodded.

Amy looked at me, irritated. "According to everything you've told me, Hsipaw's not really a tourist destination. All the less so now after the unrest. Who's going on vacation to Burma these days?"

"Exactly. We've got to generate some interest."

"With cooking classes, yoga, and a spa?"

"Why not?" Julia snapped. "If you've got a better idea, I'd love to hear it."

"Okay, don't fly off the handle. I just don't think it's a good idea. And to be perfectly honest, I can't imagine that Thar Thar would be very enthusiastic, either."

"We'll see about that."

A few minutes later Julia turned in for the night.

The next morning I heard her rattling around in the kitchen bright and early. She had slept poorly, and she spent the whole day restless and tense.

"What can I do for you?" Amy asked as we sat drinking tea around the fire that afternoon.

"You're already doing so much."

"But what else? I'm worried. You don't look good."

"Gee, thanks."

"I'm not allowed to say so?"

"I can see it plainly for myself. All I have to do is look in the mirror."

"I'm sorry."

Amy rose and put another log on the fire. "Why don't we spend the winter here," she suggested. "I can paint in the barn, you can relax, and you and Bo Bo can really connect. I'm sure it wouldn't hurt U Ba, either. There's plenty of room for everyone."

"Thanks. It's a kind offer, but I've got to get back to Hsipaw."

"When?"

"As soon as possible."

"But what's the rush?"

"Seriously?" Julia answered huffily.

"You don't even know where Thar Thar is. You don't have a telephone number or address."

"He wrote in the letter that the situation would settle down quickly and that he would be returning to the monastery."

"And what if he hasn't?"

"Then I'll go looking for him."

"Where? Are you going to schlep a baby through the jungle from one refugee camp to the next?"

Julia pursed her lips and turned away. She gazed at the flames crackling in the fireplace and rocked your cradle.

"In your condition?"

"What exactly is my *condition*?"

"You're completely exhausted. You're not sleeping well. You're off your food. You need to get your strength back." She looked to me as if expecting me to back her up.

"I've got my brother," Julia countered with a nod in my direction. "He is a great help to me."

"I know, and that's great. But what harm could it do to spend a few months here while you wait to see whether the situation really improves over there?"

"Everything." Julia stood up, stepped over to the window, and looked out on the snow. Once you have let yourself be vulnerable, she thought, once you have tasted how it feels to love and be loved, you never want to be alone again. Everything inside her was resisting that notion. Her father came to mind. He had spent fifty years separated from the love of his life. During that whole time he never got a single letter from her, never once heard her voice. Their hearts must have found some way to communicate across the continents. There was no other way to explain how their love survived such a long separation. Maybe she would one day achieve something like that, but right now every day without Thar Thar felt like one day too many.

Amy sighed. "U Ba, you're keeping awfully quiet. What do you think of all this?"

Her question made me uncomfortable. Amy had all of the good arguments on her side. And yet. My heart understood my sister. It followed a different logic, abided by rules of its own.

More than that, it was her decision to make. Far be it from me to dictate to her or anyone else what they ought or ought not to do. If she wanted to return to Burma tomorrow, I would help her do so. If she wanted to stay in America, I would be just as supportive. As far as I could tell, there was no right or wrong decision. I did not know how to answer, so I said nothing.

"U Ba," cried Amy angrily. "Say something. She might listen to you."

Chapter 31

MY UNCLE DRANK some water in small sips and paid no more attention to me. He dug a thin book out of his satchel that I had never seen before. It looked heavily worn. On the cover was the word "Anniversaries."

"What's that?" I asked.

"Some notes."

"Whose notes?"

"Your mother's."

"For me?"

U Ba tilted his head thoughtfully to one side. "I suspect so. Shortly after your arrival in Hsipaw she started again to keep a diary. Most of the volumes were destroyed in a fire. She was able to save only this one."

I felt as if I could still smell the stale smoke. "What does she mean by 'Anniversaries'?"

"It contains entries for particular days: Your birthdays. Hers. Your father's. The anniversary of your arrival in Hsipaw. The day your parents met. I would like to read a

few excerpts out loud. They describe the time at the monastery much better than I ever could."

"Where on earth did you get that?"

"Your mother gave it to me for safekeeping."

I noticed that several pages had been marked with little
scraps of paper. My uncle had prepared himself well. He
opened the book to the first marked passage.

> *May 17, 2008*
> *Thar Thar's Birthday*
> *My attempt to bake him a cake was a complete
> disaster. The oven the children had built did not work at
> all. Hard as a rock and dry as dust. Inedible.*
>
> *He says it's the first birthday cake he's ever had.*
>
> *I was more disappointed than he was. Or maybe I just
> showed it more? Sometimes it's hard to tell with him.*
>
> *Thar Thar tells me that when he was young, children
> did not get presents on their birthdays. Instead they made
> gifts and gave them to others, and they were grateful to
> the recipients for being able to give them something. The
> true joy was in giving rather than receiving.*
>
> *I think those times are long gone. Even in Burma.*

> *He's hard on himself about having left me alone in
> New York.*
>
> *Am I still angry at him about it? Sometimes.*
>
> *Do I give him grief about it? Not directly.*

The sensation of arriving. Gradually. I could hardly sit still for the first few weeks. I felt the need to be doing something all day long. It's gradually fading away.

Thar Thar is patient with me and very considerate. Everyone is taking wonderful care of Bo Bo, especially Moe Moe and Ko Maung. All the same I have some lingering concerns. The fear that someone could come and abduct us at any time. I see them standing in the yard and hauling us off—Thar Thar, me, even Bo Bo, and there's nothing we can do to stop them.

He tries to reassure me. The monks' protests are not on anyone's mind right now. There was a huge typhoon in the Bay of Bengal. Yangon and the entire Delta were devastated. Many, many people died. The government has other problems to deal with.

Even so, I pretty much never go into town. I just hope the people forget we're even here.

August 28, 2008

Turned forty today. No longer young, not yet old.

Thought about my mother and brother, but not for long. How alienated a person can be from her family. Or maybe always was.

Sometimes I talk to my father. What would he say, if he were alive, about my living in his native country? In a former monastery? Under these conditions? He would be surprised. Would he be proud of me?

Definitely.

Definitely?

Thar Thar gave me a small piece of jade that he found. With a fair bit of imagination it can look like a heart.

No one is asking me what I'm wishing for in this new year and new decade of my life. It's not that they don't care about me. Plans and wishes for the future just aren't a big deal here.

What happens happens, Ko Maung always says.

So what do I wish for?

November 21, 2008

Bo Bo's First Birthday

The children have prepared his favorite meal for him: pureed mango with sweet rice. They sang and danced for him.

He's getting so much more love and attention here in our extended family than he would have gotten living with Thar Thar and me in New York. He has a dozen caregivers here. There's always someone there to feed him, to carry him around, to play with him.

When someone takes him from me, he never fusses. He's happy about it, and I often feel relieved. I lack patience. I hope that changes.

Does that make me a bad mother?

Thar Thar can't understand what I'm worried about. To him, questions like that just make life unnecessarily complicated.

Sometimes I envy that about him.

December 2008

Two years ago this week Thar Thar and I set eyes on each other for the very first time. I remember that moment vividly: how he came down the veranda steps to greet us. His big, dark brown eyes locking onto me in their quiet way. That wonderful laugh that you would never expect from someone who had suffered all the things he did.

What I don't recall is the exact date. I think it was the twelfth of December, but it might have been the thirteenth or even the fourteenth. That I don't know for sure gets under my skin. Thar Thar says it makes no difference.

Well, it does to me.

Hsipaw, January 2009

Our first year in the monastery is now behind us.

Amy never visited, though she had promised she would.

This year for sure, she wrote.

Everyone says my Burmese has gotten really good. Moe Moe is convinced that I was Burmese in a previous life.

I learn new things every day. Thar Thar says that Burmese people find it hard to apologize or to admit to a mistake. It always involves a loss of face.

And I must take care never to criticize anyone.

He's right, I know, but I knew people in New York, too, who would never admit to a mistake, who always tried to put the blame on someone else, who couldn't handle even the slightest criticism. The moment I think I've identified a "typical Burmese behavior," a dozen similar examples from America come to mind.

We have more in common than we think.

November 21, 2009
Bo Bo's Second Birthday
Sometimes I get the feeling that he's avoiding me. Yesterday he fell and scraped his knee. He ran to Moe Moe for comfort. She was nearest to him. Still.

Shortly afterward I took him in my arms and he nuzzled into my shoulder. That felt good.

As if I needed evidence of his affection. From a two-year-old.

August 28, 2010
My Forty-second Birthday
So?

Time doesn't matter much at the monastery. Age is irrelevant.

I don't even have a proper mirror to see whether the wrinkles have increased around my eyes. Whether my hair is getting grayer. I used to spend a lot of time in the bathroom in New York looking for gray hairs and pulling

*them out. Here they mean nothing to me. Like a lot of
things that I used to find important.*

*Next week the construction on the shower and the
toilets will finally be finished. After two years! They build
entire skyscrapers in that time in New York.*

November 21, 2010
Bo Bo's Third Birthday

*We're celebrating the way we always do: cake, candles,
singing. Little gifts. He's starting to speak in longer
sentences. English with me, Burmese with everyone else.*

*He tends to be a quiet child. Not unfriendly or
unapproachable, but often self-sufficient. Always observing,
looking unflinchingly into people's eyes. At moments like that
he can look very serious and oddly grown-up.*

*When it's just the two of us—not something that
happens very often—I sometimes feel self-conscious. I have
no idea why.*

*I'm getting older, but not any more patient. Not with
him. As much as I wish it were so.*

*On bad days I even remind myself of my mother.
Dreadful thought.*

*I'm reminded of a conversation I had with U Ba a
while ago. He was claiming that we are all prisoners. We
are shackled as children. The boundaries are laid out while
we are still young. And then it takes us a lifetime to find
the limits of our bonds, and—in the best-case scenario—
to loosen them. We can never completely shake them off.*

I'm not sure that he's right, but if he is: What fetters are we placing on Bo Bo during these first years?

I don't know.

Thar Thar says it's better that way.

January 2011

Three years ago today I arrived in Hsipaw with Bo Bo. I had intended to mark the occasion somehow, but when the time came I wasn't in the mood for it. No one besides me gave it even the slightest thought. Not that they aren't delighted we're here. Anniversaries just don't mean much to Thar Thar or the children. What matters is the present moment.

May 17, 2011

Thar Thar's Birthday

Not a very nice day. Thar Thar and I fought, more heatedly than we have in a long while.

He thinks we should accept four new children. A blind boy and three girls, all of whom have trouble walking. They're no older than ten, and they require a lot of daily attention, never mind all the personal history they bring with them. Together with the four who joined us last year, that would make twenty, and that's too much for me.

What exactly did I mean by "too much," he wanted to know.

Too much responsibility, I told him.

Too much needing to help.

Too much extended family. Too little time for us.

Even just the question irritated me. To me it sounded like criticism.

Thar Thar didn't understand. The "children" were in many regards independent, he said. Several were already grown up. They could take care of themselves for the most part. The older ones looked after the younger ones. A few more wouldn't make much difference.

At some point I got so angry that I threw a cup at him. I apologized right away, but without saying a word he stood up and left and did not come back until evening.

I was ashamed of my outburst, and I didn't have any idea where the sudden rage had come from. That scared me.

My problem: aside from him, there's no one I can talk to.

August 28, 2011

I nearly forgot my own birthday.

The last few months have been difficult. I didn't want to seem coldhearted, so we accepted the four new children. They need us even more than I had feared.

I'm suffering from bouts of fever that clear up as suddenly as they appear. My doctor in Mandalay has no explanation.

Thar Thar says I'm sensitive and easily irritated. He's probably right.

I miss New York, but I can't say just what it is I'm missing. What it is I want so badly. Amy is the only person I have stayed in touch with. But still. The homesickness, if I can call it that, seems to be getting worse, not better. Thar Thar thinks I should just go there for a few weeks, but I don't dare.

What am I afraid of?

An inner uneasiness has returned. Maybe it was never gone. Maybe I had just stopped noticing it. Sometimes it all comes out at once in a burst of rage that frightens even me. No one criticizes me, but things are awkward for days afterward.

I don't understand where it's coming from. Life is actually pretty good. We're healthy. We've just about finished the plans for the café at the market. My fears that someone would come and lock us up have proved unfounded. I ought to be feeling more secure, but I'm not.

I feel instead like I'm watching a storm approach that no one else can see.

Thar Thar thinks I worry too much. He's right about that, too. But he doesn't know any more than I do what I can do to change that.

Fourth Anniversary

I wanted Thar Thar to go away with me for a few days after Christmas. Just the two of us. To Mandalay. Or Bagan. For more than three years we've spent nearly every day together, but I still feel like we're getting shortchanged. I crave time with him. ALONE.

I miss you, I told him.

I'm right here, he said.

Not in the way that I need you to be.

I can't say whether he understands where I'm coming from, but as usual he respected my wishes and immediately agreed.

Hsipaw got its first Internet café yesterday, the Small World Café. On the wall there is a handwritten sign: "Please Respect Yourself," with the Burmese translation underneath. When I ask the owner what he means by it, he hesitates and explains a bit sheepishly that it means that people should not visit pornographic sites.

Not because it's forbidden. Out of self-respect.

I tell him that that would never work in America. Most people there have a less developed sense of self-regard.

He doesn't understand what I mean.

After wasting half an hour I give up trying to open the New York Times website.

I want to send Amy an email, but the connection is too slow even for that.

That was the last of the marked pages. U Ba shut the book and packed it carefully back in his bag.

"Julia has no notes about what happened after that," he explained, "so I will have to tell you myself."

Chapter 32

THERE WAS SMOKE over Hsipaw. Ominous charcoal clouds that darkened the sky above the city. The scent of burning wood hanging in the cool, clear autumn air, drifting even up to the monastery.

Thar Thar took the moped to town to see what had happened and whether he could help.

Even at a distance he could make out the burning huts. In the south, near the river, there was an entire block ablaze. That was the neighborhood with the mosque, where most of the Muslim families lived.

Hordes of men roamed the streets armed with clubs, shovels, knives, and machetes. He knew some of the faces well, others vaguely. Most were unfamiliar to him.

The market was closed. The shops had barricaded their gates and doors. Women and children peered furtively from many a window.

No sign of any police. Nor military.

Some young monks were standing in front of a pagoda following the goings-on from a safe distance. They told him what had happened. There were lots of rumors. The night before, two young girls, Buddhists, had allegedly been raped by two brothers. According to a different version the victim was an older woman. Still a third version reported that she was a young child. In all cases the perpetrators were allegedly Muslims. This morning a vengeful mob had set fire to many Muslim houses and huts. Some had tried to defend themselves. Most had fled into the forest or across the river. Some had drowned in the attempt. The monks suspected that there were many dead or wounded.

Thar Thar drove up and down the streets, wondering what he should do. He came across a young boy hiding in the rushes under a bridge. He had seen this boy before. His family owned a stall at the market where Thar Thar and Moe Moe frequently bought rice. He stopped and climbed off his moped. "Is everything okay? Come here."

The child cowered deeper into the grass and did not move.

"You're Nyi Lay, aren't you?"

Still the child refused to move.

Thar Thar climbed down the embankment and fetched him out of his hiding place. The boy apparently recognized him and did not resist. Or perhaps he was simply too exhausted to defend himself. His arms and legs were scratched and covered with burns and abrasions. His hands and face were black with soot.

Thar Thar took him in his arms. "Hey, little guy, tell me what happened? Where's your father?"

When Thar Thar got back to the monastery a young boy was sitting behind him, holding tight with his slender arms. Both smelled of fire and smoke.

"This is Nyi Lay," said Thar Thar. "He lives with us now."

Julia saw the wounds and burns on the child's arms and legs. "What happened to him?"

"Later."

Thar Thar knelt down on a level with the boy, whose entire body was quivering. He introduced each inhabitant of the monastery one by one and explained to the boy that he need no longer be afraid, that he was safe now. No one would dare to attack a monastery. Julia dug out her big first-aid kit and started tending the boy's injuries. She cleaned his legs with a wet cloth and sprayed them with disinfectant. The boy's face twisted in pain, but he never made a sound.

"How old are you?" she asked, trying to distract him. He stared straight ahead and did not answer.

On his left hand were many broken blisters. Julia gently applied a salve to them. They must have been quite painful. "I'm guessing you're eight and you're in the third or fourth grade. Is that right?"

Silence.

"Or maybe you don't go to school at all?" Slowly she wrapped a bandage over his burned skin.

Silence.

"Do you have any brothers or sisters?"

"Julia." Thar Thar interrupted her and indicated by an energetic shaking of his head that she ought not to ask any further questions.

When she was finished, the others gathered around him and led him to the kitchen, where they made him something to eat.

Julia and Thar Thar sat down on the veranda, and he reported what he had heard and seen. People in town were saying that the arsonists were not from Hsipaw. Supposedly they were brought in on military trucks early in the morning. That was only a part of the truth. Thar Thar had seen people he knew roaming through the city and plundering their neighbors' homes.

"What about Nyi Lay's family?" Julia asked.

"There's nothing left of their home but a pile of smoking ashes. The poor kid didn't say much. As far as I understand, his father, mother, and little sister all died in the fire. His two older brothers were able to get away, but he doesn't know where they're hiding."

She buried her face in her hands and shook her head. "For God's sake, where were the police? Didn't they intervene?"

"No."

"Why not?"

"I don't know."

"And the military?"

"Nowhere to be seen."

"What can we do?"

"Not much."

"We've got to shelter him here until his brothers come back," she said.

He nodded. "That might take a while. I hope they're still alive."

"Do you think he has any uncles or aunts in the city or in Mandalay?"

"Maybe." Thar Thar pulled her closer. Only now did she notice that his whole body was quivering. She put her arms around him. Beads of cold sweat ran from his clean-shaven head down the back of his neck.

"I've got to go back to town," he said.

"Should I come with you?"

"No, it's better for you to stay with Bo Bo and the children. I won't be gone long. Maybe I'll be able to find some relatives of Nyi Lay."

Chapter 33

MORE THAN TWO DOZEN MEN STOOD at the entrance to the courtyard, many of them carrying wooden slats or bamboo stalks. Others had machetes and torches. Their longyis and white shirts were smeared with soot and spattered with something that looked like dried blood.

Thar Thar had not yet returned. Julia asked Moe Moe to take you and the new boy to the meditation hall. The others followed.

Julia waited until everyone was inside. She took several deep breaths and then approached the men.

Nothing in her life had prepared her for this moment.

If only Thar Thar could be there at her side, she thought. He would know how to handle these people whose senses were clouded by hatred. People blinded and deafened by rage and frenzy.

She did not.

He would be able to find the right words. He had faced

death so many times in his life that he would not be intimidated by a machete-wielding mob.

Unlike her.

Julia's heart was in her throat.

She stopped about ten yards in front of them. "How can I help you?" she asked in her nearly flawless Burmese, tinged only slightly with an American accent. Polite and earnest. Her voice sounded firmer and more forceful than she had thought possible.

One man stepped forward a few paces. He was a head shorter than Julia, muscular, a machete in his hands, and his face was flushed with excitement. The veins in his neck and forehead stood out like earthworms. "Why are you sheltering a Muslim?" he shouted.

"We are not sheltering a Muslim," Julia replied calmly. She felt a growing resolve that surprised even her.

"You're lying." The man was nearly stumbling over his words. "Your husband brought a boy to your monastery. There were plenty of witnesses. And that boy is a Muslim. You know it." He tightened his grip on his weapon.

Rather than retreating, Julia stepped forward until she came within an arm's length of him. He stank of fire. He stank of vengeance and violence.

"We are protecting a human being. That's all that matters to me," she retorted.

Her fearlessness caught the man off guard. A few seconds passed before he answered. "His brothers raped a girl," he shouted, though not quite as loudly or vociferously as before. His keenest weapon, his utter conviction, was showing a few small cracks.

"I know about that accusation. And if it's true, then it's a terrible crime that must be punished severely. But it is his brothers who have been accused. The boy is eight years old. What does he have to do with any of it?"

"He belongs to the same family."

"So? He's just a child."

"Hand him over."

"He's under our protection."

"Then we'll get him ourselves." It was meant to sound resolute, but you could hear the doubt mingled in his voice. He turned his head questioningly to the other men, but they, too, hesitated.

Julia crossed her arms and said nothing. She was completely unarmed and utterly at their mercy. With one well-aimed machete stroke he could have slit her throat. Or her abdomen. They could have simply pushed her aside, ignored her objections, marched into the hall, and laid hands on the boy.

She would not have been able to do anything about it.

But for some reason they did not dare to. The leader averted his eyes. Apparently he had not expected to meet any resistance. He snorted several times, turned around, and marched past the mob of men right out of the courtyard. The other men turned and followed him without a word. Julia stood watching them until they disappeared over the next hill.

The following day Ko Lwin's parents came and took him away. Without a word of protest he packed his things in a bag and followed them. The next day Soe Soe's parents appeared at the gate to reclaim their daughter. Her Soe Soe, Julia thought. Who had taught her to sew and to cook. After that came Ko Aung's parents. Toe Toe's. Even Ko Maung's. Not one of them dared to defy their parents. They exchanged embarrassed glances with Thar Thar and Julia, then disappeared.

Each time the two of them stood mute in the courtyard and watched them go. She saw how much these silent partings pained Thar Thar. She would have liked more than anything to have stood in their way. When she moved to ask Ko Maung, a grown man who had lived at the monastery for twelve years, why he was obeying like a child, Thar Thar took her arm and held her back.

Only Moe Moe hesitated. Her parents had sent her eldest brother. He rode up on a moped, and without even getting off he barked at her to pack her things.

She stood unmoving in the middle of the courtyard, silently shaking her head. He repeated his demand. She did not move.

Furious, he got off his moped and stomped over to her, a big, powerful young man towering over his sister. He rattled on at her. Insistent. The edge in his voice was unmistakable even inside the meditation hall.

Moe Moe turned her head slightly to one side. Her eyes were firmly set straight ahead. He could have beaten and kicked her; she would not have followed him.

She belonged with Thar Thar. With Julia. With you.

Eventually her brother turned around, cursed, got on his moped, and sped away.

That evening Julia was pacing the great hall restlessly. Moe Moe was doing her best to act as if nothing had changed. The strings of lights were flickering, and she had lit candles and sticks of incense. She had set offerings of potatoes, rice, and bananas on the altars in front of the Buddhas.

All the same, the silence was oppressive. Julia missed Ko Lwin's laughter. Ko Maung's always-somewhat-too-shrill voice. The clatter of pots and pans. To her it seemed that life, along with the children, had ebbed out of the monastery.

Thar Thar was sitting in front of the altars, meditating. She went and crouched down beside him. "I have to talk to you."

He opened his eyes. "Now?"

"Yes."

"Can't it wait until..."

"No," she interrupted. "We need to get out of here."

"Why?"

"Because I'm afraid."

"There's no need to be."

"How can you say that after everything that's happened in Hsipaw?"

"That's a separate thing. They won't do anything to us."

"You didn't see those men. They'll be coming back."

"I doubt it. I'm sure that everything will settle down in a few days."

"They want the boy."

"No. It was an overexcited mob. They won't be back.

"You're not taking me seriously," she answered, furious.

"What makes you say that?"

"Because it's true, dammit. I faced down twenty machete-wielding men, hatred dripping out of every pore. They could have finished me off with a single blow, and you're telling me there's nothing to be afraid of."

For a long time Thar Thar did not answer. She heard him breathing calmly, as if he had slipped back into meditation. "The monastery is our home," he finally said. "We don't have any other."

"I know, but without the children the monastery is empty. Dead."

"I'm sure the children will come back after a while," he reflected. "We just need to be patient."

Julia shook her head angrily. "'I'm sure, I'm sure.' How can you possibly be sure?" Before he could answer, she added: "You don't understand me. I am afraid! We've got to get out of here. They'll kill us all. We can come back in a few months to see whether things have really settled down."

"Where would you have us go?"

"To my brother in Kalaw."

"And then?"

"And then we'll see."

"What about Moe Moe?"

"I'm assuming she'll come with us."

"And Nyi Lay?"

"Him, too."

Julia heard a rustling and flinched. It sounded like whispering. She looked fearfully to Thar Thar. "Did you hear that?"

He nodded, rose, took a flashlight, and went outside.

She heard him gingerly descend the steps into the courtyard. Then his shout. Then footsteps in the darkness.

"Is everything okay?"

Julia edged over to the door. There were people coming up the steps. There was Thar Thar. In the glow of the flashlight she recognized Ko Maung. Bo Bo's big brother. Her best English student. Ko Maung, the helpful spirit who was always ready to lend a hand. He lowered his face, ashamed. "I'm sorry that I left," he said gloomily. "I want to be here with you."

Chapter 34

NO ONE KNEW where or how the fire started the following night. It appeared out of nowhere under a clear, starry sky.

The wood was old and dry, an ideal fuel for the flames. But that by itself could not explain how a building of that size could be reduced to ashes in so short a time. Or how the flames erupted simultaneously in the kitchen, in the meditation hall, and in the back of the building where Julia, Thar Thar, Nyi Lay, Ko Maung, Moe Moe, and you were sleeping. Or how the stilts on which the monastery stood blazed like torches. Or how even the shed and the toilets caught fire at the same time.

It may have been the chickens that saved them. Or the dogs. The cackling and barking had woken Moe Moe. Or it might have been her sensitive nose that jolted her into consciousness. She could smell the hatred at once. It seeped through all the cracks in the planks and boards. She heard it in the crackling of blazing wood.

Whatever the reason, Moe Moe woke with a cough, surrounded by smoke. She leapt up, took hold of you, and tried to run out into the open. Burning beams in the hall blocked her path. She could not breathe. Her eyes were burning. She stepped over blazing timbers and pieces of the collapsed roof. She felt the blistering heat over her whole body. At any moment her longyi might burst into flames. Or your shirt. Or your hair. Confronted by a wall of fire and smoke, she could move neither forward nor back. All at once the floor below her gave way. She fell through and landed with a thud on the sandy ground beneath the monastery. A searing pain shot through her right leg. For a moment she felt dizzy. She saw spots in front of her eyes, but she did not pass out. And she could move. As quickly as she could she crawled with you out from under the burning monastery. She rose and limped to the soccer field, where the two of you were safe from the conflagration.

Not long afterward Julia and Thar Thar emerged from the smoke. They had saved one bag. They were coughing and gasping for breath. Thar Thar had two gaping, fist-sized burns on his arms. He scanned the vicinity. "Where are Maung and Nyi Lay?"

"I thought they were with you," said Moe Moe.

Julia, too, gazed about, hoping to spot them. "Nyi Lay? Maung?" she called out. "Where are you?"

Thar Thar set off at a run, but the heat of the fire was too intense, and the blazing meditation hall was already collapsing. He could do nothing more than call loudly for them as he ran in a wide arc to the other side of the building. "Nyi Lay? Maung?" he bellowed time and again. "Nyi Lay? Maung? Please answer."

Chapter 35

U BA FELL SILENT. The sun was already getting lower in the sky. A light breeze had come up, and the air was noticeably cooler. I shivered and got goose bumps. Now I knew why I did not like the smell of burning wood. Why tall, raging flames always made me uneasy.

I wanted to ask about Nyi Lay and Ko Maung, but I was afraid of the answer. "Were the two of them able," I chose my words carefully, "to save themselves?"

"No."

"What happened?"

"No one knows for sure. They may have been struck by a falling beam. Or they may have succumbed to the smoke. Your parents found them amid the ashes of the monastery the following morning. Wrapped in each other's arms."

I had no memories of Nyi Lay or Ko Maung. Even so, I had to wipe my eyes with my sleeve. My uncle reached out for my hand. I could see that he was on the verge of tears. "You know, Bo Bo..." His voice was broken up.

"You know, Bo Bo..." he tried again, but couldn't finish the sentence.

I scooted closer to him and wished I could curl up with him the way I used to whenever I was sad or frightened. Just the scent of him and the warmth of his body were enough to convince me I was safe. Now we were sitting side by side, and for a moment he leaned his head on my shoulder. I put my arm around him. Before us stretched the nearly empty valley. Mountains as far as the eye could see. No sound but a few birds and insects and the wind in the trees. The loneliness of it soothed me a little. I was glad not to have to see anyone other than my uncle.

"Didn't the firefighters come?"

"No."

"Why not?"

"I don't know. Why are there people who refuse to help another person in need? I wish I knew the answer."

"What did we do?"

"You fled to me that very day. A potato farmer in Hsipaw owed your parents money. They used it to purchase train tickets to Kalaw. I was horrified when you suddenly appeared in my yard with just the one bag. Your mother's longyi and blouse were blackened. Moe Moe's face was covered with soot. You were clinging to your father like a newborn monkey. I could see the burning monastery in your eyes. Do you remember anything from that journey?"

"No." Or maybe I did, but it wasn't anything I would have been able or willing to discuss.

How could a fire start in a house in the middle of the night when everyone was sleeping?

"I guess someone set the monastery on fire?"

My uncle shrugged.

"Fires don't just spring up out of thin air," I insisted. "Nothing happens without a cause."

"Don't you think it was arson?"

"Most likely."

"Do you know who it was?"

"No. No one was ever charged."

"U Ba, tell me, could what happened in Hsipaw ever happen here in Kalaw?"

"No."

"Are you certain?" I asked, relieved but wondering whether I could trust his answer.

"Completely certain."

"Why not?"

"Because . . . because . . ." He was grasping for an explanation.

I waited and thought about it. Most of the kids at my school were Buddhists, but there were also Christians, Hindus, Muslims, and even Gurkhas. We argued a lot, but I don't remember us ever arguing about who believed what. But we were kids. Grown-ups might be different.

I thought about our neighbors, who always said hello, who were always friendly, who helped us out with eggs, rice, or water when we needed it, and I wondered whether there was any reason why they would suddenly descend on us and set fire to our house. I couldn't think of any. But maybe Nyi Lay would not have been able to think of one either until it actually happened. Maybe his neighbors had also always said hello and helped them out with eggs, rice, and water. Until the moment when they decided to slaughter his parents and his little sister.

"Because…because…it just could not happen here," my uncle said, interrupting my thoughts. "I have lived in this city for nearly eighty years, and to the best of my knowledge it has never once in that entire time come to blows between Buddhists, Muslims, or Christians. I do not recall there ever being so much as an argument. Kalaw is different."

"Different how?"

"Just different.

"U Ba," I reproached him, "what kind of answer is that?"

My uncle suppressed a groan and a sigh, just as he sometimes did when his stomach hurt or when he had to fart. He turned away and gazed silently into the distance. In the end he pulled me in very close. "Then listen closely, my dear Bo Bo," he said almost imploringly. "It can happen anywhere. In any country, in any city, in any village in the world. Is that a better answer?"

I backed away from him, horrified. "No. No, that's not a better answer at all."

"It can happen anywhere we fail to see others first as people. Where instead we see brown, black, or white; Buddhist, Muslim, or Christian. In any country, in any city, in any village in the world, there is only one power that can protect us from these atrocities, Bo Bo. Only one that we can truly trust. Promise me you will never forget that."

"Okay." I cannot remember my uncle ever speaking so seriously and urgently to me. "What power do you mean?"

"Love. And the courage to follow it."

I waited, but instead of continuing, he looked me right in the eyes. He was trying to tell me something for which words failed him.

But I did not understand and wanted instead to ask him what kind of love he was talking about. The love between an uncle and his nephew? Between a mother or a father and their child? Between siblings? Between a man and a woman? Or were there other forms of love I knew nothing about?

As if he had read my mind, he suddenly said: "The love that needs no name and knows no limits. The love that makes us greater and more beautiful because it prompts us to think of others before ourselves. Because it invites us to be bigger than ourselves, and because it has no end. It is the light in the heart of darkness."

U Ba moved around as if about to rise, but the long sitting had wearied his muscles. He propped himself with all his strength against one of the tree's roots, but still he could not get up. My uncle crouched on the ground, helpless as a beetle on its back. I jumped up and offered him my hand. Slowly I eased him up.

"Thank you," he said, clinging to my arm.

Breathless. Uneasy.

It was high time for us to be heading back. I packed our things. U Ba took my arm and we set off. Although it was downhill nearly all the way, he found it more difficult than the way there. Again and again we needed to take breaks, during which we simply stood side by side without a word. The memories that accompanied us now did not put wings on our feet. They weighed instead like stones on our hearts, and even for my uncle it was obviously difficult to let go of them, though he had claimed to be an old hand at that.

I felt as if I was in two places at once. Hand in hand with U Ba, I was walking along a path back to Kalaw. At the same time I was in Moe Moe's arms. I heard her labored breathing. Smoke stung my eyes. I saw my mother reaching out for me. My father's tears. His voice.

Nyi Lay, Maung, where are you?

Please answer.

An endless, wordless train ride.

These were memories like no others I had known.

More, so much more.

It was dusk by the time we got back home.

I lit a fire and put water on for tea and rice. My uncle had collapsed exhausted onto the couch, where he was slowly recovering. "Please come here," he suddenly called out.

"I'm just making some tea."

"It can wait."

I went into the living room and crouched down beside him. "What is it?" I asked, worried. "Are you okay?"

He took my hands. His were cold. "You know, my dear Bo Bo, every one of us has scars," he said quietly. "Some of them are visible; others are not."

For a long time I had thought that I would rather have a less visible wound. But now I was thinking that the invisible wounds might be the harder ones to bear. But of course it didn't matter. No one gets to choose their wounds.

It had gotten dark. I went to turn on a light, but U Ba indicated with a shake of his head that I should leave it off. He didn't want candlelight, either.

We sat across from each other, and I could make out only his silhouette. All at once I sensed what he wanted to tell me. The moment I had so long been waiting for.

"U Ba, how did I get the scar on my cheek?"

He spoke more quietly than usual, and I leaned in to hear him.

"Your scar," he said, "is from your mother."

I had known it all along. A part of her. And I always would be. "Is hers as big as mine?"

"She doesn't have one."

I didn't understand. "But you just said that I got it from . . ."

"A scar is not hereditary. It is not a thing that one generation passes to the next. She inflicted it on you."

A few seconds passed before his words really sank in.

Inflicted.

In-flic-ted.

"How?" I whispered.

"No one was paying attention," he replied.

His voice made clear to me that that was not the truth. Or not the whole truth. One look into his eyes would have told me more. Now I knew why we were sitting in the dark.

"What does that mean?"

"It means that each one of us, your father and I included, bears some of the blame."

He was being cagey. "Tell me what happened."

My uncle turned away.

"Please, U Ba."

"You were still little..."

"How little?" I interrupted him.

"You had just turned five."

"Where were we?"

"In Kalaw, here at my house, at the table over there in the kitchen. You were playing with a very sharp knife. Your father was outside. I was cooking with your mother and Moe Moe. You wanted to help out." He was having difficulty getting the words out.

I waited. "Please, U Ba."

"None of you were doing very well. The fire at the monastery, the departure of the children, your escape from Hsipaw. All of it had taken a toll.

"Moe Moe had fallen completely silent. She hadn't uttered a single word for days.

"You were a different person. Gone was the cheerful, easygoing child with the ready laugh, the boy so able to amuse himself. From morning till evening you would tear through the house or the yard. Heedless of all warnings, you would climb along the porch railing, or you would run after the chickens. As if you had only to run fast enough in order to forget everything that had happened. Only in your father's arms or on his lap would you ever find peace, but not even he could always contain you. And of course he was quite preoccupied with troubles of his own.

"The loss of his home and the death of the two boys had smitten him to the core. He tried to be there for you, but he was not really up to it. This once muscular man seemed to have lost half his weight overnight. His face was gaunt; his eyes were sunken. He would often just sit on the sofa or on the stoop, staring off into the distance, absent. To me it seemed that something inside him was broken.

"Your mother was no better off. She wept frequently and blamed herself harshly for having failed to save Nyi Lay and Ko Maung. Her infrequent sleep was troubled by nightmares, and she was a bundle of nerves. She feared the entire time that the police would come and arrest Thar Thar or her or both of them. Or that someone would set fire to the house. She would sit bolt upright in the middle of the night and check to see that everyone was there, safe and sound. Her temper was short, and she quarreled frequently with your father about how they would ever carry on. She wanted to stay in Kalaw, to build a house here, or maybe in Yangon. She even considered a move to New York. He wanted to play it by ear, to move back to Hsipaw in a few weeks or months. For her that was completely out of the question."

My uncle took a deep breath. "We were busy in the kitchen. She told you to put the knife down immediately, but you did not listen."

Again he paused. I sat perfectly still. The whole house was quiet, as if even the moths and flies, the chickens and the pig wanted to know what happened next.

"She told you a second time, but again you ignored her. Then she shouted at you. I had never heard my sister shriek like that. She was tripping over her words, so completely beside herself she was, as if out of her mind. You looked at her, eyes wide, and still you did not obey."

"And then?"

"Suddenly you put the knife in your mouth. I do not know why. Maybe her screaming had frightened you. Maybe you wanted to spite her. Maybe you had no idea what you were doing. I simply cannot say. In one swift motion your mother reached across the table. Moe Moe froze.

"Your father came bounding up the stairs, but by the time he reached the kitchen it was too late. Before he or I could say a word, your mother had grabbed the knife and taken it away from you."

"That's not the kind of thing that leaves a scar," I objected.

"She pulled it sideways through your cheek. Edge first."

Part Three

Chapter 1

FOR A WHOLE WEEK I felt nothing more. Nothing at all. My left, scarred cheek was numb.

Dried up.

Withered like the shriveled leaves of the banana tree in our yard.

I could press on it from the inside with my tongue, or I could poke at it with a sharp fingernail. It made no difference; I felt nothing.

At school I would tap my cheek from time to time with my hand, as if to make sure it was still there. When I ate or drank I worried that the food or water might run back out of my mouth. During the lessons I never said a word. The other children noticed right away that something was wrong, and they left me in peace.

Then it started to hurt. At first it was a slight tugging or burning, a feeling I had become familiar with over the years. But then it started to hurt terribly. After two days I asked U Ba to have a look in my mouth. He shone a flashlight in there, but he couldn't see anything wrong. Both my cheeks looked the same, he claimed, aside from the scar, of course. He thought I might have a toothache or an inflamed jaw.

When there was no sign of improvement he brought me to see a doctor, but he couldn't find anything either. My teeth were not only in good condition, but as healthy as could be, the doctor declared with satisfaction.

That night I woke up to a throbbing, piercing pain. My cheek was burning as if I had laid it on fiery coals. It could hardly have been worse when my mother actually pulled the knife through my flesh.

I didn't want to wake my uncle, and I couldn't think of anything to do but to count as fast as I could: Onetwothreefour-fivesixseven . . . fifty . . . one hundred . . . two hundred . . .

When I got to a thousand, I woke him up anyway.

At the hospital they gave us some pills that were supposed to ease the pain. They had no effect at all. Nor could the doctors offer any explanation for my suffering.

Not knowing what else to do, my uncle took me to an astrologer and medicine man of Indian descent who, according to U Ba, had once, long, long ago, helped his mother when her crippled feet had swollen overnight and were causing her terrible pain.

His name was U Thar Khin, and he lived on the other side of Kalaw. We walked clear across town, and it took us nearly an hour. Every step, every movement, pained me.

The man must have had a green thumb. Roses, daisies, and hibiscus were blossoming around his yard. White and yellow orchids hung from his porch. Poinsettias and asters grew in pots on his steps.

My uncle led the way up the stairs.

In the entryway we climbed over stacks of cookie tins, boxes of laundry detergent, little sacks of rice, soda bottles, and cheroots. It was clear that many of his patients paid in kind.

U Thar Khin was lean and tall, with the longest nose I have ever seen. He wore a white longyi, a white shirt, and on his head a white turban like those favored by the Pa-O. His long white hair was peeking out from underneath it. I'm guessing he was older than U Ba, and I had the impression that his vision was no longer the best and that his hearing was still worse. When you spoke to him you had to bend down right next to his ear.

He listened closely to everything my uncle said, nodding now and then. Eventually he led us into his treatment room, a small, empty space with bare walls. U Thar Khin lit a few candles, and the air was soon filled with a strange, sweet fragrance.

I couldn't really imagine that this old man, of all people, would be able to help me in any way.

He walked in circles around me several times, stood face-to-face with me, gazed into my eyes, poked at my neck and my jaw, ran his hands over my chest and my stomach. He had me open my mouth and stick out my tongue.

Then he asked me to lie down on the floor and close my eyes.

I hesitated and looked to my uncle for guidance. He nodded silently. I lay down reluctantly on the wooden planks.

U Thar Khin spread a blanket over me and crouched on the floor above my head. He wanted me to rest my aching cheek in his hand and to let him bear the whole weight of my head. Again I hesitated. I did not like to let anyone touch my face and least of all my scar.

With his other hand he gently began to massage my neck. I flinched, but his skin was warm and softer even than my uncle's. He told me just to keep breathing, to keep my eyes closed and to try to think of nothing. At some point I stopped resisting and let my head sink into his hand.

I tried to keep still, but it wasn't easy for me. The moment I closed my eyes, images would appear that I did not want to see. Just like in the evening, when I was trying to go to sleep.

"Close your eyes and listen to what the birds are telling you."

I closed my eyes. "I don't hear any birds."

"Concentrate."

I heard crackling and snapping on all sides. The neighbor's baby was crying. Chickens were cackling. Barking in the distance. Birds were also singing, but they weren't telling me anything.

"Do you hear them now?"

"No."

"What are you worried about? Why are you so upset?" he asked. "You just need to be a little patient with yourself."

"What's wrong with me?" I asked, trying not to sound frightened.

"I don't know."

"But you are the doctor."

"You are the only one who has the answer."

"Me?"

"Who else?"

I was certain he was mistaken.

Time rolled by, and at some point I began to settle down. Now he took my head in both hands, held it firmly, and turned it slowly from one side to the other, humming a tune as he did so, quietly at first, so that it sounded as if he was sitting far away, maybe even in another room. Gradually the sound got closer, and I really did manage to stop thinking about my mother.

Very gently he pulled me closer to him. He let my head rest in his lap, and he laid his hands on my stomach. Their warmth was so comforting that I wanted to take hold of one and never let it go. Then something very surprising happened: I started to cry. It wasn't actually the usual kind of crying; I didn't sob or wail, but tears were running down my cheeks. Rather than feeling sadder, though, I found myself starting to feel better.

I actually fell asleep, and when I woke up, I had forgotten where I was. Who was holding my head. Who was humming that tune to me. I felt my cheek, but it no longer hurt.

"Your nephew will feel better for a while now," U Thar Khin explained to my uncle in the loud voice of a person who cannot hear well. I had sat up again. "But I cannot say how long it will last." He scratched his head. "He may come to me anytime, but I am afraid I cannot do anything more permanent for him."

Chapter 2

U THAR KHIN PROVED TO BE CORRECT. The pain in my cheek crept back after only a few days. Fortunately it was not quite so severe as it had been. It was not unbearable, so I decided not to mention it to my uncle.

I ate almost nothing. I was weary and sensitive. Just the sight of a dead beetle could make me sad. I slept poorly and in the mornings I was so exhausted that I didn't want to do anything at all. I would most have liked to spend the whole day in bed, but then U Ba would have worried more about me, and I wanted to avoid that. So I would get up, pack eggs, toast, and a banana for lunch, and then set off for school. As soon as I left the house I would forge an excuse for myself, give it to Thu Riya, and then go to Ko Aye Min's place. At this time of year he was often away leading tourist hikes, so I was generally alone in his office, and that suited me just fine. I didn't want to answer any questions. I didn't want entertainment. I didn't even want to watch soccer or play video games. I just sat at his desk, watching flies. Or cockroaches. Or staring at the bare wall.

For hours.

For days.

The whole time I kept returning in my thoughts to a single word:

Inflicted.

In-flic-ted.

A scar is not hereditary, not something you pass from one generation to the next, U Ba had said.

I thought about my father, who was missing a finger on his right hand. Had he lost it in an accident? Or had someone *inflicted* that injury upon him? I had never considered that possibility before then.

Or what about Ma Cho Cho? She limped because one of her legs was shorter than the other. The story was that an oxcart had rolled over it while she was playing as a small child in her village. An accident. But maybe something had been *inflicted* on her, too.

Or Ko Htun Min from school. He stuttered. People said he had always stuttered. But is a child born a stutterer? Or is stuttering *inflicted* on a person? I did not know.

Suddenly I could think of so many people, young and old, whose various injuries and scars might at one time or another have been *inflicted* on them. Some earlier in life, some later. It was not a comforting thought. Not in the least. The longer I dwelt on it, the more dreadful it seemed. To distract myself I went to the market, hoping to find Ma Ei.

She was sitting at her mother's snack booth, playing on her phone, and she was happy to see me. "How's it going?"

"Good," I lied.

"No school today?"

"No."

"Do you want something to eat? A soup, maybe?"

"Sure," I answered, although I felt sick to my stomach and was not at all hungry.

With a sieve she lowered a handful of noodles into a pot of boiling water. A few seconds later she poured the noodles into a bowl and added broccoli, cauliflower, a few carrot slices, bamboo sprouts, tofu, and little pieces of cooked chicken. She poured a steaming broth over everything and sprinkled it with a couple of pinches of dried chili pepper. She remembered that I liked it hot.

"Thanks so much. It's very kind of you." I blew on the noodles and waited until they had cooled slightly, then tried a spoonful. It was still very hot.

Ma Ei watched me with curiosity. "You're not really hungry at all, are you?"

"Sure I am."

"You're not a very good liar," she said with a laugh.

Her laughter eased my sorrow.

"What's wrong?"

"Why should anything be wrong?"

"You're just . . . different somehow."

I shrugged and felt my eyes welling up again. It was awful. Ever since U Ba had told me the story of my scar, I was prone to frequent and inexplicable bouts of tears. It was embarrassing, and I lowered my eyes.

Ma Ei said nothing. Her hand moved slowly across the table to mine. For a brief moment the pressure in my eyes increased.

"Can I help you?" she whispered.

Yes, please, I wanted to answer.

Please.

But I had no idea what she could do for me. I didn't even know where the tears were coming from, so I just shook my head.

She stroked me at first across my healthy cheek and then softly across my scar. That was something only U Ba was allowed to do. She had never done that, and it just made everything worse. To be touched, I thought, just makes everything worse.

"Can I ask you something?" I said.

"Of course. You name it."

"Was anything ever *inflicted* on you?"

She tilted her head to one side and looked at me for a long while. I didn't even try to read her eyes. A person who is full cannot take anything in, even if they try.

"You ask very"—she searched for the right word—"unusual questions. What do you mean by *inflicted*?"

"That ... that ..." I weighed my answer. "That someone hurt you terribly."

She considered it. "On purpose?"

I nodded.

"Let me think about it. When I was five, my father died. He was run over by a military truck. They claimed he had been drunk and had stumbled out in front of the vehicle. That was a lie. My father never drank. He was a carpenter and every year for my birthday he would carve a little animal for me. I miss him every day. But maybe that's not what you mean."

No, that wasn't it. She had wooden animals from her father, not scars. On second thought, maybe it was close. Now I understood the dark shadow that lay in her eyes, even when she laughed.

I heard the words of my uncle: Everyone has scars. Some are visible; others are not.

Still: Her father's death had been an accident. Fate. Very sad, but still different from my scar.

I shook my head.

Her phone rang, and she turned it down without looking to see who was calling. She rubbed her nose in thought. "Inflicted? Hm. I don't think so. Fortunately for me. Maybe I'm too young for anyone to have done anything cruel to me."

Some sentences hurt more than others.

"Why do you want to know?" she wondered.

I would so have liked to tell her about a little boy who was playing with a knife. About a mother who was *beside herself*. About a father who came bounding up the stairs too late.

But that would never do. She could never know where my scar had come from. That had to be my secret. Forever.

And U Ba's. And my parents'. I didn't want anyone in the world to speak ill of my mother. Or even to think ill of her.

"What about you?"

I shrugged my shoulders and said nothing.

She misinterpreted my gesture. "You don't know? Maybe you're right. We probably don't realize until later whether or when something has been inflicted on us."

When I got home U Ba did not even bother to ask me about my day at school. I suspect he knew very well that I was spending my time elsewhere. He made a bit of a fuss over me and told me I should rest. He would do the shopping and cooking for the next few weeks.

But resting was not so easy. I felt ill at ease in the house now. In some odd way it had become unfamiliar to me. My scar would pull every time I caught sight of the table where U Ba, Moe Moe, my mother, and I must have been sitting. Every day I invented some new excuse for eating on the couch. Or the porch. Or in the yard.

A fire was no longer just a fire.

A knife no longer just a knife.

A scar no longer just a scar.

When my uncle was cooking and he would cut open a pepper with a sharp blade I would feel sick to my stomach. There were things I just couldn't stand to see anymore.

I wasn't sure whether I really believed in ghosts. Some days I did for certain. Other days maybe not. But I had the feeling that my uncle and I were no longer alone in the house.

"You believe in ghosts, don't you?" I prompted him one day.

"It is not a question of belief."

"Have you ever seen one?"

"Of course not. If you can see it, then it is not a ghost. But just because you cannot see a thing does not mean that it is not there. You cannot see air, for instance. Why do you ask?"

"Because lately I've often had the feeling that I'm not alone in a room even when I'm the only one around."

"And indeed you are not alone. None of us ever is."

"What do you mean?"

He thought for a minute. "My wife, for instance. She has been dead for more than fifty years. I have not so much as a photograph of her, and my memories of her face and her voice are gradually fading. But of course she is with me. When I wake in the morning she is often sitting by my bed. She even used to hold my hand, though she does that only rarely now. When I am restoring a book she likes to stand by and watch."

"How do you know?"

"I feel it. Ghosts are something one feels."

"Is she here right now?"

My uncle paused briefly, turning his head this way and that, as if looking for her.

"Do you hear her?" I whispered.

He smiled. "No. One does not hear ghosts, either. She is not here just now. Sometimes she disappears for days. I have no idea where she goes. I know only that I can always count on her. She always returns."

"Does she speak with you?"

"No. But I speak to her."

"Who else is there?"

"My father. My mother. A neighbor and his young daughter, both of whom drowned some time ago in the river. The woman who occupied the house before me. There are many. The dead populate our lives whether we want them to or not."

Maybe we are surrounded by more and more ghosts as we get older. Or maybe older people can sense them better. I didn't know who was around me. I only know that it felt creepy never to be alone anywhere.

I was most at ease out in the yard. I felt better outdoors than sitting in the house. Better to be hanging laundry, weeding the garden, planting vegetables, or feeding the chickens or the pig.

The ants were not much help to me at this point. Their hustle and bustle, their unwavering sense of purpose, left me more unsettled than I would otherwise have been.

As an alternative, I took to counting the leaves on our neighbor's eucalyptus tree. That was a good distraction. By the time I got to one hundred I would lose track of which leaves I had already counted, and I could just start from the beginning.

Same with the stars in the night sky.

From time to time U Ba would look to see that I was still there. As if he was afraid I might just disappear.

So passed the hours.

So passed the days.

And the nights.

Chapter 3

DOES IT TAKE A WICKED PERSON to do a wicked thing? Or does it sometimes happen that a good person does something wicked? And if so, does that wicked act mean that that person is now wicked?

Slicing a child's cheek open with a knife is definitely wicked.

And yet, now that I knew how I had gotten my scar I felt even more longing for my mother, not less. I felt closer to her. Much closer. Some days I missed her so much that I could not think of anything else.

As if the injury she *inflicted* on me was not driving us apart but binding us together. For all time. How could that be?

Did she ever miss me?

I had so many doubts, so many questions. I wanted to know what had happened after my mother had taken the knife away from me. Who had taken care of me. And of her. When had my parents moved to Yangon. Where Moe Moe was. Whether in the end it was actually all my own fault. My karma. That would have been a good explanation, but something inside me resisted that thought. I didn't dare ask my uncle a single one of these questions. I couldn't imagine ever saying them out loud. As if someone had stolen the necessary words from me. I couldn't even have written them down.

My mind was in a terrible disarray. A tumult of thoughts, stories, and images thundered through my head.

I saw myself sitting on a bus. By the window. Alone. My parents stood outside, waving to me. They were laughing, but not cheerfully. I didn't want to leave them, and I started to cry. The bus slowly pulled away, and now my mother no longer wanted me to leave. I could see it in her face. She shouted something, gesticulated, ran alongside the bus and pounded on the door. But it was too late. The driver would not stop. We drove faster and faster. She ran behind us for a few blocks. Eventually, exhausted, she could no longer keep up.

I saw myself sitting alone in a doorway and waiting. And waiting. And waiting.

I saw myself and my mother walking through a market. There was an awful throng. She held my hand tightly. Suddenly she let go and we got separated. All I could see was her outstretched arm groping around for me. Seconds later she was swallowed up by the crowd, the way a raging river carries off a bit of wood.

One evening my uncle and I were sitting at his desk. I was helping him restore one of his books. It was tedious.

The bits of paper kept falling out of the tweezers. I carelessly let some glue fall on the pages. Both of us were elsewhere in our thoughts.

"I went to see U Thar Khin again today," U Ba said abruptly.

"Why?"

"Because I am worried about you."

"You don't need to be."

He gazed at me over the top of his reading glasses. "Do I not?"

"No."

"You promise?"

"Yes, I'm fine," I lied. "My cheek no longer hurts. It feels completely normal again."

"I am glad to hear it," he replied skeptically.

All at once we heard loud voices in the yard. Steps. I wanted to go see who was there, but U Ba told me not to move. There was only one person brazen enough to come to the house even at this hour. I knew, too, as soon as I heard the heavy footsteps on the stairs.

At the door stood a young soldier. He made no move to remove his boots or enter the house. "U Ba?" he asked sternly.

"Present," my uncle responded in a loud voice, as if issuing a command. I had never heard him speak that way.

At once the soldier stood somewhat straighter.

"I have a message for you from Colonel Tin Shwe," he declared. "The colonel regrets to inform you that for reasons of national security the military is compelled to seize ownership of properties previously in your possession. You can expect a small compensation. Headquarters will settle on the amount in the near future."

U Ba looked at him with a serious expression. "Thank you. Please be so kind as to inform the colonel that I..." Before my uncle could finish his sentence, the soldier turned on his heel and descended the steps.

"That you...?" I wondered aloud.

"That I... that I..." Instead of finishing the sentence, he just smiled. In his eyes was neither anger nor disappointment, only a calm that did not seem to fit with the soldier's news.

"U Ba, is something wrong?" I asked, worried.

"... that I am relieved and grateful that proper order has been restored."

"What order?"

"The old order. Nothing is worse than when things are not where they ought to be. When each person knows his place, there is peace. Otherwise everything gets quite mixed up, and that causes only confusion."

I had to think for a long time about what he said, and eventually it gave me an idea. A person's place.

Where did I belong?

With U Ba.

With my father.

And with my mother.

I lay awake for a long time after my uncle had started to snore beside me. I spent hours during the night refining my plan.

Chapter 4

I FELT AS IF my left cheek was going to explode. The skin was taut, and I could feel my pulse throbbing in it. It was terrible. The first light of day fell through the cracks in the wall. U Ba was sound asleep. I rose, dressed, and slipped into the living room. I stuffed a second shirt into my bag. Underwear, a book, and the little stuffed bear that U Ba had given me years ago.

On a scrap of paper I jotted down my parents' number and address from my uncle's phone and put that with the rest of my things. I took ten thousand kyat from his money tin. That ought to cover my ticket and something to eat and drink along the way. Then I sat down and wrote him a note.

Dear U Ba,

> *Forgive me for leaving you alone.*
> *I need to see Mama. I think she needs me.*

My place is with her now. And with Papa.
I'm very, very sorry.
I don't know when I'll be back.
Please don't worry about it.
And please don't be angry with me.
I love you very, very much.
Yours,

Bo Bo

I set the letter on his desk and weighed it down with a tin of milk. I found it terribly difficult to sneak out on him like that, and I had a guilty conscience. But I knew what his answer would have been if I had asked for permission.

I hesitated for a minute. Could I really do that to him? No. But I had no choice. Before I could change my mind I grabbed my things and set off for Ko Aye Min's office.

As I had hoped, he was not around. On his computer I pulled up a map of Yangon to see what part of the city my parents were living in. The neighborhood was called Golden Valley, and it was near the city center, not far from a lake and a big embassy.

The train rolled out of the station, blowing its whistle several times to clear the pedestrians from the rails. Just like every morning at this time. A few months ago they nearly ran over a man who had fallen asleep on the tracks.

I scurried down the embankment, ran alongside one of the cars, took hold of a handrail, and jumped aboard. For a while I stood on the lowest step, looking out over Kalaw. We were crossing the river that Thu Riya and I sometimes swam and fished in, and we were passing Ko Aye Min's place. I thought again of U Ba. The yard. Our house. I would miss everything, even the chickens and the pig. I felt darkness engulfing my heart.

When Kalaw's last buildings had disappeared from view, I found the conductor and gave him the money for the ticket. Luckily for me, he did not know me and did not ask why I was traveling all on my own or why I had not bought my ticket back at the station. He was probably delighted at the chance to pocket the cash.

The cars were not particularly crowded. I found a free seat all to myself. At the next station a mother and her two children sat down next to me. She smiled kindly, took some crackers out of her bag, and offered them to me. I thanked her but soon rose to look for another seat. I felt like the only one on the whole train who was traveling without a family, even though that was probably not true.

We reached Thazi early that evening. The night express from Mandalay to Yangon was full. I walked the length of the train, clambering over sleeping passengers and their baggage, but I couldn't find a single free seat. A family with three children let me squeeze in with them.

Gratefully I lay down on the floor between their benches. I used my bag for a pillow. The car shook and rocked. I

felt every crosstie and I started to count them. I was enjoying the rhythmic clack—clack—clack. At some point I fell
asleep.

When I woke it was light. I stretched and reached for
my bag but found only a piece of cloth. It was filthy, and
it stank. Someone had stuck an old towel under my head.
I sat right up and looked around. The people lying next to
me were unfamiliar; the family must have gotten off somewhere along the way. The car was full of sleeping people. I
searched under the neighbors' seats. I stood up and walked
around the car, checking under every seat. I climbed up
on benches and searched the luggage racks. There was no
trace of my bag. I was starting to feel frightened, and I went
through the whole car a second time, examining each passenger closely. Certainly it was neither of the two young
nuns behind me. Nor the old woman next to them. Maybe
one of the young men with their hair bleached blond. Or
the man on the seat in front of them, who was not sleeping
at all but regarding me through lowered eyelids.

What would a person look like who would rob a child?

If I had been able to look each one of them in the eye, I
would have found him, but I could hardly wake all the passengers and subject them to that.

In my search for the thief I covered the whole train from
end to end. Twice. It was no use. For all I knew he had jumped
off long ago. I felt cold and nauseated. I had not memorized
my parents' phone number or address. Yangon, of course, was
a big city. How was I ever going to find them there?

I huddled on the steps of an open door. The warm air slipping past whipped at my longyi. If only there had been a person with a name and a face to be angry at. But I wasn't angry at all, just disheartened and alone.

It was dusk by the time we reached the outskirts of Yangon. The train was delayed by several hours. All at once it lurched to a halt. I looked out the window, exhausted. To the right and left people were walking beside the tracks. There was not a platform in sight. We waited. Some of the passengers started to pack their things and disembark.

Conductors came through the carriages to explain that the engine was broken and would not be going any farther. But we were only a mile or two from the main station, and we could go the rest of the way on foot. All we needed to do was follow the tracks.

The families I had been sitting near for the last several hours gathered their bags and boxes, climbed down from the carriage, and headed for the station. I fell into line with them.

A few hundred yards along we turned aside, stepped through a gap in a hedge, scrambled through some undergrowth, and found ourselves on a wide, brightly lit street.

It was loud.

And crowded.

And hot. Much warmer than in Kalaw. Sweat ran down my face and neck. My dirty shirt clung to my skin.

Everyone else apparently knew exactly where they were going, and they went off in all directions. Pretty soon I was standing there alone at a giant intersection without even a vague idea of what to do. I was hungry. I was thirsty, and I was so tired that my eyes were falling shut. I asked a woman the way to the city center and went in the direction she indicated. When I couldn't go on I hopped on a bus at a light and stood in the open door until the conductor discovered me two stops later. I jumped off and continued again on foot.

I found a small street where the sidewalks were packed with food stalls. I squatted down at the last table of one of the stands. Pretty soon a boy showed up, no older than me, with long hair, a green longyi, and a white shirt that was dirtier even than mine.

"What'll it be?"

"I'm hungry." U Ba always says that one discovers a person's true nature when one is in need.

The boy took a menu from the next table and handed it to me.

"I don't have any money."

He thought for a minute, turned around, and walked over to a woman who was preparing food over an open fire. They spoke. She gestured with a wok and scowled in my direction. After a while he returned with a plate of fried rice. He set it on the table in front of me without a word.

"Are you thirsty?"

I nodded.

He brought me a bottle of water.

"Thank you," I said.

He said nothing. He just stood there watching me.

"What are you staring at? Haven't you ever seen a scar before?"

"Does it hurt?"

"No."

He was quiet again.

I was sick to my stomach with hunger, and I started to wolf down the food.

"It tastes great," I said through a full mouth.

"Are you alone?" he asked.

"No," I said, without giving it much thought.

"Why don't you have any money?"

"Because."

"Where's your mama?"

"Away on a trip."

"And your papa?"

"Him, too."

The boy thought about it. "I don't believe it," he decided after a while. "You're completely alone."

"Am not," I replied furiously.

The woman called to him and pointed out new customers a few tables away. "Do you want more?" he asked before turning to go.

Though I was still hungry I shook my head no. I didn't want to be greedy.

"What's your name, anyway?"

"Bo Bo. Yours?"

"Htun Htun."

He wiped the table for the other guests, took their orders, and then passed them along to the woman at the wok. He got two beers out of an ice chest. All the while he kept looking back over to me and grinning.

I ate everything on my plate and waited for him to come back.

At some point there he was again. "My mother says that you can sleep with us if you want."

I shrugged, as if I didn't really care where I slept.

When all the guests had left, the woman and her husband started to clean and stack the tables and stools. The boy was also helping out, so I pitched in, too. Together we lugged several buckets of garbage two blocks away, where we dumped them into a trash heap that was teeming with rats.

The family spent the night under a tree on the edge of a park. The branches hung over the path like a roof. They had spread a tarp on the sidewalk and arranged some newspapers and burlap sacks on it. Three small children were already huddled asleep in the middle of it. There were people with big hearts and little ones, with sound hearts and damaged ones.

There were people on whom something had been *inflicted* and there were still others on whom *somewhat more* had been inflicted.

We lay down on two sacks beside Htun Htun's siblings. It was so warm that we did not need a blanket.

I was completely exhausted, but at the same time too wound up to fall asleep. On top of everything else, my cheek was hurting so badly that I could hardly stand it. I looked from side to side.

"What's troubling you?" whispered Htun Htun.

"What do you mean?"

"You can't even lie still."

"So?"

"Your parents are dead, aren't they?"

"No," I contradicted him.

"Sure they are. I have a friend whose parents are also dead and he can't sit still, either. Don't you have any uncles or aunts you can stay with?"

"My parents aren't dead."

"So why aren't you with them?"

"What's it to you, anyway?"

"Did you run away or something?"

"No." I thought for a minute. "They ran away."

Htun Htun turned to me and rested himself on one elbow. I could feel him staring at me in the dark. "Both of them?"

"Yes."

"Why?"

"How should I know?"

"Parents don't just disappear like that."

I turned away.

He tugged on my shoulder: "Should I ask if you can stay with us? It would be no problem. You could help out waiting tables and washing dishes."

"No. I want to see my mother. I haven't seen her in a very long time."

"Why not?"

I didn't want to lie. I wanted to tell him what had happened, but it was impossible.

The truth.

I could have told him in three sentences. In two. In one. But I couldn't get the words past my lips. The mere thought of it made me queasy. I didn't have any words for what had happened. And so I told him about a mother who was an actress, from America, where she had so much work that she had no time to see me. Even though she was always promising to visit me and my uncle in Kalaw, she always ended up having to go to Singapore, Los Angeles, or London in order to make movies. I told him that I hadn't seen her in seven years and was hoping now to surprise her on her birthday. And I told him there were people who would steal even from children, but I'm guessing he knew that already.

When I was done he said nothing for a while. I started to worry that he had already fallen asleep, but his breathing was too irregular for that.

"Is she famous?"

"Who?"

"Your mother, of course."

"Yes. In America."

"Very?"

"Yes," I reassured him.

"Your father, too?"

"Not so much, but he always travels with her."

"As her bodyguard?"

"Something like that."

"I get it." He thought for a while. "Listen," he finally whispered, "I have an uncle who drives a rickshaw. He knows every street in the city. Maybe he can help you find them. I'll take you to him first thing tomorrow."

Chapter 5

THE MAN IN QUESTION did not particularly appreciate being woken so early in the morning, and even less so once he learned what his nephew had in mind.

"Golden Valley is far," he grumbled. "Tell your friend he should take a bus or a taxi."

"He hasn't got any money."

His uncle cursed. Wearily he stepped off the rickshaw and retied his longyi. He put a hand on his nephew's shoulder and gave it a hard squeeze. "Then you tell your mother that she owes me a dinner, deal?"

Htun Htun briefly scrunched up his face, then smiled and winked at me.

His uncle turned to me. "What's the address?"

"Forty-two."

"Forty-two what?"

I shook my head.

"You don't know the street name?"

"Something with *I*," I said sheepishly.

"Inya Lake Road?"

"No."

"Golden Valley is a big place."

"There's a lake right nearby, and an embassy."

"Which one?"

"I . . . I don't remember exactly. It looked pretty big on the map."

He cursed again. "The American?"

"Hm, yeah, I think so."

"Do you at least know your parents' names?" he asked sarcastically.

I told him everything I knew about them and then some: their names and that my mother was American (and a famous actress) and that my father played guitar and was missing a finger on his left hand; that my mother was very tall and very beautiful and that she had a smile that would warm your heart.

He rolled his eyes, sighed deeply, and shook his head. "Hop on."

He turned to his rickshaw, took a few powerful strides, and jumped on. There weren't yet many cars on the streets, and soon enough he was pedaling hard to get over a bridge that passed over the train tracks. He had the most muscular calves I had ever seen, but still he was huffing and puffing.

We had been riding for about half an hour when we stopped at a food stand by the side of the road. He climbed off the bicycle and went over to a woman who was squatting at a table and chopping vegetables. He ordered a tea and the two of them chatted for a while without paying any attention to me.

In her display case there were several cans of My Boy condensed milk. I counted the letters, then the cans: "one ... twelve ... twenty-four."

Then I started all over again.

"She knows your father," he said when he finally came back. "He drinks a tea here now and then. He doesn't live far."

"How does she know he's my father?" I asked skeptically.

"Maybe because there aren't that many Burmese men in Golden Valley who are missing a finger but still play guitar and who are married to a foreigner, smarty-pants."

We turned onto a narrow street that led up a hill. He pedaled standing up and using all his strength. I offered to step out and walk along beside him, but he brushed it off. All the houses in the street stood behind high walls topped with barbed wire. Any time I caught a glimpse of a window, it had bars on it. Like in a prison.

At a kiosk he asked a second time. A man came out, gestured, pointed up the street and then to the right.

"Everyone knows your father, but no one knows your mother."

He ought not to have said that.

We went to the next intersection, and when I saw the street sign I remembered right away: Inya Maing Street. "This must be it," he said, pointing to a white two-story house surrounded by a wall and a garden full of shrubs and trees. We stopped in front of a green iron gate. Number forty-two. I climbed out and burned with shame that I couldn't pay him.

"Thank you," I said. "That was—"

"Next time you can pay double." He interrupted me and laughed. "Good luck!" Then he turned and rode off without ever looking back.

"Thank you," I repeated quietly.

Chapter 6

THE GATE WAS CLOSED but not locked, and I slipped through it into the yard.

In the shelter of the bushes I crept through the garden to the front door, where I hid behind a column. The door was open. In the kitchen I could see two women chatting and cooking. I was just thinking about calling to them when I heard a third voice from the second floor.

I recognized her immediately.

One of the women, pills in hand, hurried up the stairs. A short time later she came back down again and disappeared into the kitchen.

Without a sound I stepped inside and flitted across the entryway to the staircase.

My legs felt heavier with each step.

I wanted to turn back.

I wanted to hide.

I wanted to go back to U Ba.

From above I heard someone shuffling papers.

My heart was pounding as if I had just run up the 272 steps to the pagoda in Kalaw.

Or up some giant celestial stairway.

There were many rooms off the main hall. One of them was open.

I tiptoed to the door.

The room it opened on was big and long and full of books. They lay in piles on chairs and on the floor. Just like at home.

I stepped inside.

At the other end there was a couch along the wall and a desk in front of the window.

There was my mother, typing on a keyboard.

She sat with her back to me.

I stopped in my tracks.

"Mama?" I whispered.

She kept on typing.

"Mama?" I said, louder this time.

She froze. Perfectly still.

The chair turned in my direction.

Inch by inch.

"Mama?"

I took one step toward her.

Then another.

She stood up. Braced herself with one hand on the desk.

I stood still.

We were no more than a few yards apart. Four, maybe five.

And seven years.

And one scar.

At least.

I don't know how long we stood facing each other.

A telephone rang.

Someone called for her.

She didn't move.

Louder now.

Still she didn't move.

"Bo Bo."

I wanted to run to her, but I couldn't move. Not a single step.

Carefully she approached me, as if I were a shy animal.

Biding her time.

Deliberately.

As if she feared that I might flee at any moment.

She was at once so familiar and so strange to me.

My hands needed time. My nose. My eyes. My ears.

Every part of me needed time.

Almost every part.

Now we were inches apart, and I flung my arms around her.

I felt dizzy. Everything was spinning. The bookcases, the chair, my mother's face.

She caught me as I fell.

Chapter 7

WHEN I CAME BACK to my senses I was lying on the couch.

My father was sitting beside me.

"Where's Mama?"

"Resting."

"Is she feeling ill?"

"No, she was just tired."

Why was he not telling the truth? "Is it my fault?"

"Nothing is your fault."

"Everything is my fault—"

"Bo Bo, stop," he said, interrupting me. "Why do you say that?"

Because I thought it was true. I didn't have a better answer.

"Can I go to her?"

"I think she's asleep."

"Can we look in on her?"

He rose and took me by the hand. I was grateful for his help. We went to a door at the other end of the hall. My father opened it carefully. The windows were wide open. A gentle breeze moved the white curtains. My mother lay on a bed and was indeed asleep. Her skin was paler, her lips redder, her hair blacker than I had imagined. I thought she was even more beautiful than U Ba had said.

Then my father closed the door again and led me into a room across the hall. There was a wide bed, a dresser, a bookcase, and a desk. From the ceiling hung a wooden fan. There were colorful paintings on the wall, and the sun reflected off the highly polished wooden floor. The room had its own bathroom with a toilet, a shower, and a tub. I had never seen such a beautiful room.

"This is where you'll sleep," he said.

I flinched. "Here? Won't we all sleep in the same room?"

The question seemed to embarrass my father. "Hm, well, actually . . . it's a big house, you know, it is not like in Kalaw. We have plenty of room. Mama and I have our bedroom, and you have your own."

He didn't mean it to hurt. But at that word I found myself overcome with such a deep sadness that my eyes welled up again. I didn't want my *own* room. I had no desire to sleep alone.

He must have seen the disappointment in my face. "I mean . . . we will see later."

We stood looking at each other without a word. "Are you hungry?" he asked after a while.

"No . . . or maybe yes, after all."

We went down to the kitchen. The two women were there, chopping vegetables. They looked so much alike that I could not tell them apart. My father introduced us. They were sisters, and they lived together in a room off the kitchen. We stared at each other. As if they had never seen a twelve-year-old boy. As if I had never seen twins.

I had no idea what I wanted to eat. They suggested mango with sweet rice. I offered to help, but they didn't want me to. My father and I sat down at a long table in an adjacent room. A short time later one of the sisters brought me a fresh peeled and chopped mango and a bowl of delicious rice. U Ba and I had never prepared it so well.

My father watched me but didn't eat anything himself. "I waited for you at the train station yesterday afternoon."

"The train got stuck."

"So I heard."

"How did you know . . . ?"

"U Ba called when he found your letter."

I should have thought of that. "Is he angry with me?"

"He was worried." My father regarded me with his big, dark eyes. "We were, too."

"I'm sorry. Forgive me."

"You should probably give him a call later."

"Yes," I said while devouring my mango. I had barely finished it when the sisters offered me a second one, which I gladly accepted.

"What are those two doing here?" I whispered after they had disappeared back into the kitchen.

"They're from Hsipaw, and they need work. They help Mama and me around the house and in the garden."

"Is Moe Moe no longer with you?"

"No, unfortunately."

"Why not?"

"She got married last year and she lives with her husband's family in Bago."

"Do the sisters cook for you?"

"During the week. They have the weekend off. Then Mama cooks, or I do."

"Can Mama cook?"

"Of course. She's a very good cook."

"Me, too."

My father nodded. "I know."

"What does Mama do, actually? Does she work?"

"Yes. She's a lawyer and a consultant."

"What's that?"

"She gives advice to companies that want to invest in Burma, and also to the government before they pass new laws."

"And they listen to her?"

"Sometimes."

"And what do you do?"

"I help Mama."

"Giving advice?"

He paused a moment. "No, I wouldn't put it quite like that."

"How then?"

His only answer was an evasive smile.

"Don't you work?"

"Oh, I do. I teach English every afternoon at a monastery school."

When I had eaten everything down to the last grain of rice, I was overcome with a great weariness. From the kitchen I could hear the ticking of a clock.

"You must be exhausted from your long journey and your night on the street."

I nodded.

"Do you want to lie down?"

I nodded again.

He got one of his longyis and a clean shirt that was much too big for me, and he brought me to my room. Exhausted, I lay down on the bed.

"Are you okay resting here?" he asked with a gentle smile.

I nodded. "Yes. Can you stay a little while?"

"Of course."

He lay down right next to me; I felt his warm breath on my skin. He stared at the highly polished floor as if there were something interesting to see there. I followed his gaze, but I didn't notice anything remarkable.

"Are you still angry with me?"

"Why on earth would I be angry with you?"

"Because I didn't want the harmonica anymore."

"Oh, no, I'm not angry at all." He stroked my arm. "Don't you worry. I understood why you were so furious with me. I guess I would have felt the same way."

"Really?"

"Yes. I am sorry I did not explain to you why I had to leave. I thought it was still too early for you to know . . . It was . . . it was a mistake . . ." His voice trailed off; he paused for so long that I was starting to think he had forgotten what he wanted to say. "I'm very happy that you have come."

"Sure? I was afraid you would be angry, because I just—"

"No." He interrupted me and turned to face me. "Believe me, I am really glad you are here. But the next few days will not be easy. For any of us."

When he had gone I lay there in the middle of the bed. Even with my arms stretched out in both directions I could not feel the edge of the mattress. There was room enough for two U Bas beside me.

At least.

Nothing was easy.

For any of us.

It was too warm for a blanket, but without my uncle I felt as if I was missing something to hold on to. In the bathroom I found two big, thick towels. I rolled them up together and held them close. I fell asleep with the towels curled in my arms.

Chapter 8

MY PARENTS' HOUSE had a large rooftop terrace. There was a fountain with some water plants. There were two hammocks and several pots of red, white, and blue bougainvilleas and geraniums. There was a wildly over-grown arbor. Under it was a table, a bench, and two chairs.

That's where we ate dinner. Someone had set the table and lit a few lanterns. My father and I sat at the table in silence, waiting for my mother.

I was so excited that I couldn't sit still. I fidgeted in my chair, counting and re-counting the seventeen cashews in the small bowl in front of me. My father was restless, too. I could tell by the way he was bouncing his legs. I hadn't ever seen him do that.

We heard her coming slowly up the stairs. My father jumped up and went to meet her. He took her by the arm and led her to the table. He insisted that she sit to my right.

My mother was wearing a red and black longyi and a light blouse. She had a white frangipani blossom in her dark hair. Her movements were slow and deliberate, at this particular moment perhaps not quite as graceful as a dancer's, but still wonderful to watch.

I was struck by her long, thin fingers. They reminded me of my own. On her wrist was a bracelet like my father's, a red band with two small jade stones.

She took a cloth napkin and spread it on her lap.

"How are you doing?" She spoke slowly and softly, as if she were still half asleep. All the same it seemed to me that even our voices were similar.

I was afraid of saying the wrong thing, and I hesitated with my answer. "Good," I finally replied.

"I am happy to hear that."

Silence.

"And how is U Ba?"

"Also good."

"How lovely."

I thought that she could actually just have called and asked him herself, but that seemed unimportant at that moment. We could just as easily have been talking about the chickens, our pig, or the weather in Kalaw. I wanted to hear her voice.

"Is the house still there?"

"Of course."

A long silence.

"Thar Thar tells me that you're a good cook."

"It's true."

She fell silent again, and I wondered what I could ask her. It couldn't be anything stupid or inappropriate. Above all I didn't want to upset her with an awkward question. Why did you act as if you didn't know me that time on the phone? For example. That clearly would have been a bad question, even though it was the one I was dying to ask.

It took me a while to think of something else. "Do you play harmonica?"

My parents looked at each other. A smile flashed across my mother's face. "No. Why do you ask?"

"Well, I thought...maybe you and Papa play music together."

"That's not a bad idea," she replied a bit sluggishly. She sounded something like my uncle's wavering cassette player. "Unfortunately I'm not very musical."

"I'm not, either," I said.

"That's not true," my father contradicted. "You were making great progress in Kalaw."

My mother took a sip of water, and I had the sense that her hand was quivering. But I might just have imagined it.

The sisters set a steamed fish, vegetables, and a bowl of rice on the table. My father did the honors.

"Do you like fish?" my mother asked. She took her fork. She did not touch her knife.

"Very much," I replied.

"What's your favorite food?" she wanted to know.

I suppose there are other mothers who don't know their children's favorite dishes, but still the question made me sad. "I like fried rice. Fish curry. Thin pancakes with sweet milk sprinkled with grated coconut. But actually I like pretty much everything. I'm not so picky."

The fish was very tasty, but my mother hardly touched it.

I noticed now how thin she was. She probably never ate very much.

Now and then I would catch her stealing a glance at me, but I pretended not to notice.

My father was still bouncing his legs.

The sisters cleared the table and brought out a plate of watermelon. My mother took only one piece, and she left half of that uneaten.

"You'll have to excuse me. I'm not feeling very well," she said. She started to get up but sank back into her chair. My father came to her aid and then went with her downstairs. It was a long time before he came back up.

In the meantime I sat eating the melon and trying to spit the seeds into a bowl on the table. Most of them missed. I thought about U Ba. He knew what I liked to eat.

My father sat back down and tried to smile at me. He didn't quite manage it.

"I want to live, I want to give," I started to sing hesitantly, and saw how his expression relaxed.

"I've been a miner for a heart of gold," he joined in quietly, "... that keep me searching for a heart of gold ... And I'm getting old ..."

"I want to live, I want to give," I repeated while he drummed on the table with his fingers. We sang the whole song, and when it was over his fingers still kept moving.

"What's wrong with Mama?" I wanted to know.

He stopped drumming. "She has an upset stomach. It happens now and then. I'm sure she'll be feeling better tomorrow."

"Why does she speak so strangely? Does that have something to do with her stomach?"

"No." My father turned his head from one side to the other, as if looking for something. "It's . . . how can I explain it . . . she's having a difficult time. She had to take some pills before dinner. She was worked up after seeing you."

It took a while for that sentence to sink in, word by word, like water on the dry earth in our yard.

My mother was worked up after seeing me.

Until that moment I had not given a single thought to how our reunion might make her feel.

Not one.

Inflicted shot through my mind. My injury was to some extent her injury, too. If for me a knife was no longer just a knife, what must it be for her? When I felt sad and full of longing because I had seen a mother and child at the market, how must something like that make her feel?

"Maybe I can help her."

My father looked at me, surprised.

"How can you help her?"

I didn't have an answer for that. Or at least no answer I could put into words. Just because you can't see something doesn't mean it's not there, U Ba had told me. Just because I can't put what I know into words, I thought, doesn't mean that I don't know it.

The longer I thought about it, the more confident I felt that I really could help her.

Chapter 9

MY FATHER AND I were having breakfast alone on the terrace. My mother still was not feeling well, he said. She wanted to spend the day recovering in bed. It was not unusual for her and nothing I should worry about. There was fresh fruit on the table, yogurt, toast, various jams, and a bowl of mohinga. I took some of the fish soup. My father ate only some mango and papaya with yogurt.

"Is your scar hurting?" he suddenly inquired.

I choked on my soup. My father had never spoken to me about my injury.

Seeing how it confused me, he added: "U Ba mentioned that it had been hurting a lot lately."

"That's true. Sometimes it even wakes me up at night."

"Last night, too?"

"No. It's gotten better."

"Starting when?"

"On the journey here it was still pretty bad." I thought about it. "The night before last, too. Yesterday it was bearable."

"And now?"

"Nothing I can't manage."

"Do you mind if I have a look?"

I turned my head and showed him my left cheek. He leaned over and examined it closely. I could not remember him ever looking at it before then. "Did you see a doctor about it in Kalaw?"

"Yes. I even went to a hospital, but nobody there was able to help."

"Mama regularly sees a dermatologist who also does plastic surgery here in the city. He's helped her several times with her irritated skin. Maybe we could ask him for an opinion."

I doubted he could help me, but I nodded anyway.

After breakfast my father wanted to take me to the Shwedagon Pagoda, but he had to make a call first. When I could hear that he was talking, I went to my parents' room and opened the door.

Sunbeams fell in through two windows. A fan turned on the ceiling. My mother was sitting upright in bed. She wore white pajamas. In front of her was a tray with a teacup and some fruit. She had black circles under her eyes.

"Good morning," I said.

She smiled when she saw me. "Good morning, sweetheart. Come in."

I stepped in and closed the door behind me. "How are you feeling?"

"Good." She was a bad liar. Like her brother. Like me. "But I didn't get enough sleep."

"Why not?"

She shrugged. "It took me forever to fall asleep, and then I kept waking up. At night ants turn into elephants, if you know what I mean."

"Yeah, I know," I said and took a couple of steps toward her.

"Sit down."

I sat on the edge of the bed. There was a pile of books on her nightstand and several packets of pills on top of that.

"What about you? Did you sleep well?"

"Yes."

All at once she reached out her hand to stroke my head. I flinched involuntarily and pulled my head back a little.

Some things cannot be hurried.

She wiped the sleeve of her pajamas across her face. That's the same thing I always did when I felt tears coming on.

"I'm sorry," she whispered.

"Bo Bo." It was my father calling. "Where are you?"

My mother and I looked at each other. Her eyes were slightly clouded, as if concealed by a thin veil. Even so I could read them as clearly as my uncle's.

On any other day I would have been very impressed by the Shwedagon Pagoda. Its golden stupa, three hundred feet tall; the countless temples and altars with their tiny bells and flags; the small and large Buddhas; the crowds of people crouching everywhere, praying or meditating; the families who had come to picnic. My father led me to the spot dedicated to people born on a Wednesday. He told me that both my mother and I had come into the world on a

Wednesday. We scooped water out of a fountain and poured it over the Buddha who watched over the fates of anyone born in the middle of the week. All the water had worn his features down. He looked as smooth as a river stone. My father closed his eyes while he poured. I, too, wanted to make a wish, but I couldn't think of anything. My mind was elsewhere.

My mother's eyes. They weren't shining.

They had revealed to me how full of fear she was. And longing.

They had revealed to me how sad she was. And how happy.

How uncertain she was, and how distant. And how close.

There was so much my uncle had not told me about her, I thought.

When we got home late that afternoon my mother was sleeping again. My father disappeared for a while into their bedroom. When he emerged he reported that we would be dining alone that evening.

He led me into his office. It was next to my room and much smaller than my mother's office.

There was a guitar leaning against the wall opposite the door. Above it hung a little altar. In the middle sat a Buddha flanked by red and white flowers. I suspected that my father used this room for meditation, too. On the shelves were books and two framed photos. In one of them you could see an old monastery. In front of it stood a group of young people with serious faces. Beside them my mother and father with me in his arms.

The other photo showed my mother looking just as U Ba had described her. Her eyes radiated strength, and her smile could have warmed your heart...I barely recognized her.

Behind the picture frames I noticed a harmonica.

"Is that mine?"

"Yeah."

"May I?"

He nodded.

I took it, dusted it off, and blew into it. It sounded just as tinny and unmelodic as the first time around, but that no longer bothered me. I knew I just needed to practice. Then my father and I would be able to play together again.

He sat down on the floor, and I joined him.

"Why did you name me Bo Bo?"

"Don't you like your name?"

"Oh, I do, but I wondered if it was true that I was named after the cartoon character Bo Bo."

"Who said that?"

"Everyone at school."

"No. It was my best friend's name. He was extremely brave and courageous. And he had a big heart. Like you."

I looked again at the picture of my mother. "Mama used to look different." It just slipped out.

His face twisted into a forced smile. "You, too, no? What kind of life would it be that left no trace on us?"

He folded his legs and straightened his back, as if he would start meditating at any moment. Instead he fixed his eyes on me. "Did U Ba tell you that Mama and I were in Kalaw?"

"No," I answered, surprised. "When?"

"Last year. Just before your birthday."

"You were in Kalaw?" I repeated, incredulous. "And you didn't come to see me?" I felt a mixture of anger and disappointment, and I didn't know which emotion had the upper hand. "Why not?"

"We couldn't manage it."

"What couldn't you manage?" The anger was increasing faster than the disappointment. I could have cried with rage.

"Visiting you. Mama stood on the street in front of the school and watched you in the schoolyard during recess. We were planning to meet you at the gate. But then we had to turn back, and we flew home the same day."

The thought of me playing in the schoolyard while my mother stood fifty yards away was so painful that I did not know what to say.

"Two times before that we made it as far as the airport in Yangon. We made it to the gate, boarding passes in hand. But we couldn't manage it. At the last minute she lost heart."

"But why? I...I would have been...so happy. I...I would have..." All at once I began to stutter.

"I know. She was afraid to meet you face-to-face. Don't you understand that?"

"No!"

"A mother who slices open her five-year-old son's cheek. She completely lost control, and to this day she can't explain why."

I didn't want to be angry with my mother. I was so delighted finally to see her again, to be with her. At the same time I felt something taking shape inside me. Something dark that I could not describe. Sorrowful anger. Angry sorrow.

Seven years.

More than half my life.

"What part of that is difficult to understand?"

"You were across the street from the school?" Why hadn't I seen them? Why hadn't I sensed that they were in my vicinity?

My father said nothing.

"Why didn't *you* call out to me?"

"That would not have done anyone any good."

"It would have done me some good," I answered defiantly.

"No," he countered, trying to sound calm even while his voice was quivering. "It would not have done you any good, either." The only other time I had heard him this upset was at the end of his last visit to Kalaw. "Trust me."

"What makes you think you know better?" I shouted angrily.

"Because I know better."

That's no answer, I wanted to object. No answer at all. But I did not dare to contradict him again.

We both stared mutely at the floor.

"Your mother is not well."

"So then she is sick after all?"

"To a certain extent, yes."

"Has she been to a doctor?"

"Of course. Often. Several."

"There's nothing they can do for her?"

"She's taking medicine. Otherwise it would be worse. But there are ailments that neither doctors nor pills can cure. At best they can ease the suffering."

"Is she going to die soon?" I asked, horrified.

"No. Her body is healthy. It's her soul that suffers."

"What does she do about it?"

"Not much. She lies in bed. Sorrow can be like a puddle or like a cloudburst. But it can also be as endless as the sea in which a person eventually drowns."

I swallowed.

"Her greatest fear," my father continued, "is that something similar will happen again."

"But I would never make her so angry again."

"That's not the issue." He sounded calm again, but no less serious.

"Has she ever attacked you?"

"No, why?"

"Because you said she was afraid it might happen again."

"I am certain that nothing of the kind will happen again. But neither you nor I can understand this fear, no matter how hard we try. When a person has been certain that she would never, ever do a certain thing in all her life, and then she does it, she loses a fundamental confidence in herself. What happens once can happen twice, don't you see? Maybe not everyone would feel that way about it, but your mother does."

"Is that why you visited me only once a year?"

"Yes. I was afraid to leave her alone. Her mood can shift very suddenly."

"You're with her all the time?" I asked, doubtful.

"Whenever she needs me," he answered. "And because I never know exactly when that will be, I prefer to be close by."

"That's very kind of you."

"That's how it is when you love someone above all else."

Chapter 10

THE CROWS WOKE ME around dawn. I got out of bed and looked out the window. Monks marched in long lines through the city, asking for alms at each door or gate. The two sisters stood at our entrance, ladling a scoop of rice into each monk's *thabeik*. The line went on forever, as if the monks were all circling back for seconds.

Unsure what I should do so early in the day, I was thinking I would have a look in my mother's office to see if I could find anything to read, when I noticed a wooden chest beside my bed. In it I found slender, leather-bound volumes without labels. Someone must have brought them into the room during the night. Curious, I picked out a couple and started leafing through them.

Yangon, March 8, 2015

Dear Bo Bo,

I wish I knew how you were doing!

Yesterday our new neighbors invited us to dinner. The man is from New York, and he's working at the American Embassy. His wife is from the Philippines. They have two children, a boy and a girl. The boy is your age.

He reminds me a little of Bo Bo, your father whispered to me during the meal.

I have no idea what he was thinking. I'm sure he meant no harm. Quite sure. A careless remark. From him of all people.

I couldn't stand to stay at the table after that. I made some excuses and apologies and then left. It was rude of me, but there was nothing else I could do. It was not the first time that I had stood up and left in the middle of a meal. I suppose it makes some people think that I'm moody. They are mistaken.

When I do something like that, it's not just because I feel like it; I am driven by dire necessity.

One time I experienced something that my doctor later called a flashback. To this day, a year later, I find it difficult to write about.

It was triggered by a small boy who was crying in pain and who could not stop. I was sitting on the street at a teahouse. He was playing in the cooking area just a few yards away. His father accidentally tipped over a kettle of boiling water and some of it landed on his bare feet. It must have been extremely painful.

His wailing brought me right back to Kalaw. All at once I was sitting in my brother's house with you and Moe Moe; for all I could tell at that moment, I was actually there! The table where we were chopping vegetables. My tottering stool. The sooty kitchen ceiling. I could hear your voices as if we were in the same room. I smelled the freshly chopped garlic. I could see you playing with the knife. I heard myself shouting at you. I felt myself leaning over the table and...

Moe Moe's horrified screams, your crying, the blood on the table, on my hands, on your face. There it was all over again.

My heart began to race. I felt dizzy and very hot. I gasped for breath and even lost consciousness for a few seconds.

For the next few days your father was the only one who could calm me down. His quiet nature and his love for me, his patience and the way he cared for me.

I am a prisoner even if I don't live behind bars. I can go wherever I want and say whatever I want. Still, I am not free. I feel so fragile. My mood swings are unbearable.

I am my own prison—and there is no way out.

I make things hard for everyone.

I tried to ask your father how he manages to put up with me. He didn't understand the question.

Not even after I asked a second time and provided a fuller explanation.

As if not putting up with me was inconceivable to him.

He says that he already left me alone once in New York because he thought his country needed him.

He regrets it to this day.

I don't know what I would do without him. He is my anchor.

I have long thought that love is something like a plant. You have to tend it and protect it, especially when it is young, when its roots are still shallow. Otherwise it dries out and shrivels up. You have to give it what it needs in order to thrive. But sometimes it manages to fend for itself, and then it can grow in the least hospitable places and against the longest odds.

Now I need to go to bed, my brave little Bo Bo.

Love,

Mama

Yangon, March 9, 2015

My dear little Bo Bo,

Can you sit still for ten minutes?

I cannot. Your father meditates for a whole hour every morning and evening, but I can't manage even ten minutes. Sitting quietly, doing nothing, thinking of nothing; it's not one of my strong points. Instead of relaxing me, it just makes me more nervous. It amplifies my fears, not my courage. It leaves me feeling lonelier.

All the same, your father thinks that meditation can heal my heart. I think he's being overly optimistic. I doubt there's anything that can heal me.

I used to be such a strong person, or at least I thought I was, and in many cases, the thought alone is sufficient.

Now I often feel extremely weak. One day I'll be fine, I can work and be very productive, and the next day I'll have trouble getting out of bed. I'll feel so ashamed that I can't imagine leaving the house. My mood can change overnight, or even from one moment to the next. Little things can trigger the swing: the sight of a knife, a scar on a taxi driver's hand, or even just a child in his mother's arms.

I am my own greatest puzzle.

There's no one I mistrust more than myself.

I have not forgotten how fragile a thing trust is, even trust in ourselves. How precious. How much light it needs. How much dedication. How dark it becomes when Falsehood spreads her wings.

My friend Amy says that every person is her own mystery. It is our lifelong responsibility to come as close as we can to solving the riddle of ourselves. A definitive solution is out of our reach.

I used to contradict her. I was convinced that I knew myself.

I think often of my mother, your grandmother, whom you have never met. Her temperament, too, was very volatile. As a child I could never understand why. She spent a lot of her time in a darkened bedroom. Eventually I came to think of it as the room where Pain dwelt.

How awful it would be if we were doomed to repeat not only our own mistakes, but also those of our parents.

If only I could be with you!

A thousand kisses!

Mama

Yangon, October 10, 2015

Dear Bo Bo,

U Ba arrived from Kalaw yesterday. He tells me that you've learned to ride a bike. And to swim. I'm so grateful to him for everything he's teaching you.

Will I ever be able to explain to you why your mother and father haven't been there for you?

In my thoughts I am with you every hour of every day, but what good does that do you?

I can see time leaving its marks on U Ba. He is hard of hearing now. And his eyesight is failing. Sometimes I wonder how much longer he'll be up to the task.

The dream is always the same: We, you and U Ba, your father and I, and several children from the monastery, are all together on some kind of wooden fishing boat. I'm cooking in the galley, and I'm careless with the fire. All at once the boat catches fire. Pretty soon the

*whole thing is in flames. We all jump overboard, but I
don't know where you are, where your father is, or my
brother. Fiery timbers collapse into the water, where they
continue to burn. I dive deeper and deeper. It gets darker
and darker, and I've lost you all forever. It's all my fault.
And that's when I wake up.*

*The dream will haunt me all day long. There is no
torture more cruel than knowing that you have caused
a calamity and that there is nothing you can do to set it
right.*

*We gather so many things in our lives. Not
just furniture, books, or clothes. Also offenses.
Disappointments. Unfulfilled wishes. Unrealized dreams.
Unrequited love. Guilt.*

Where can we put it all?

*Reading these lines, I notice that I have only questions,
no answers. I'm sorry. I wish it were the other way
around.*

*I hug you and squeeze you and wish never to let
you go,*

Mama

Yangon, December 21, 2017

My dear, sweet Bo Bo!

*The past few weeks have been hard on me. Just like
every year around your birthday.*

Not a day goes by on which I don't ask myself how I could have done that to you. Who did that to you.

It was me—and it wasn't.

Just like I'm an American—and I'm not.

Just like I'm Burmese—and I'm not.

It was me. Period.

It's just that I don't know what part of me it was.

Where did that come from? Where has it been hiding since then? Will it ever reemerge?

It feels so foreign to me, and so repulsive.

But it's there. Was there. Will maybe be there forever.

If you only knew how it shames me. How I feel as if I'll never be able to make it up to you.

There are many days when shame keeps me in bed.

There are days when I can't look into a mirror, because I can't stand the sight of myself.

Without your father I would not be able to bear it.

Without him I would no longer be here.

He says that we are not condemned to remain who we are.

We may not, like a snake, be able to shed our old skins, but still we change from day to day.

How can I expect you to understand me when I can't even understand myself?

All I can do is ask that one day you will forgive me.

All I can do is

And that's where the letter breaks off. Those were the last lines on the last page of that volume.

I leafed through several other notebooks. There was an entry for every day. Sometimes it was only a line or two: *Please forgive me . . . How can I ever make it up to you? . . . What I wouldn't give if only . . .* Sometimes they were several pages long.

Apparently my mother had written a letter to me every day. I did some quick math: over seven years that added up to two thousand five hundred fifty-five letters.

Occasionally she would add a small drawing. A birthday cake with candles. A Christmas tree. Three birds on a branch. A table set for three. Everything in red.

I lay down on the bed. She was her own greatest riddle, she had written. I was not a riddle to myself, but maybe I just hadn't thought enough about myself yet.

For a while I felt empty and numb. I just lay there staring at the fan that hung from the ceiling. At some point I got up and went into the bathroom.

There was a big mirror over the sink, and I stood there looking at myself for a long time.

Dark red. A long, deep cut: as wide as a matchstick. Stretching from the corner of my mouth almost to my ear. And just like me, it got bigger from one year to the next. My scar grew with me. Just like my ears, my nose, my arms and legs.

If I turned my head to the left, I couldn't see it. If I turned to the right, then it drew my eye the way a misshapen nose would, or a cleft lip. As if that flaw were my face's only feature. I leaned toward the mirror and looked closely at myself. A long nose. Dark eyes. Full lips. A scar.

A very long, ugly scar. I got the feeling that the longer I looked at it, the smaller it got, though of course that was only my imagination. I could stare at it for the rest of my life, and it would never disappear.

There was no Bo Bo without a scar. There never would be. It was mine—but it was not me. It was just one part of me.

I thought about my mother's two thousand five hundred and fifty-five letters.

I thought about the hours, days, and weeks that she spent in bed.

One cut, many scars.

Mine was visible; hers were not.

I undressed and turned on the water. I had rarely washed myself under a shower before then, and never under a hot shower, at least not that I could recall.

The water trickled over my body. I set it hotter and hotter until it burned on my shoulders.

The mirror started to fog up, and I gradually disappeared behind a milky white curtain until there was nothing more to be seen of me.

Chapter 11

AFTER SHOWERING I lay down on the bed again and fell asleep. When I woke it was already late morning, but I felt in no way refreshed. There was a throbbing in my head. The bright sunlight falling through the windows hurt my eyes.

My parents were not in their rooms. I searched all over the house for them until I found them on the terrace. They were standing at the railing with their backs to me. My father had his arm around my mother, and she was resting her head on his shoulder. Their outlines merged into one. My mother looked even smaller and thinner standing next to him.

I was happy this was not one of the days when she would lie in bed for shame, and I hoped that today she could bear to look at her own reflection in the mirror and that she saw how beautiful she was.

Neither of them noticed me right away. I walked lightly to the table and sat down under the arbor. Leftovers from breakfast were still on the table.

For a moment I considered whether it might be better for all of us if I went back to Kalaw, but that was a bad idea. At that moment there was no place I wanted to be more than in that house, even if it wasn't easy.

And my mother needed me.

My parents turned around and started when they saw me.

"Where did you come from?" my mother asked. She looked better rested and more alert than she had on the other days.

"I hope you slept well," my father added.

He eyed me with a look of interest, and I felt certain that he had put the letters in my room.

"Yes," I said. "I always sleep well."

All at once he was in a hurry, saying he had to take care of some things in the city, that he would be back late in the afternoon. He wished us both a pleasant day, and before I had a chance to respond or to ask any questions he walked quickly down the stairs.

My mother and I were alone on the terrace.

I was so excited that I didn't dare say anything or even look at her directly. I watched her movements out of the corner of my eye. She turned to the railing and waved to my father in the courtyard.

Was she feeling like a prisoner right now?

Would she stay with me or excuse herself and retreat again to her office or bedroom?

"Do you have to work today?" I asked cautiously.

She took her time with the reply. "No," she said at last, coming over to the table. "May I join you?"

I slid over on the bench and tried as nonchalantly as possible to turn to the side so that she would not see the injured half of my face.

She sat down on one of the stools.

There was so much I wanted to ask. There was so much I wanted to say.

Though it crossed my mind that I might be fooling myself. Perhaps we already knew everything that really mattered.

She brushed a strand of hair out of her face and smiled uncertainly. "What shall we do? Is there anything in particular you would enjoy?"

U Ba had never asked me a question like that. I shrugged my shoulders without a clue.

"You don't know what you'd like to do?"

I shook my head.

"Okay, forgive me. That might have been a silly question."

For a while we sat by each other in silence. I was accustomed to that from U Ba and my father, but my mother's silence sounded different from theirs.

"Do you have a favorite subject in school?"

What gave her that idea? There was nothing I had less desire to talk about just then than school. "No."

"Not one?"

"No!" I had not meant for it to sound unfriendly.

"I didn't like to go to school, either."

When I did not reply she asked whether I was hungry.

"No."

"Do you always say no?"

"No."

We both laughed, she more than I. "That would of course be too bad. What questions would you answer with a yes just now?"

The question of whether I was afraid that she would stand right up and walk away. Her mood could change from one moment to the next, she had written. And anything could trigger the swing. I was afraid that even one false step from me would be enough.

Or one unfortunate memory.

The sight of the knife and the breakfast table before us.

But of course I didn't say anything like that. "You could ask me whether I'm doing well," I said instead. It wasn't the whole truth, but part of it.

"How nice. I'm pleased to hear it."

"And you?"

She furrowed her brow and tipped her head thought-fully from one side to the other. "Can I answer the same as you, or would that not count?"

"Only if it's true." It just slipped out before I had time to think about it.

The smile disappeared from her face.

I felt as if we were walking along a narrow, rotting board, like the one that led across a river near Kalaw. I was always afraid to cross it because I could not tell whether it would bear my weight and whether I would be able to keep my balance.

"Why should it not be true?" She didn't sound angry or irritated, more just surprised and maybe a little disappointed.

"Because...because..." I started to stutter again. I could think of reasons, but none that I cared to mention.

My mother stood up.

"Where are you going?" I asked, terrified.

"Just to the bathroom, sweetheart. I'll be right back," she replied, walking to the stairs.

I wanted to follow her. I stood up but thought better of it at the last moment. A twelve-year-old following his mother to the bathroom. As if I were a toddler. I waited impatiently for her return.

When she came back she set a few pictures on the table. The first one showed a young boy on a moped wedged in between my parents. He was holding tightly to my father with both hands while my mother had her arms wrapped lovingly around him.

"Is that me?"

She nodded.

My mother and I were in all of the pictures. Sometimes my father was there, too. In one of them I was sitting with her on a staircase, with my head resting on her lap. She was stroking my hair and looking very happy.

In the next one we were playing soccer in front of the monastery. Then we were walking hand in hand through a market. She was carrying me somehow on her shoulders. The mother and son in these pictures were very much at ease with each other.

I noticed that my mother was happier and happier with each picture we looked at.

"Do you remember any of that?" she asked hopefully.

I didn't want to disappoint her. "Yeah," I lied. "Lots."

"How I always used to spin you around?"

"Yes."

"The songs we used to sing together?"

"Of course."

"Our outings to the waterfall?"

"Absolutely."

"What else?" my mother looked at me expectantly.

Nothing. I remembered nothing. "How we played with Moe Moe," I answered, taking a stab in the dark.

"Oh yes, we had a lot of fun with her," she said, sighing with relief. "I'm delighted you still have so many happy memories."

She sat down next to me on the bench, took a piece of bread from a basket, and dipped it in her coffee cup. Like her brother.

"You need to eat something." My mother took a knife and a second slice of bread, on which she spread a dark brown cream. She handed it to me.

For her sake I took a bite. It was some kind of viscous chocolate. It did not look at all appetizing, but it tasted okay. "Thanks."

She poured me a fresh orange juice, spread more chocolate cream on yet another slice, and then covered it with thin banana slices.

"We could play something," I suggested.

"Oh, God, it's been ages since I've played anything. What do you and your friends like to play?"

Should I tell her that I don't have any friends at all to play with in the afternoon? Most of the boys in my grade spent all their free time on video games, and they rarely invited me to join in. "Mobile Legends," I answered.

"What's that?"

"A game you can get on your cell phone."

"I don't know it. Don't you play soccer?" she wondered.

"Oh, sure. Sometimes at recess."

"What do you play with U Ba?"

"Chess."

"Unfortunately I don't know how to play. Do you ever play cards?"

"No, actually . . . How about hide and seek? The sisters could try to find us."

That sounded good to her, so we went downstairs. The two of them knew the game, of course, and we agreed that we would hide only in the house and not in the garden. The two women disappeared, somewhat baffled, into the kitchen, and we heard them counting loudly.

My mother and I looked at each other a bit helplessly. Under the table wasn't much of a hiding place. Behind the door wasn't good, either. We wrapped ourselves in the curtains in the living room, but it didn't take long for the sisters to find us. The curtains weren't long enough. Our feet gave us away. They started counting again, and I thought of the big closet in the hallway on the second floor. I signaled to my mother to follow me up the stairs. Quietly we opened the closet doors. We crept inside, hid behind blankets, rain-coats, and jackets, then pulled the door closed behind us.

It was hot and cramped and pitch dark. She was lying half in my lap, but I couldn't even make out her silhouette.

Her warm breath on my skin. Hers was not the only racing heart.

We huddled closer together so that no one could see us even if the door was opened.

The sisters came upstairs. We could hear them search-ing through all the rooms. We kept still as mice. They went onto the terrace, but they soon came back inside and went downstairs to search the first floor again.

I called out loudly: "Peep." They came right back up-stairs. One of them opened the door, but she didn't notice us behind all the things, and she closed the door again. All the while I clung tightly to my mother. My left leg had fallen asleep, but still I didn't move.

If she was feeling like a prisoner now, I thought, then at least she was not alone.

The sisters called our names, but we didn't answer, and they went back downstairs.

My mother gave me a squeeze. "I would give my life if I could undo it," she said suddenly into the darkness.

"I know, Mama."

"But I can't."

"I know," I whispered, feeling around for her hand.

At that moment the two women came back upstairs and stood right in front of the closet, whispering about us. What was my mother up to now? They had seen a lot of strange things in this house, but this beat all. This high-spirited behavior was quite unlike her. It must have something to do with the boy. Hopefully Thar Thar would return soon, or who knew what kind of monkey business they would cook up next?

I held my hand over my mother's mouth so that her laughter would not give us away. At some point it was too much, and her chuckling was quite audible.

We tumbled out of the closet at the feet of the sisters. It was some time before they got over the shock of it.

They had no desire to play another round.

"We could go to the city together," I suggested.

My mother was not excited by that idea. "It's so crowded and loud. Why would you want to go there?"

"I have a debt to repay," I said, and explained how I had spent my first night in Yangon and how I had gotten to their house.

The taxi dropped us off in front of a hotel called the Strand. My mother suggested we get something to drink there. A man with a black jacket and an elegant longyi held the door for us. Standing in the reception area were several men who greeted us with a bow. Someone had set the air-conditioning too high, and I got goose bumps from the chill. On one wall there was a huge mirror. We paused and gazed solemnly at ourselves, as if at two strangers. I came up to her shoulder. I looked at her eyes. Her mouth. I thought we resembled each other as much as I had always imagined we would. My mother's face was expressionless, like a mask. I turned my head to the side. There was no mistaking my scar at this distance. I had never known that I could look so stern, and I started to smirk and to make faces. My silliness broke her trance, and we both started giggling, at first softly, then louder and louder.

There was no prison that could hold her forever, I wanted to tell her.

There was no more reason to be afraid.

Not of me.

Not of herself.

She should never again dislike herself.

No one ever should.

I did not want to sit with her in a freezing hotel. I wanted to walk through the streets with her the way other children did with their parents.

We went out again and walked down a side street where two boys my age were playing soccer. The ball landed right at our feet. She trapped it neatly, took two or three quick steps, then passed it to me. I was too surprised to react, and it rolled past my feet into the open sewer.

That was embarrassing. I fished the stinking ball out of the ditch and gave it back to the boys.

"I'm much better than that on the playground at school," I assured her.

She looked at me askance, the way I imagined parents looked at their children when they weren't sure they were telling the truth.

I took my mother by the hand, and on we went. At an intersection we turned onto Maha Bandula Road. It was packed with people. Teahouses and little restaurants had set up stools and tables along the sidewalk. There were merchants on every corner hawking newspapers, mangoes, pineapples, or even screwdrivers and padlocks. I liked the crowd. It reminded me of market day in Kalaw.

It was too much for my mother. At the next intersection she led me into a bakery, where things were a little quieter. We ordered a scoop of vanilla ice cream for each of us and an espresso for her, then we went and sat down.

She took a paper napkin, rolled it into a ball, and tossed it expertly into a trash bin at least ten feet away.

"That was luck," I said.

"As if! I used to be a good basketball player, you know." She rolled another ball and sank that one, too.

I gave up after three tries.

She laughed and wanted to know just what we had been doing during all our gym classes.

"Well, we weren't tossing balls of paper into trash cans, at any rate," I answered.

We enjoyed our ice cream. I tipped the cup and waited for the last bit to drip into my spoon.

"Do you want another scoop?"

"No, thanks."

My mother ordered another espresso. "What do you wish for?" she asked suddenly.

"What kind of wish?" I replied, surprised.

"Any kind."

I could not understand her question.

"I've never given you anything for your birthday. I'd like to make that up to you."

The offer was kindly meant, but still it confused me. For which birthday? I wondered. My twelfth? Or my eleventh? My tenth? What about my ninth, eighth, seventh, and sixth? I would gladly have celebrated all of them with her. I would have loved to open a present from my mother every year. There never had been one.

Make it up to me? Where should we begin? With the mornings I went alone to school while the other children were accompanied by their parents? With the afternoons a few years ago when I was the only one with no one to pick me up? As if there were any way to make up for things like that.

"No, thanks," I said. "I've got everything I need."

"There's nothing you're wishing for?" she asked skeptically.

"No." At least nothing any present could satisfy.

She smiled. "You're like your father."

The way she said it, I wasn't sure whether it was meant to be a good thing or a bad.

My mother wondered how I was intending to find the rickshaw driver I owed money to. Did I have any idea how many such drivers there were in the city? Of course I didn't. But I had a very clear memory of the restaurant I had eaten at and where I had slept. It was next to a little park right around the corner from a pagoda that I had caught sight of from Maha Bandula Road.

We set off. It didn't take long for me to find the place. Htun Htun was already working. His face lit up when he saw me. We sat down at one of the free tables.

"I could use something to drink," I said.

"Me, too," she replied.

In a moment there he was in front of us.

"Is that her?" he whispered into my ear.

"Yes."

"Wow, she really does look like a famous actress. Was she happy to see you?"

"Oh, definitely!"

My mother thanked him for taking such good care of me when I was in a tight spot, and we ordered tea and soda. He kept his eyes on her the whole time. His parents, too, were staring at us unabashedly. When he brought the drinks he leaned over to me and said: "I'm sure I've seen her on an old poster at some point. My mother, too."

"Entirely possible," I whispered back. "Maybe the one with Leonardo DiCaprio."

"I think so."

Lies arise out of hardship; stories, out of imagination.

"What kind of secrets are you two keeping?" my mother asked.

"None. None at all." Htun Htun and I couldn't help but laugh.

"That's not how it looks."

"Really, we're not," I protested, and we giggled some more.

"The tea is delicious."

"Would you like another?" asked Htun Htun.

"No, thank you."

"Something to eat?"

My mother shook her head, but I was not ready to leave, so I claimed to be very hungry.

My friend brought us a menu. I did not care at all what I ate, and I ordered a fried rice. It tasted even better than I remembered.

"Would you like a bite?"

"Sure." Rather than picking up her silverware, my mother waited for me to feed her.

I pushed some rice onto a spoon and made sure to get some vegetables and egg with it, then put it in her mouth.

"Yum. Very tasty."

Htun Htun was delighted. He disappeared for a moment, then came back with his parents. They had their cell phone with them, but they didn't dare to say anything.

"Can we take your picture?" he asked.

My mother looked at me, surprised, questioningly.

"Of course, why not," I said, pretending that I, too, was surprised by their interest.

Htun Htun posed with us. First his mother and then his father also wanted to get into the picture. Finally they asked me to take a picture of all of them with her. They posted it immediately on Facebook and proudly showed us their post.

We gave Htun Htun ten thousand kyat for his uncle. He thought that was too much and gave us five thousand back. He would not accept my mother's money for the drinks and the food. It was a birthday present, he explained.

"What kind of birthday?" she wondered.

"Don't say anything to her about birthdays," I whispered to him, rising quickly before anyone else started asking questions. "She doesn't like to be getting older."

Chapter 12

I COULD HEAR my father's voice, even on the second floor. He was still on the phone when I came into the dining room. "We have an appointment with the dermatologist at four," he said when he hung up. "I'm sure he'll be able to help you. We need to leave in half an hour."

Suddenly my mother stood in the doorway. "I'll take him."

My father turned to her, surprised. "You?"

"Yes."

"To the dermatologist?"

"I know."

He fumbled for words. "Sweetheart ... are you sure?"

"Yes."

"Should I come, too?"

"No."

He looked first at her, then at me. As if it were up to me.

"Have you thought carefully about this?" With each question his voice got lower, more doubtful. With each answer, my mother's voice was more determined.

"Yes."

"We could go all three of us, and I could wait outside."

"No. Bo Bo and I can handle this ourselves," she declared confidently. Then she turned and left the room.

My father stood in the middle of the room. His worried expression alarmed me. He was working on a reply and realized only now that it was too late. He paced back and forth awhile. Restless.

My mother and I took a taxi. She wore huge black sunglasses with reflective lenses. I could see myself in them, and they covered half her face. It made her look a little like a prisoner after all.

I wanted no part of any of this. I did not want to go to a doctor. Neither with her, nor with my father. A scar was a scar. What was a doctor going to do about it? So what if it sometimes hurt pretty badly. I had to learn to cope with it. No doctor could help with that.

"Mama?"

"Yes."

"Can't we just go back?"

"No."

"I could go by myself. I'm not a baby."

She shook her head.

"Really. Besides, it doesn't hurt at all anymore."

She shook her head again.

I would have liked to say more, but she gave me the distinct impression that she was done talking about it. We said nothing else for the remainder of the ride.

Dr. U Thant Htein's office was tucked behind a dingy entryway on a side street not far from the Sule Pagoda. There was a handwritten sign next to the entrance: "Dermatologist/plastic surgeon." I didn't even know what that was.

We waited in a narrow, windowless room. Even so, my mother kept her sunglasses on.

The room was full of patients. The face of the man squatting next to me was deep red and completely dry. His skin was flaking off like the bark of a eucalyptus. A girl about my age was sitting across from us. The skin on her right hand was burned. Her fingers looked like little twigs.

I would have liked just to stand up and get out of there.

We didn't have to wait long. The doctor greeted my mother amiably and inquired about her health. He asked me to take a seat on a chair opposite him. My mother sat behind me. He took my chin in his hand, turned my face from side to side, and examined it thoroughly. His breath stank of stale smoke. With each passing second the whole situation became increasingly unpleasant. "It doesn't look good," he said, shaking his head.

He dug a flashlight out of a drawer and pointed it at my face. He had me open wide so that he could shine it into my mouth while he pressed down my tongue with a piece of wood. "How on earth did you ever come by this?" he wondered out loud.

My breath faltered. The question caught me off guard. "I...I...well...I..."

"That was me," said my mother before I had a chance to say anything else.

"An accident?" he asked, almost casually, while still examining my scar.

A shiver ran through my body, and I turned toward her.

With both hands she slowly removed her sunglasses. "No, not an accident."

With each word her voice grew more brittle. Even from this distance I could see her heart trembling.

"When he was five," she took a deep breath and paused briefly, "I cut open his cheek with a knife."

Apparently there was also a kind of hardship so severe that a person could no longer lie about it. U Ba had never mentioned that one to me.

For a moment the doctor assumed that he had misunderstood. "Wait, you cut open your son's—"

"Yes," she said, interrupting.

His gaze wandered from my mother to my scar and back again. He let his arms drop, and he sank into his chair without a word.

Without a single thought, I jumped up and went over to her and wrapped my arms around her. I pressed her head to my chest and held it firmly while kissing her hair.

No, I did not want the doctor to take another look at the scar.

No, I did not need any kind of salve.

No, I did not want to make another appointment.

I did not care at all whether the doctor could understand how difficult this situation was for us.

Nothing was simple. Not for anyone.

I took my mother by the hand and led her without another word out of the exam room, through the waiting room, and into the street. We walked right past all the people on whom something had been *inflicted*, whether by chance or fate or some other person. She just followed my lead.

I guided her through the foot traffic, expecting at any moment to see my father emerging from the throng. He was standing in a doorway, partly concealed by a press of people. Just then I lost sight of him. We stopped, and I called out to him, but he didn't answer. Was he hiding? Or had I just imagined him?

We hustled down a boulevard and crossed at an intersection without checking for traffic. Cars honked, a man shouted something after us, but we hurried along until we came to a park.

I wanted to keep going but she was spent, and we let ourselves fall onto the grass, exhausted, as if we had been running for our lives through half the city. We lay there stretched out side by side. I heard her wheezing and gasping for breath.

Minutes passed. We both continued to struggle for breath.

In my mind I was still sitting across from the doctor, smelling the stench of stale smoke on his breath, hearing his question and my mother's answer.

That was me.

That was me.

That was me.

The picture in my mind became blurred, everything went to black, and then another image faded in: my uncle, my mother, and I are sitting at the table in our house in Kalaw. She stands up, then sits back down, argues with U Ba. I'm not listening. She falls into a rage. She's beside herself and shouting at me. The metal of a sharp blade between my lips, on my tongue. It's pleasantly cool. Then I feel a piercing pain, the sweetish taste of blood in my mouth. My father charges in, my uncle screams, the table lurches through the room, I fall from my stool and land headfirst on the wooden floor.

I had never remembered this moment until now, and it felt as if I was experiencing it all over again. A second time. A third time. And a fourth.

I started to sweat. My face felt hot, and I was having trouble breathing despite my efforts to inhale and exhale as calmly and deeply as I could.

One-two-three.

One-two-three.

Even counting didn't help.

"Mama?"

She said nothing.

I reached for her hand, and I could feel how forcefully the blood was still pulsing through her body.

"I want to go home."

When she didn't answer, I sat up. Her eyes were closed, and I was afraid she had passed out.

"Mama?" I said, alarmed. "Please, say something."

She did not respond. I sat beside her and laid her head on my lap. It was burning hot. Strands of hair clung to the sweat on her brow. She was shivering, as if from a fevered chill. She was worse off than I was, and I had no idea what was wrong with her or what I should do about it.

Were we demanding a courage of ourselves beyond the strength of our hearts?

There was no way I could go to look for a doctor. Under no circumstances was I willing to leave her lying there alone. Sitting on the lawn around us were several couples, young and old, picnicking, reading, or cuddling and paying no attention to us. I called loudly for help. A man leapt up right away and came over to us. Others followed. Soon we were surrounded by a crowd of curious onlookers, one of whom claimed to be a doctor.

He knelt down beside us, checked her pulse and her temperature, and said that we needed to get her to a hospital as quickly as possible.

Suddenly I heard my father's voice behind me. "She doesn't need a doctor," he said under his breath. "She needs us."

He put his arms around me. I leaned my head against his chest and buried my face in his shirt, as if it had again been a year since I last saw him. I hoped and hoped that he would just hold on to me like that.

Someone was taking pictures of us on his phone. Someone else growled at him to knock it off.

And then my mother regained consciousness. She looked at the many unfamiliar faces, and at first she did not know where she was. I stroked her hand and my father whispered a few sentences in her ear that I could not make out.

The doctor offered her something to drink. A boy offered her some pastries. She thanked them but waved them off. She struggled, trying to stand up, then sank back down onto the grass.

My father and I helped her up, lifting her gently. With one of us on either side we walked in tiny, tentative steps toward the street, though I was barely able to stand on my own.

Chapter 13

MY MEMORY of the next few days is spotty. My mother and I lay side by side in my parents' bed, sleeping most of the time. Whenever I woke I would hear her quiet, even breath. I would take her hand and fall back asleep. Sunbeams would fall into the room and then disappear. It would get warm and then cool. Ravens would call and then be silent.

Whenever I opened my eyes there would be a pitcher of water and a plate of bananas and fresh-cut mangoes on the nightstand. But I was neither hungry nor thirsty.

Now and then one of us would get up, go to the bathroom, and then fall back into the bed without exchanging so much as a word.

The only thing I heard from my father was his soft footsteps whenever he brought fresh water and fruit.

It was a sleep unlike any I had previously experienced. It did nothing to relieve weariness. It had no beginning and no end.

I slipped dreamlessly in and out of it.

Even so, something was happening inside me. I felt my strength gradually returning. A long time must have passed before I felt thirsty again. Then hungry. Quietly I rose and slipped out.

I could hear noises below, a soft murmuring from the kitchen. It was not the sisters' voices. We had company.

Curious, I crept down the stairs. My father was leaning over the sink, cleaning a fish.

Next to him stood my uncle.

"U Ba!" I cried, running to him and putting my arms around him. He gave me a big hug.

"Tighter," I implored him. He was hugging me with all his might.

I wanted to know how he was doing, how long he had been there, how long he would be staying, but the two of them insisted that I first have something to eat and drink. My father took a homemade soda out of the refrigerator. U Ba sat down beside me. I had the feeling he was waiting to tell me something.

The thought crossed my mind that my parents must want to send me back to Kalaw. I was to blame for my mother's collapse. If I had not come to Yangon, if she had not taken me to the dermatologist, none of this would have happened. Who knew what other catastrophe I might trigger. I didn't want to make a prisoner out of her, but I didn't want to go back, either. My mother was right that the city was loud and crowded and, compared with Kalaw, not very attractive. All the same, it was where I wanted to be.

I looked at my uncle. "Did you come to take me back?"

"No," he replied. "Why would you think that?"

"Really and truly?" I asked warily.

"Really and truly," my father said. Seeing the doubt in my expression, he joined us at the table. "On the contrary. Mama and I wanted to ask you whether you would like to stay with us in Yangon."

I was too surprised to answer.

"We would be very happy to have you here." He waited for a reaction, but I still had no idea what to say.

"There's a very good school close by," he continued. "The instruction is even in English. There's plenty of room in the house."

He misunderstood my silence.

"You can take your time and think about it."

"I don't need to think about it." I looked at U Ba. Could I leave him alone in Kalaw? Who would go shopping for him? Who would cook for him? Do the laundry? Massage his feet? It would not be easy for him to get along without me. "What about you?"

"I could spend a part of the year with all of you here in Yangon. When it gets too hot, I can retreat to Kalaw. During the holidays you can come visit me and stay as long as you like."

"But you don't like to travel," I objected.

"For you I will gladly do so," he answered with a loving grin.

I heard my mother calling from upstairs. I jumped out of my seat and bounded up the stairs two at a time. "U Ba's here," I called out before I even got to the door.

The long sleep had done her good, too. I could see in her eyes that today was not one of the days when she would loathe herself.

She was overjoyed when she saw her brother! She laughed in just the way U Ba had described.

My mother put on a light jacket and suggested we all go out to the terrace. She stood there blinking in the sun, walking the length of the terrace and back, gazing in silence and awe at the blooming flowers, as if she had expected never to see them again.

Then she lay down in the hammock and asked me to join her.

I looked doubtfully at the metal posts from which the ropes hung.

"Don't worry, they'll hold you," my father promised.

I climbed into the hammock with her. He gave us a push. The material stretched but didn't tear, and we rocked gently from side to side. Above us a blue, cloudless sky. My father went downstairs to fetch some drinks. U Ba sat down and watched us from the shade of the arbor.

My mother lifted her arm and pointed to her wrist, the red bracelet with the two small jade stones. "Do you know what that is?"

"A talisman?"

She nodded.

"And it brings good luck?"

She regarded the bracelet thoughtfully, playing with the two stones, then looked at me. "Yes," she said, "so much that I have no idea what to do with it all."

"Did Papa give it to you?"

"No. I bought three of them from an old man at the Bogyoke Aung San Market. One for your father, one for myself—and one for you. Would you like this one?"

"Where is the third?"

"In my desk drawer. That one can be mine, then."

"And U Ba?"

"We can buy a new one for him tomorrow."

Reassured, I held out my hand. She took the bracelet off, wrapped it around my right wrist, and adjusted it for me.

She smiled and wanted to say something, but I put a finger on her lips. I did not want to hear anything just at that moment. All I needed to know I saw in her eyes. Her bright, shining, beautiful eyes; they were talking to me.

Everything was good.

Or as good as it could possibly be.

Acknowledgments

Several people play a role in the creation of any novel. In this case I wish to thank Winston, my friend and travel companion in Kalaw. For the past twenty-five years he has accompanied me from one end of Burma to the other, tirelessly explaining his country and culture all the while. In a similar way I am likewise indebted to Tommy. I have met and conversed with many people over the years and made many friends who have sparked ideas that in one way or another have had an impact on this book.

In particular I express my gratitude to my Burmese publisher, Waing Waing, to Jens-Uwe Parkitny, Franz-Xaver Augustin, Thintlu, Htein Lin, Kyaw Zaw Moe, Bert Morsbach, Ma Ei, Hans Leyendecker, Soe Paing, Sunshine, Jim Connors, Pyone Kathy Naing, Luc de Waegh, and Sister Martha.

Dr. Christian Jährig was a great help and inspiration in researching Julia's illness.

My friends Stephan Abarbanell and Ulrich Genzler witnessed the development of the manuscript and nurtured it with their questions, suggestions, and very welcome encouragement.

Writing a novel is a lonely occupation, but publishing is a team effort, for which I feel a bond of gratitude in particular to Hanna Diederichs, my wonderful editor, as well as to the entire Blessing Verlag. I thank Tilo Eckhardt, Margarete Ammer, and Doris Schuck as well as their staffs for their support and for the passion with which they promoted the release of this book. I also would like to thank my wonderful US editor and publisher Judith Gurewich and her amazing team at Other Press for their enthusiasm and support over the ten years we have been working together. Judith is an incomparable editor, with her analytical mind, full of passion and understanding for the author and the characters of a novel.

I owe her as well as all the people at Other Press a lot.

My son, Jonathan, with his comments as accurate as they were critical, as well as with his praise, was extraordinarily helpful.

As always, I am most especially grateful to my wife, Anna. This book, too, would never have been possible without our many, sometimes contentious conversations and discussions about the narrative, without her advice, her patience, or her tireless encouragement on the many, many days of doubt.

The Art of Hearing Heartbeats

When a successful New York lawyer suddenly disappears without a trace, neither his wife or his daughter Julia has any idea where he might be – until they find a love letter he wrote many years ago to a Burmese woman. Intent on solving the mystery and coming to terms with their father's past, Julia decides to travel to the village where the woman lived. There she discovers a tale of unimaginable hardship, resilience and passion that will change her life for ever.

A poignant and heart-warming love story, *The Art of Hearing Heartbeats* will reaffirm your belief in the constancy of the human heart.

The Art of Hearing Heartbeats is the million-copy international bestselling prequel to *A Well-Tempered Heart*.

A Well-Tempered Heart

'This is the kind of stunningly perfect novel that changes lives' Caroline Leavitt, *New York Times* bestselling author

Julia Win, a successful Manhattan lawyer, is at a crossroads in her life. Despite her wealth and privilege, she is exhausted and unhappy – a lost soul. She returns to Burma, the homeland of her father, where she encounters an anguished mother whose life is shattered when her two boys are taken from her to fight in Burma's civil war.

Both women embark on their own journeys of self-discovery, experiencing heartbreak, horror, love and, ultimately, redemption.

This mesmerising novel explores the most inspiring and passionate terrain of all: the human heart.